Praise for
The Absence of Nectar
A National Bestseller

"Lyrical and full of sensuality . . . it's impossible to stop reading it. With its horrific but oddly muted violence and hint of Southern Gothic, *The Absence of Nectar* is a fine and original contribution to the suspense genre."
—*The Washington Post*

"[A] dramatic and well-structured psychological thriller."
—*The Durham Herald-Sun*

"The strength of Hepinstall's second novel lies in the quirky characterizations."   —*Booklist*

"Hepinstall tells this . . . story in language so lyrical it could be poetry instead of prose . . . She pulls the reader into a languid, sweltering summer and then fills that summer with heart-racing terror, made more frightening by the matter-of-fact manner in which it is presented. So effective is this world she's created that even the incredible requires no conscious suspension of disbelief; the reader can't resist believing . . . Preternaturally mature Alice is as memorable a child as Scout in *To Kill a Mockingbird* . . . *The Absence of Nectar*, with its absorbing story, its insightful examination of relationships and human behavior, and its powerful writing, proves that the success of that first novel was no fluke; Hepinstall has done it again."
—*BookBrowser*

continued . . .

Praise for
The House of Gentle Men
A #1 *Los Angeles Times* Bestseller

THE ABSENCE
OF
NECTAR

Kathy Hepinstall

JOVE BOOKS, NEW YORK

THE ABSENCE OF NECTAR

A Jove Book / published by arrangement with
G. P. Putnam's Sons

PRINTING HISTORY
G. P. Putnam's Sons edition / September 2001
Jove edition / September 2002

Visit our website at
www.penguinputnam.com

ISBN: 0-515-13363-9

A JOVE BOOK®
Jove Books are published by The Berkley Publishing Group,
a division of Penguin Putnam Inc.,
375 Hudson Street, New York, New York 10014.
JOVE and the "J" design are
trademarks belonging to Penguin Putnam Inc.

PRINTED IN THE UNITED STATES OF AMERICA

10 9 8 7 6 5 4 3 2 1

To my father, dear friend, and favorite storyteller,
Jack Hepinstall

Acknowledgments

My thanks go out first to Terry Brooks, whose inspiration and faith turned things around for me.

Maria Massie, Stacy Creamer, and Phyllis Grann believed in this novel and ensured its survival. I owe them a great deal. I would also like to thank Noelle Murrain, Beth Thomas, and the sales reps who got this book to the stores.

My partners Todd Grant and Alda Abbracciamento showed great support and patience during the editing phase of this book, and Robyn Komachi went out of her way to help me publicize my first novel. I can't thank them enough. Thanks to Grace Cooley, Leon Swaine,

Gussie Townsley, Velmer Smith, Mary Cleveland, the Merryville Historical Society, and the Museum of West Louisiana. Thanks especially to my mother, Polly Hepinstall, whose arcane knowledge of woodsy things, great eye for detail, and general support and love always strengthen my manuscripts.

Thanks to my brother and sisters: Randy Hepinstall, Becky Hepinstall, and Margaret Plsek. Thank you, Sheri Peddy, Shonie Cooley Warden, June and John Grams, Catherine Hamilton, Madge Noble, and Laura and Noot Landry. Thank you, Granny Cat and Suki, Lynn Branecky, Sandy Jordan, Sarah Casey, Sherman Judice, and Marc Olmsted. Thank you, Adrienne Brodeur, Anne Dingus, Ray Lazenby, Matthew Snyder, Dawn DeKeyser, Melinda Haynes, Beth Anderson, Chris Blum, Court Crandall, Kirk Souder, Marie Smith, Sharon Miller, Rohitash Rao and Stephanie Zelmer-Rao, Andrew Wilson, Gina Biancarosa, Melinda Kanipe, Laura DellaPenna, Valerie Jerome, Nancy Sundquist, Liz Foster, Thad Russell, Elizabeth Wika, Shari Long, Dan and Deborah Morrison, Woody Kay, Mary Ann Frerman, Phoebe Kelley, Deb Hagan, Ed Godwin, Joan Lyons, Dan Cain, Mike Hughes, Dan Wieden, Susan Hoffman, Eric Silver, Todd Waterbury, Shyam and Vidya Madiraju, Peter Wegner, Mike Woolf, Juan and Judy Perez, Mary Gay Shipley, Nancy Nelms, Jeremy Ellis, Chris Graves, Susan Nicholas-Graves, Edna Johnson, and Janet Murphy McKee.

Thank you, Candy Davis, for the early editing help. Thank you, Melinda and Deb, for the "warm room" in which I wrote part of this book. And thank you, Alex Kronman, wonder boy, for inspiring us all.

One

All these years later, there remains a scar on my face. Very thin, and light in color like a beekeeper's glove. My stepfather, Simon Jester, was standing at the stove one day, flipping an egg. I walked up behind him and said something. Startled, he whirled around.

"It's only me, Simon," I said, already afraid of the look in his eyes.

Instead of answering, he pressed the edge of the hot spatula against my face. My mother, who insisted that her children call her by her first name, Meg, found me later on the porch and rubbed a white cream into the long, thin blister. "It's the heat, Alice," she murmured, still rubbing.

"Makes him touchy." That was only a half-truth, Meg's specialty. Simon's madness wasn't a slave to temperature alone. However, I am convinced that it was the soaring heat of a summer afternoon—together with my brother's unforgivable betrayal—that made Simon finally decide to kill both of us.

That day I stood before the mirror in a bathroom that reeked of Simon's aftershave, gazing carefully at myself, looking for evidence that Simon had poisoned my toothpaste, my pillow, the milk I'd held to the light that morning. My eyes were clear. The pupils weren't dilated. My lips weren't blue. No yellow tint to the skin. No tremors. I leaned forward and bared my teeth. My gums weren't bleeding. The mist my breath made on the mirror looked benign. And yet my body could fail at any moment. My heart could stop.

It was early June. The grass stood high around the fence posts where my brother had forgotten to trim. Clover and black-eyed Susans. Oleander in bloom. Ladybugs, grasshoppers, crickets. My bare feet could not touch the lawn without collecting living things, but I knew that there was something wrong with the ecosystem of that yard, that house. Stepfathers are not meant to conspire against their new children, and if they do, mothers are meant to put a stop to it. But my own mother would not believe the truth about Simon, was dead set against it, annoyed by its heat and its color.

I finished my inspection in the bathroom mirror and went out on the back porch, where my brother sat polishing his glasses. His hands trembled and the nervous tic around his eyes was worse than I'd seen it in a long time, but he seemed to have shaken himself out of the strange daze he'd been in since that morning, and for that I was relieved. I sat down beside him and said: "The jig is up, I guess." I said it very casually and with an air of weariness, hoping my tone would calm my brother.

"I know," he said.

"We've gone too far."

"I've gone too far."

"Doesn't matter who did what."

Boone looked over at our mother, who sat on a cypress glider facing the porch, holding her swollen stomach, her back to her dead bee colonies. She seemed lost in the memory of those bees. Their variable buzz. Their perfect functions. Their desperate urge for order, which had churned seasonally into wax and honey. The last of them had died before the daffodils opened, and the frames in the hives had crusted over with a fuzz that proved on closer inspection to be their decaying bodies. Meg, however, still tended to speak of them in the present tense, as though they still worked and buzzed and stung her unprotected hands. She wore a shapeless green muumuu and arched her bare feet each time the glider moved her forward. Even from that distance we could see the glow that her pregnancy put on her face. The triumph. She waved at us languidly, and Boone shook his head in disbelief.

"Why won't she help us?" he whispered.

"She doesn't think anything's going to happen."

"God." He ran his fingertips over the bushy curves of his eyebrows and put his glasses back on. He looked at me and his eyebrows twitched. A brief tic smoothed by an afternoon breeze. He touched my arm. "Do you hate me?"

"No."

"Really?"

"Simon was just waiting for an excuse. If it wasn't what you did, it would be something else."

"Please, Alice. Go talk to her."

"What good will it do?"

"Maybe she'll finally believe us."

Boone was fourteen—two years older than I was—but he didn't understand what I did, that it's easier to shake a snapping turtle from a barbed hook than a woman from her savior. Just to please him, though, I waded through the grass toward my mother, sending gnats dancing up and grasshoppers in their crazy directionless bounces. Here and there in the grass lay the abandoned artifacts of my mother's beekeeping: white gloves, a nylon veil, a hive tool, a smoker turned on its side and spilling charred burlap. At this time the bees should be gathered around the perimeter of the rain barrel, collecting water for the steaming hives. Now all of the bees were dead. Except . . .

Meg slid over on the glider and showed me the back of her hand. "Look," she said, delighted. "A bee!" It crawled between her fingers, through the pink valley between her knuckles, circled back around and moved up her fourth finger to the diamond on her wedding band, balancing precariously on the tiny gem whose real value was always in question. It was a wild bee—not one of Meg's Italian bees that used to roam the countryside aching for nectar. Nonetheless, she admired it on her finger as though her diamond had suddenly swelled.

"He's my new friend," she said.

The bee was covered in yellow pollen. It turned around again on the ring and flew away. My mother sighed sadly, because she hated to be left.

I said to her: "Simon's going to kill us for what Boone did. I can see it in his eyes."

She didn't answer me. Instead she picked up my hand and pressed it against her stomach. Against my palm I felt the pressure of the baby's kick.

"Can you feel it?" she asked. "That's your brother."

"Half brother. If it's a boy."

"Oh, it will be a boy. Simon wants a boy."

"Did you hear what I said, Meg? About Simon?"

"Simon just likes to talk. He likes to scare us. He'll be all right after dinner, when it's cooler."

"Cooler? That doesn't matter. He'd plot my death sitting on an iceberg." I took a deep breath. "Don't you want to know what happened this morning?"

"No." Meg said the word in a sad, gentle way.

Underneath my hand, the baby kicked again.

"Won't be too long now," Meg murmured.

"Until we die?"

"Sweetheart . . ." Meg's voice was soft and sad. "Nothing bad will happen." She brushed back my hair. Pulled me closer so I could feel her scent: an immature sweetness, like the fluid of a honeysuckle. She moved her feet and the glider rocked. I looked down at her stomach. A bully, no doubt, this baby. Temperamental in the womb. Annoyed by the dull light coming through the stomach wall. The heat of the embryonic fluid. The pull of the umbilical cord.

Gently I shook off Meg's embrace, left the glider and walked back through the grass.

Boone was missing from the porch. He had probably gone to his room to shiver. The wild bee that had crawled over Meg's fingers now hovered on the railing. It had lost

its way in the search for sweetness and was now sniffing at
the perspiration my brother's palm had left on the wood. I
wondered if it had already flown through the quiet beeyard,
among its dead fellows.

I looked back at Meg. She was rocking back and forth
and holding her belly.

I turned and slapped my palm against the railing. The
bee died under my hand with all its bustling intentions, and
I left its crushed body there, pollen from one stomach, nectar from the other. I went into the house and was passing by
the den when Simon called to me. My heart dropped suddenly at the sound of his voice.

He was propped up in his recliner, an empty china plate
on his lap, inspecting the tines of his fork with squinted
eyes, turning the fork over and over in the afternoon light
that poured through the drapeless window. His black hair
was gathered in a rubber band, pulled back from his head
so tightly that it revealed a mole near his ear and another at
his hairline. His goatee hosted crumbs. He turned so that
he could regard me with his close-together eyes. "Where's
your mama?"

"Outside."

"When's dinner?"

"Whenever you want."

He looked up at me and I could see the line in the skin
between his eyes. A wrinkling that meant an angry mood.
One of his sleeves had turned red earlier that day. Wincing,
he lifted his arm and pointed in the direction of the kitchen.
"Got any more of that cake in there?"

When I nodded, he said, "Bring me some."

I went into the kitchen, where a drop of blood still clung
to the peach in the fruit bowl, and two drops had dried on

the floor near the sink, and one had run like a tear down the front of the white oven. A gash of blood had left an anchor shape across the window curtain, and a small brown streak of it still lingered on the rose-colored soap.

I found a knife and cut Simon a piece of cake, thinking about his plans. I knew he had access to poison; out of terror and uncertainty, I had read all his books on that subject, properties and effects and case studies, and I knew that within our home, garage and yard, half a dozen deadly poisons could be found: strychnine, arsenic, calcium cyanide, fluorosodium. Thallium in the dated products. No more poison than usual for a family who had mice and roaches and gophers to contend with, along with the now dead bees. A family who had silver to polish, floors to clean, cabinets to stain.

I went back into the den and handed Simon the cake. I watched him tear off little chunks of it and put them in his mouth. Swallowing the pieces like pills. Jamming his fingers into it, pressing so hard they left indentations. His hand trembling. This man. A bully to cake and children. He looked up at me, his eyes crowded close to the line between them. More lines in his forehead. "You still here?"

"Where would I go?"

"Away from my sight, if you don't mind."

"I don't."

"Hold on."

He looked at me a long time, perspiration running down his face. A crumb fell out of his mouth and onto his plate, and he flattened it with the tip of his finger. "You and Boone think you're funny, don't you? What you done this morning."

"How about what you did?"

"I didn't do nothing wrong. Tried to help somebody. A poor little girl with half a brain."

"Some help."

"What do you know? You ain't even my child. Neither is your brother. You don't have one drop of my blood . . ."

I looked at his sleeve.

". . . and so you're not my . . . you know . . ."

"Natural children?"

"That's right, Smart Girl."

I left him without waiting for my dismissal and went back into the hallway, my senses so heightened that I could feel the darkness against the part on my scalp, and when I ran my hand along the wall, I discovered tiny uneven patches in the paint that no other human in the world could have felt.

Boone was sitting on his bed in the room he and I shared. He was shirtless in the heat and looking at a black-and-white picture of Persely Snow he'd cut from the crime section of the newspaper and copied at the city library. The poor quality of the Xerox left the famous teenager looking even more maniacal. Eyes wild, hair tangled. Teeth bared like an animal. No flesh tones to make excuses for the expression. Even as the hour of our deaths drew near, Boone remained entranced. His fingers traveled down her face, forehead to eyes to defiant smile. I had tolerated his devotion for years, but now I wanted to seize that picture and tear it to shreds, for this girl had entered our lives with a vengeance and had caused us nothing but trouble. She had recently escaped her flimsy state institution for the seventh time and was now hidden on a small island in the middle of Lake Shine. Now I imagined her pacing around in the brambles, looking up at the sky, waiting for my brother.

Boone whispered: "What did Meg say?"

"She said that we were right all along. That she married a maniac. That she's going to shoot him in the back of the head. And sell his demon child."

"That's not funny, Alice."

"Why'd you even ask? You knew what she'd say."

He lay back on the bed, the picture of Persely Snow facedown on his chest. "Meg can't help it. She's not like other mothers."

"No kidding." I sat down on my bed, hugged my knees, then flopped back against the mattress, frightened and angry and sad for all the things I would miss on this earth. Hula hoops. Handmade belts. Necklaces made by twisting the insubstantial stalks of clover. The hard black shell of a licorice gumball. The yellow wig of a young dandelion. The gray wig of an old one. The slide on the school playground. The peculiar and random spread of live-oak branches. The dome of a purple snow cone, inviting the ache of a pair of front teeth. I hated Simon Jester for wanting to take these things away from me with his poison. I was a tomboy and an expert on American Indians and a straight-A student, and I deserved to live.

And if I did have to die, I couldn't bear the thought of doing so without finding out Simon's secret. Where he'd come from. And what he'd done to his first family.

"We should feel sorry for Simon," Boone said suddenly.

"I don't. I hate him."

"He's one of God's creatures."

"Remember that when you're drinking your tea."

He wasn't listening anymore. He was looking at the picture again.

I folded my arms and glared at him. *And how about*

Persely Snow, Boone? The girl you love. Who killed one person and tried to kill another. Is she one of God's creatures, too?

I wanted to say this, but I held my peace.

A round six o'clock Meg comes into our room, flushed and wet like a woman just pulled from a lake. If she has lived her afternoon according to habit, then she has spent it on the cypress glider, humming to herself, gazing up at the blue summer sky, rejoicing in the stagnant clouds and mourning the ones that leave her.

When she opens the door, Boone hides his picture of Persely behind his back.

"It's only me," she says.

"Oh." He takes his picture back out. "I thought it was . . ."

"No. He's in the den." Meg has applied lipstick to her bottom lip and then rubbed her lips together for the haphazard coverage of a color I've seen on winecup flowers. "Could you help me with dinner, baby?" she asks me. Reluctantly I rise and follow her into the kitchen, past the den where Simon may be sleeping or plotting, reading or praying or rubbing his bloody arm.

The kitchen smells of Clorox. The white oven gleams. The peach in the fruit bowl has been scrubbed clean of blood drops. The curtain has a big water stain where the red shape used to be.

I prepare the rice myself, rinsing out the utensils first and reaching way back in the cabinet to find the hidden salt. Another package of salt sits on the counter, which Simon can poison all he wants. I use only my guarded crystals. While the water boils, Meg busies herself at the stove, her pregnant belly causing me to have to lean forward to stir the chicken dish.

Just before dinner Simon comes in. He's changed into a clean shirt and his black ponytail is caught inside the back of his collar. He walks up behind my mother, puts his arms around her stomach and kisses her neck. Simon has been deeply suspicious about whether the baby is his, but now he suddenly seems to believe all of Meg's tearful denials, and he murmurs into her ear: "How's the queen mother?"

Meg giggles and turns around. She puts her arms around him and he says, "Ow, be careful."

"Sorry, sweetie."

"He been kicking?"

"Hard."

"That's my boy."

He kisses her cheek. His hands slide from her stomach to her breasts, and Meg says: "Oh, Simon."

"How long till dinner?" Simon asks.

"It's almost ready."

"I'll help you dish up," he says meaningfully.

I bring him a stack of plates, which he yanks away from me with a grunt, then I stand there watching him dish up our meal. Chicken Meg, we call it. Shredded chicken mixed with bell peppers and tomatoes.

"What are you looking at?" Simon asks me.

"Nothing." Sweat runs down my face. If I blink it away, I might miss a sudden movement of his hand.

"Alice," my mother says, and without thinking, I turn my head away from Simon.

"What?"

"The rice is burning."

I take the rice off the stove and turn off the flame. When I turn back, Simon is putting the full plates on the table, and my heart speeds up and my knees tremble with fear. In those few seconds, Simon could have added an ingredient that carries no spice but arrests the nervous system or thins the blood or kills the light in my eyes. But I do not betray my emotions as I dish up the rice—safe and white—and put it in a separate green bowl, then set it on the table.

Boone comes in and we all sit down. My brother looks at the rice and then at me. I give him the signal. Two long blinks and two short ones. The Morse code of survival. It means that Simon has not been near the rice, and so it is safe to eat. Not so the Chicken Meg, and I broadcast this fact with three short blinks. We've been using these signals for weeks, growing lean and sad as the food we love ends up down the disposal.

My mother pours the strawberry lemonade, which is sweet and red and safe. I've kept the mix in a secret place in the bedroom. Ten minutes ago I watched Meg make the lemonade; Simon hasn't come near it. I blink at Boone.

Simon looks at my mother. "Say the prayer."

She takes my hand and Boone's and begins: "Lord, thank you for another day. Lord, teach us patience. Lord, thank you for always being good . . ."

As she speaks, my eyes open just enough to see what Simon's up to. He's sitting there drumming his fingers on the table. I wonder if he washed the blood off his arm before he put on the fresh shirt. "Okay, that's enough," he says, interrupting the part of Meg's prayer that has to do with mercy. "Everybody eat."

We begin. No one speaks. Meg and Boone and I eat delicately, as if we can placate the situation by handling the food gingerly enough. White rice slides through the tines of our forks.

Simon picks up his teaspoon and begins eating from the sugar bowl—his most disgusting habit. Presently he looks up, glaring at us.

"Why aren't you eating the chicken?" he demands, spitting white crystals.

"We don't like chicken," Boone says nervously.

"Bullshit. I've seen you eat it before."

"Come on, kids," says Meg. "Just eat a little. It's really good."

"I'm tired of it," I say.

She looks hurt. In life-or-death dramas she has room to flinch from small discourtesies. This is the magic of Meg.

Simon jumps out of his chair and rushes over to Boone, his shadow coming out ahead of him and announcing him too late. He grabs the back of my brother's neck and forces his head down into his plate. Boone struggles, his fork still in one hand.

I leap from the table and grab Simon's wrist. "Stop it! You're hurting him!"

Simon pushes me, and I fall back to the linoleum floor. By the time I jump to my feet, it is already over.

When Boone's face finally comes up, it is covered with Chicken Meg, his glasses heavy with it.

Simon sits back down and crosses his arms, watching Boone clean his glasses and then go over his face with his napkin, wiping away a long, thin piece of tomato that is shaped like the blister Simon once gave me with the edge of his spatula.

Meg is blinking. I imagine her head as a beehive, a

quiver of terror in the very center that does not radiate outward to the other bees. Judging by the expression on her face, the beehive remains calm, though she wrings her hands.

"Please," she says.

Simon ignores her. "Eat your damn food," he tells Boone and me. "Both of you. After what you did today, you're lucky to eat at all."

In this year, in this house, things happen and nothing stops them. In the living room God's Bible sits open on Simon's chair, where he'd been leafing through it, bloody. This part of Texas can't save us. We eat our chicken.

After dinner Boone and I go back to our room and wait to die. I lie on my twin bed; he flops on his across the room. We don't say anything for a few minutes, caught up in our own processes, vigilantly regulating our bodies, waiting for a falter in the heart, a dizzy sensation, a headache or a breath that brings sudden agony. Sweat is dripping down our faces. Too much sweat? We stare at our hands.

In the darkness I think of the Indians I've been reading about at the library. How they died so bravely. Crazy Horse was stabbed while struggling against his captors. Mangas Coloradas was invited to a peace conference and bayoneted by white men. Roman Nose fell in battle. And Sitting Bull died in a hail of bullets, slumping to the ground as his white horse danced.

I breathe in and out, trying to shift my mind from death to Spencer Katosky, the boy I love, but instead my thoughts wander to Meg. I want to hate her and also her new baby, who is half Simon and therefore half despicable, but something in me forgives them.

Boone picks up Persely Snow's picture again and puts it on his chest so she can smile down at his seizing heart. I roll my eyes a little but keep my voice steady. "How do you feel?" I ask him.

"Kind of sick."

"Sick like you're scared, or sick like you're poisoned?"

"I don't know." His voice is shaky. "What if Simon put strychnine in the Chicken Meg?"

A reluctant expert on poison, I shiver now as I imagine the effects of that nightmarish drug. The stiff neck, the spasms of the arms and legs, the involuntary arching of the body, the horrible smile. "Strychnine is bitter," I say, remembering what I've read in the books, trying to soothe my brother with my quiet voice. "We would have tasted it."

"How about cyanide? You know, what Meg uses on the sick bees. Simon could have mixed it in the lemonade."

I shake my head. "First of all, Simon never got near that lemonade. And second, I think that kind of cyanide turns into a gas when it touches moisture."

He thinks a minute. "Carbolic acid."

"Your mouth would be burning."

"Curare?"

"Doesn't hurt you if you swallow it. It has to break the skin. Has Simon shot you with a dart lately?"

"Alice, I think I'm dying."

He looks pale. I go over to his bed and begin rubbing his arms. "You're fine, you're fine. Think of Persely. She needs you." I rub his arms harder and say what I know will galvanize my brother: "She can't survive on that island without you, Boone."

At the thought of this, he lets out a groan and lunges off the bed. I lose my balance and we fall down in a heap together.

"Get up," I say, trying to extract myself. "We've got to get out of here. Get up. Get up!"

"I'm trying."

I hear footsteps coming up to the door, and Boone and I stiffen as the knob turns and light spills onto the floorboards in an anvil-shaped gash.

It's Meg. We sigh in relief.

She closes the door behind her, staring down at the floor, at our tangled-up bodies. She says nothing but holds one hand over her stomach and pushes the other against Boone's mattress so she can kneel on the floor. Her belly presses against my arm and I can feel her baby kick. The real baby Simon craves. The one with his blood. His face. His madness. I picture a line forming between its tiny eyes, its face turning red at some perceived grievance there in the darkness of the womb.

Boone and I are still tangled up, motionless, silent. My mother runs her hand through my hair, then through his. I am still half angry at her, but glad to be alive and awaiting her sweet endearments.

Tears begin to roll from her eyes and a look crosses her face, one of such torment that I think she has taken poison herself. One of the corrosives, perhaps. She smoothes our hair again, takes a deep, painful breath, leans down to us and whispers a word that I know must cause her unbearable grief.

Run.

Chapter Two

My mother's relationship with Simon Jester had begun in the late spring of the previous year. He must
have seemed like a god to her upon first glimpse. Like a
vague yet steady shape among all those roiling waves.
She was coughing. Her skin was turning blue and she
had no breath in her lungs. She reached for him through
green water, clawing at his face, pulling his hair, clutch-
ing the collar of his shirt. Perhaps she even bit him. As I
remember that scene now, I pretend she is fighting him
in our defense. Hurting him for us.

* * *

Our real father was a sweet-tempered man who never raised his voice. I used to watch him as he sat at the kitchen table, working crossword puzzles with one hand and eating an apple with the other. He could eat that apple until the core was nothing but the slenderest of twigs, all the while holding it so lightly that it didn't buckle in on itself. He was that gentle.

Sometimes after dinner he would go outside in the backyard with us and play softball. Our old dog, Numbhead—who had been hit by a go-cart as a puppy and was consequently too stupid to do anything but carry around a hapless live toad in his mouth—would set down his little friend so he could chase balls. My father never took his turn at bat. He was strictly the pitcher. That is what I remember the most about him, the little step he took when he threw the ball underhanded, how gently he released it. Grace in motion, he was. The Laird twins from across the road would drift over, standing together in their matching paisley jumpers, their tan Buster Brown shoes dark at the toes from popping tar bubbles in the street. Brother and sister, they were unattractive children with unruly expressions and nests of curly red hair, already showing the odious personality traits that would only worsen with age. Prone to setting off firecrackers, tormenting living creatures and going through their neighbors' trash, they kept their mother in a constant state of raw emotion. Once they had been sent to their rooms for two days for dropping their cat down a cistern to see if it would land on its feet.

The twins would hold hands and watch us play. "Your dog is stupid," they'd tell us as they watched Numbhead look for the ball. "He doesn't know a single trick."

"He knows how to land on his feet," I once replied hotly. "Not like your cat."

"Alice," my father said, his voice so soft it barely reached me, "don't tease them about their dead pet. They're only five years old."

They had an older sister, Lucinda, who had once been the pride and joy of the Laird family—beautiful, sweet, talented. She'd had a terrible accident while riding her horse one day, and now occasionally we saw her sitting slumped on a quilt in the front yard, her eyes unfocused and looking past her brother and sister as they tortured some poor insect to death—a praying mantis, a locust, a long-legged spider.

Boone loved all children and would try to include the diabolical pair when he sat with Lucinda on her quilt and read her stories from the Bible or showed her his prize possession—his butterfly collection. The butterflies were a motley crew, for Boone could never bear to kill one in a jar of ether. Instead he found their bodies in meadows and on the tops of old sheds, sucked dry in spiderwebs, and in one case, in the middle of a white vinca bloom, quite dead, as though drinking or sleeping. Often they were missing wings, antennae, legs, or that precious colored dust that once made them able to shadow centipedes with the patterns of their flight. I thought it quaint, the idea of Boone rescuing and honoring torn and beautiful things; the twins simply looked depressed over the fact that dead things no longer suffered. At the time neither Boone nor I could know that one day those twins would play a major role in our undoing.

Our father began to come home late from the office. He seemed ashamed by his excuses, reciting his hectic day in a stumbling fashion as he sat at the dinner table, gently stabbing at his sweet potato as if probing his own story for leaks. Something was different about him, something I couldn't quite define.

One night I went to kiss him and smelled something different. Lavender. Or lilacs. One of those scented blooms.

Meg had been trained by her beekeeping to detect the least change in the atmosphere. A catch in the humming, or a different tone. Sluggish flight. Nectar's listless gathering. I would find her in front of the bathroom mirror, trying on new shades of lipstick one after the other. Dozens of shades, some of which had dropped from the bathroom sink to the floor, even into the toilet. Once, when she turned to me, I saw several colors competing for the spare property within the boundaries of her lip line. One more shade was clinging to a front tooth.

"I need to look prettier," she said.

"You're beautiful."

"You don't know that. Only a man knows if a woman looks all right."

She would come in early from tending the bees so she could wash and roll her hair, then shake it out just before she saw his moon-colored Chrysler pull into the driveway. She'd hold dinner until nine, ten o'clock, waiting for him. The days passed and she began to lose energy. Her showers took an hour and a half. She stopped rolling her hair. After she made hamburger patties out of raw ground meat, she no longer washed her hands under the faucet, instead wiping the blood off on her knit pants. Once she broke down crying because she couldn't get the twist tie off a bag of pretzels. I knew that she was desperate over my father's increasing distance, but I didn't know how desperate until one night in September.

I was sitting on my twin bed on my side of the room, playing with Boone's softball as he wrote another letter to Persely Snow on manila paper.

He had never met the girl but had cared for her deeply for some time, ever since she had been judged insane and therefore not responsible for the crime of putting cyanide in her parents' Tang. Her mother had died in a horrible fit, and her father had been hospitalized for nearly a week. But what made Persely Snow famous was her habit of escaping from the mental hospital time and time again.

The sheriff's office would be called out, and the search dogs. The media would have a field day trying to keep track of Persely Snow sightings as people sat out on their front lawns, drinking apple wine and talking about her. Persely's daring attitude, her blond curls, her large and slightly turned-in front teeth and her few defiant statements to the press had made her a local hero. (One newspaper clipping collected by my brother shows her chin jutting out, eyebrows arching in the klieg lights. The headline: GUESS WHO JUST ESCAPED AGAIN?) She would roam among the population until someone called the police—although this stool pigeon was a rare individual, for according to popular opinion, anyone who could do that to her parents had to have a good reason: a fact that Persely herself alluded to at her trial. The last person to turn her in had his car windows smashed out the next night.

Persely Snow had a strange habit of comparing herself to the character of Cooper in the movie *Hang 'em High,* and so of course the local theaters showed the movie every time she escaped. In one newspaper interview (escape No. 2), Persely revealed that she hated the Texas police because they did not live up to the standards set by Cooper. "Cooper was a lawman. But he was about justice. Tracking down those bastards that hanged him and left that ring 'round his neck. He'd pull down his bandanna and show 'em the ring. Then they'd resist arrest and he'd end up having to kill 'em. These Texas cops ain't nothin' but rednecks. Homo rednecks. They don't care about justice. They just drive around arresting innocent people and sneaking into pastures and giving it to cows up the whatfor." As a result of such insults, every cop in Texas hated Persely Snow, and each time she escaped, the police made it their first priority to bring her to justice.

My brother had caught a glimpse of her picture in the newspaper on the day of her trial, and something about her expression had left him haunted and touched. "Someone hurt her, Alice," he told me. "I can tell by the look in her eyes." Too young to admit his interest in her might have shades of a deep attraction, he disguised his passion with religion and began writing to Persely in the hopes of saving her soul. *God loves you,* he'd write. *God will forgive you if you only ask. You are God's child.*

"If she's God's child," I asked, "don't you think God must be sniffing His Tang every morning?"

Boone collected every article on Persely he could find, arranging them in a big binder, underlining new information. "You know what's funny?" he said once. "It never says where she poisoned them."

"What's it matter where they were poisoned? What does any of it matter?"

"I don't know. I just want to know . . . everything about her."

When Boone would hear of her latest escape, he would call the newspaper and use the money he earned sacking groceries to take out a small classified ad:

To P.S. NO WALLS CAN HOLD YOU. BUT GOD'S
LOVE CAN. MEET ME AT HOLLOW COVE ON LAKE
SHINE. SATURDAY AT NOON. FROM BOONE.

"What makes you think she'll read the ad?" I asked. "I mean, she's got better things to do. Like eating grass and frothing at the mouth and, you know, being a maniac."

"I told her in my letters to look in the classifieds the next time she escapes."

"Maybe she's never even read your letters."

But my brother believed in magic, and so if Saturday came and Persely wasn't yet captured, we got on our bicycles and doggedly rode down the old abandoned highway to Lake Shine. Once there, we would untie the old motorboat from the dock of our friend Mr. Walt and search Hollow Cove in vain for the sight of a crazy girl with wild golden hair and a Cooperesque squint.

On this night Boone was working on yet another letter. I looked over his shoulder. The address Boone was writing on the envelope had a distinct upward slant.

"That's not straight," I said, pointing.

"It's not supposed to be," said Boone. "The address is slanted up toward the stamp. Under the stamp I write a secret message, then I lick the stamp just around the edges and put it on top." He moved his hand so that I could see.

I squinted. The letters were tiny. Finally I made out the words: *I want to meet you. I have Ding Dongs.*

"What makes you think she'll find that?" I asked.

Boone carefully licked the edges of the stamp and pressed it to the envelope. "She's very smart."

"If she has to read words that tiny, she'll become a near-sighted poisoner."

Boone sighed. "Even with glasses, she'd still be beautiful."

Suddenly we heard a distinct thump from our parents' room. Boone threw down his pencil and I leaped from the bed. We rushed into the other room and found our father kneeling on the floor, holding our mother's head in his lap.

"Call an ambulance, honey," my father said to me.

Boone sat between our father and me in the waiting room of the hospital, a dismal area with orange plastic chairs, too many ficus plants and a television set mounted on brackets in a corner. The people sitting around us looked frightened or confused. It was as if the great gout of the world's misunderstandings had gathered in this room. Inside the operating rooms, the bright lights would give answers.

As the paramedics had carried my mother to the ambulance, the horror of her situation had zipped like lightning through Numbhead's stupidity, and using his only means of friendship, communication and comfort, he had tried to take into his mouth one of her hands, which dangled limply from the stretcher. One of the paramedics had thought he was trying to bite her and had kicked him. His yelp of pain seemed to somehow be Meg's as well, and it haunted me as I sat with my hands knitted together.

My father had thrown on the pants he'd worn to the office that day, but he still had on his pajama shirt. He folded his arms, sighed, then repositioned them. Rocked back and forth. Crossed his legs.

"What's wrong with her, Daddy?" I asked.

He didn't answer me for several moments. Finally he said: "She took sleeping pills, baby. Lots of them."

"Then why doesn't she just sleep?"

My father's expression turned vaguely angry. "Alice. I saw the IQ tests you took at school. Don't pretend to be stupid."

I shut up and folded my arms. Boone was sniffing beside me. I touched his knee and he cried harder.

But my father had focused on something else. A woman in a blue dress, who had just entered the waiting room. My father jumped up and hurried toward her. He tried putting one hand on her waist and then the other. He didn't seem able to understand what to do with her, where to touch her. Her dress was very bright and would have disturbed Meg's bees. My father finally rested his hands on her arms and looked toward the swinging doors with a guilty expression, as though God Himself would come through the doors, scrubbed up to the elbows and livid at my father's sin.

I watched them. I wanted to cry but was afraid the source of my tears would not be recognized—that my father would assume I was crying for Meg and try to put his cheating hand on my shoulder.

Four days later my mother came home from the hospital, and she and my father settled into their old relationship as though nothing had happened. He came home on time. He ate his food and asked about our day. Delighted, Meg kept the empty sleeping-pill bottle on the windowsill, as if it were the container for some kind of rouge that had finally cast its spell. Boone was ecstatic that we were all back together, but I was too wise to believe the harmony would last. Although I had long ago passed the age where drawing pictures was considered precious, I drew one anyway and gave it to my father. It was a picture of our family, holding hands. A softball flying through the air above our heads like a bird. Numbhead, through the magic of my colored markers, looking handsome and intelligent. No one in a blue dress for miles.

My father left on a clear, temperate afternoon in early February. I sat out on the front steps, watching him put things in the trunk of his car. Numbhead had retrieved his unwilling toad from the crack between the cement walkway and the foundation of the house and sat watching my father with the toad in his mouth. He panted a little, opening his jaws slightly so that I caught a glimpse of a webbed foot and a wide, unblinking eye.

Meg sat on the kitchen floor for two days and wouldn't move.

"Meg, don't worry," said Boone, holding her hand. "He'll be back."

When we finally prodded our mother into getting off the floor, she went straight to bed and didn't leave it for two months, her body motionless under the sheet, her bare feet peeking out, toenails losing color in patches. Boone tried to entertain her, reading to her from the "Dear Abby" column and propping the frame of his butterfly collection against her night table so he could show her the latest acquisitions.

"Boone," I said one day as we sat out on the front lawn,

"mangled butterflies and advice from 'Dear Abby' about guests who stay too long aren't doing the trick."

"What are we going to do?" he asked.

"I don't know."

The twins wandered over.

"Where did your daddy go?" the girl asked me.

"He took a trip."

The boy twin came up behind her and handed her something that wriggled. The girl made a fist to stop the wriggling, tighter and tighter.

It was time for the spring inspections of the bee colonies, but Meg wasn't up to it. Boone and I put on the white bee overalls and the draped hats and went to check on them ourselves. The frames were crusted with propolis and were difficult to pull out. Many of the bees had died over the winter. Poor ventilation or the late frost. We checked the brood patterns and fed the bees with sugar syrup, as the supers were light with honey. Even though our inspection was rough and unpracticed, we knew the colonies weren't thriving. Perhaps the presence of queens wasn't enough. Perhaps the bees needed fathers.

Boone and I had our own ways of coming to terms with the abandonment. Boone simply cried: for himself, for me, for Meg, for our broken family, for our father and for the woman who had stolen him, for all sad circumstances; for Lucinda, whose brain could not distinguish between butterflies and snow cones; for the poor misunderstood Laird twins; for old women with bad backs whose children never called; for the waning tribes of Africa.

I burned my father's clothes. His shoes and his pima-cotton shirts and his socks, and that pair of khaki pants that had collected pollen on the cuffs as he threw that softball so elegantly. I did not feel sorry for the world or imagine that God was crying. I felt sorry for myself and I hated my father for the way he left us—one step, graceful, easy, un-derhanded. His family rolling off his fingers and arcing through the air.

I had always loved Indians, but now I went to the library and checked out stacks and stacks of books about them, finding an odd sense of shared torment in their long and horrible plight. The Trail of Tears. Sand Creek. Wounded Knee. Cholera blankets. Firewater. Holocaust. Old men, women, children, no one spared. Sitting Bull fell. His white horse danced.

Numbhead lay at the foot of Meg's bed and wouldn't get up. Boone and I couldn't believe that a dog too stupid to come out of the rain could have such an insight into grief.

"Numbhead sure is being loyal to Meg," I said. "I'll bet that toad is happy to have a few spit-free weeks."

"I think the toad feels peaceful in Numbhead's mouth," said Boone.

"Is that why it has fits now? And why it tries to hop away every time Numbhead sets it down?"

"Numbhead is a little bit like Jesus," said Boone.

"Please," I said, "don't tell me someone with Numb-head's brain came to save the world."

By the time we got Meg out of bed, we were poor. Every once in a while an envelope would arrive from my father, our address written in very thin blue ink. The stamp upside down or sideways. The check inside didn't amount to much, and neither did the remains of the past year's honey crop.

Boone worked double-time bagging groceries for tips after school, and I started working in the yards of the nice neighborhood that bordered our scruffy one. Real cedar fences instead of bushes between the yards. St. Augustine grass, green and lush. Sprinklers shooting water in sparkly half circles. Rows and rows of azalea bushes and manicured gardens whose weeds weren't meant to be pulled by the owners. I knocked on doors, offering my services at a dollar an hour. I edged around trees with a handheld clipper, set bricks back where they should be, scrubbed the cement squirrels that perched atop birdbaths. Swept driveways. Yanked on weeds that snapped in half and spat milk on my hands.

Once a slight, bespectacled man waved me over from several houses away and asked, "Can you do some work in our yard, too?"

I looked around at his beautiful lawn, his handsome redbrick house. I could barely breathe. This man was Spencer Katosky's father, and this was Spencer's house.

"Sure, I'll do it," I said, listening to my heart race.

"How much do you charge?"

"Nothing. I mean, a dollar an hour."

I had loved Spencer from afar for two long years. He was in the class ahead of me in school, and the sight of him had become increasingly magical: his fragile, sickly body, his tousled red hair, the slight lift of one shoulder, the pale skin, the sad look in his eyes. As though he'd just witnessed an old man celebrating his birthday alone. Spencer had tried to join Boone's swim team the summer before, and I had seen him struggle through two meets, his breast-stroke crippled, his backstroke sinking, his butterfly stroke a discordant shriek in the hum of blue water. Spencer would emerge dead last, razzled by asthma and chlorine, amid whispered taunts. Water would run off his long fingers as he held his hands self-consciously over the crotch of his swimsuit, and I would die of love for him.

Finally he quit the swim team, or was forced out by his parents or the coach. I never got the whole story. All I knew was that the strong, smooth swimmers who were left couldn't move me.

My passion for Spencer extended to the country of his origin. Poland. Land of historically shifting borders and invasions by burlier men. Folk art, feverish handshakes, wayside chapels, bituminous coal. A love of poster exhibitions. A language in which the *r* is always trilled. An infrastructure as wounded as Spencer's style of swim.

Funerals. Quilts. Sulfur dust on coat sleeves. Lakes and mountains. The sad refugee.

One day I looked up from my yard work and froze. Spencer Katosky had come out of the house and was regarding me with his arms folded. Now he approached me and watched me work, one shoulder slightly lifted, his arms still crossed, a little red in his eyes as if the chlorine had followed him home like a bully and lived with him all winter.

"You go to my school, right?" he asked. His voice was tentative.

I shrugged. I looked up at him, wondering if the loss of my father showed on my face, if it would hurt Spencer's heart to know about it.

"Can I help?" he asked, and for a moment I was sure he had heard my thoughts. Then he nodded down at the spade in my hands.

The thought of him pitching forward dead over the stubbornness of a deep-rooted weed was too much for me. "No, I'm fine," I said. I watched him go back into the house. Then I used the spade to carefully dig up a particularly vicious-looking weed. I brought it home and transplanted it to a little clearing in our backyard, then dragged Numbhead over to it by the collar and held his head so that he could focus. "See that weed, Numbhead? That's not for you to chew on. That's a sacred weed from Spencer Katosky's yard."

One day Mrs. Laird saw Meg crying by the mailbox, crossed the street and embraced her, then gave her the name of a shrink. Mrs. Laird, whose daughter had sustained major brain damage, whose husband had fled, whose twins had recently frightened off a copperhead snake and a nest of yellow jackets, and whose life revolved around themes of tragedy, abandonment and rank evil, was no stranger to professional help.

Her doctor would see our whole family for fifteen dollars a session. A sliding scale, Mrs. Laird called it.

"Sliding scale," Meg breathed, impressed.

"Sounds like a fish," I said.

The fish had a suit, a gravity clock, some framed degrees and a leather sofa. We all sat upon it, Boone and I by the armrests and Meg in the middle. The counselor told us there are certain themes that start up clumsily in childhood

and then become wily enough to hide in otherwise unconscious acts once adulthood is reached. A distant father dis-
appears and reemerges as a lover; a negligent mother takes
over the fragile id like mint crowding an herb garden. Or
something like that. "You must love you for you, Meg,"
said the counselor. "That's the ticket."

I knew what the ticket was. Meg needed a new husband,
and I had my own way of getting one for her. A method my
saintly brother would have disapproved of, had he known.

That night I left my bed, tiptoed over to my dresser and
took out the giant marble my aunt Garnet had sent me from
North Carolina. It was as big around as a Ping-Pong ball,
and the insides swam with vague color. I stole out of
the bedroom, out the back door and into the backyard. The
night was chilly and clear, and my footsteps attracted the
feverish attention of Numbhead, who jumped up and down
and whined until I shushed him. I found a hammer, put my
marble on a stump and crushed it with the hammer, my
heart sinking over the loss of the irreplaceable gift from
my favorite aunt.

I walked through the beeyard and threw the green fragments into the Burford holly bush that bordered the edge of
our property, for Boone had his God, and I had mine. The
pagan god of pure dumb superstition, a savage god favored
by some Indian tribes, made of time and space, demanding
a sacrifice for every benefaction. I sacrificed my favorite
marble, whispering my request under that thin moonlight:
Please let Meg find a man.

I blamed myself for what followed.

* * *

One day in late April, Persely Snow escaped again. Boone hesitated before placing the ad; we were low on money.

"Oh, just do it, Boone," I said at last. "Maybe this will be the lucky day she follows us home and kills us."

Saturday arrived and Persely was still free. We convinced Meg to go with us to Lake Shine. "Even if we don't see Persely," Boone said wistfully, "it's such a nice day. You need some sunshine, Meg."

Lake Shine was a great green body of water a few miles away, dotted with islands and teeming with fish. Our family had visited many times, and my father had kept a small motorboat tied up to Mr. Walt's dock. He'd let us keep it there; he was lonely and kept the boat in perfect shape on the unspoken condition that we would always knock on his door and say a few words to him.

We piled into Meg's station wagon and headed for Lake Shine. After a few minutes Meg turned on the radio, and we listened to the music of the Andrews Sisters on the old highway out to Lake Shine. Cows grazed in the fields on either side of the highway; we passed the abandoned Shell refinery, and the little bait store south of the railroad tracks. The yellow lines in the highway had faded, and in parts the asphalt had peeled away. Once we arrived at the lake, we parked and took a dirt path that wound around the bank and up the small hill where Mr. Walt lived. His house had the look of something once pampered and then abandoned. Wisteria vines had rampaged unchecked across the fence, then had come back down to half-strangle the air-conditioning unit. A bird walked the edge of a birdbath that was no more than a big plastic pipe and two cultivating discs. Newspapers lay scattered on the porch. An old dog scratched his ears.

Mr. Walt was a sixty-two-year-old man who scuffled his feet with a certain jazzy rhythm, though his life had been full of tragedy. He had outlived all six of his children. Two had died soon after birth, one drowned, one died in Korea, one succumbed to cancer, and the last one, who drove a big rig cross-country, had wrecked one night while trying to shell a pistachio nut. Mr. Walt's wife had died in his arms in 1965, and now her grave made a rectangle in the Bermuda grass that filled his backyard.

Mr. Walt's heart was going and his skin was pale, yet when he saw my mother, he lit up. He'd always had a crush on her. "Where have you been all this time?" he asked. "Where's Dan?"

We stood frozen a moment. Silent. He looked at Meg's face and seemed to understand everything. "Come on in," he said, "and see Grace."

We trudged through the house and went out back with him to visit his wife's grave. He sank to his knees and pointed. "The pansies are gonna be gone soon. Gonna replace them with snapdragons. And I'm gonna repaint the cross."

The cross said: WE WILL MEET ON THAT BEAUTIFUL SHORE.

Mr. Walt looked back at my mother and an expression of guilt suddenly crossed his face, to be so attracted to her while his knee was only six feet away from the crossed arms of his beloved wife. Boone seemed to sense his distress and took Meg by the arm and said that we had to be going. Mr. Walt led us down a path to his dock, where the old motorboat still bobbed on the water. "I took it out a couple of times over the winter," he said. "Just to keep it up. And it's full of gas."

We all climbed in and Mr. Walt stood waving as Boone started the motor and guided us out into the river channel. My father had taught Boone how to run the boat years before, and he naturally fell back into it now. I smiled at my brother and he smiled back. His hair had grown a little past his ears, and a welcome breeze pulled on it. He looked around. "I read that Persely Snow used to swim here before the trial," he said. "Which cove, you think?"

I didn't answer him. The day was beautiful, and the subject of Persely Snow had long ago begun to wear thin.

Meg was wearing a one-piece swimsuit and a wrap-around skirt. She adjusted her scarf and her sunglasses, pursing her lips at the scattered light on the water. "Fun," she said.

"Meg," I said. "Mr. Walt likes you."

She shrugged.

"Why don't you like him?"

She looked at me, then made a fist and gently tapped her chest. "He's sick," she said. "He'd leave me."

She fell silent and I let my hand trail over the side of the boat to collect spray. Although the water had no strong currents aside from near the dam, it still had a way of pulling people down to the bottom. Last August two boys had drowned. One went to my school. Once, at a school dance, I had watched a plain, bespectacled girl walk up to him and ask him to dance. "I can't," he'd said, pausing to smile at his friends. "My leg hurts." I felt sad as I imagined this rude boy drowning, for his rudeness made him all the more real to me. I'd had dreams of him walking along the lake's silty floor, his hair no less blond, as homely fish swam up to him and swam away again, rebuffed.

After twenty minutes, Never Island came into view. In

bygone summers, we used to tie off to an old tree stump, and my father would sit with Meg while Boone and I climbed the banks. We considered Never Island our own, because the banks were too steep for picnics, and fishermen preferred the area next to the dam. Once Boone and I had walked through the dark woods of the island and found a flat clearing in the middle.

I watched the island as we arced around it, Boone expertly guiding the boat around the stumps.

We headed toward the far end of the lake, past the marina where the yacht club docked, past the state park, past the coves the Baptists had bought for their summer retreats. Meg threw her head back, gazing at the clouds. She leaned back until her head was in my lap, her hair tickling me. The last color she'd put on it had grown out two inches, and I could see the boundary where her false color met her true one. She looked up at me and smiled.

Boone cut the motor when we reached the mouth of Hollow Cove. He checked his watch. "Five minutes to twelve," he said.

I began to sing a song I'd practiced in my head. "I'd like to buy the world a Coke, and teach it harmonyyyy . . . I'd like to buy the world a Tang, because my name's Perselyyy . . ."

"That's so mean," Boone said.

The cove was deserted except for a man fishing near the bank, knee-deep in the water. Thigh waders and a shirt with cutoff sleeves. I could barely make out his features. A black ponytail, a goatee.

"Catching anything?" Boone called.

The man held up a stringer of fish, a bunch of bait stealers. Sunfish, probably. We would have thrown them back.

But we waved at him anyway, giving him a thumbs-up, because the day was sunny and the water was perfect and our mother was slowly coming back to life.

We drifted back and forth for half an hour. The man caught several more little fish. The sun beat down on my head. Boone squinted at the shore, his eyes moving back and forth.

"Persely's not coming, Boone," I said at last. "I'm sorry."

He lowered his head. "I don't understand," he said softly. "I could help her."

I felt bad about my earlier song, and so I said, "Of course you could."

"Of course you could," Meg echoed. She was looking at the fisherman.

"Well," I said. "We might as well go for a swim, right?"

"I guess," said Boone at last in a defeated voice. He lowered the anchor, took off his glasses and dove into the lake. Meg went next, her wide bottom disappearing into the green water, then her pale legs and feet. I dove down deep, feeling the all-over Jell-O embrace of a lake whose chill is kept a secret from the hot, shining surface. Instead of pushing back up for the surface, I swam down deeper. It felt good to work my arms and legs and force the breath into my lungs, and I swam down until I could grasp a handful of green plants and carry them back with me. I broke the surface and held the plants above my head triumphantly.

Boone looked at me, treading water and squinting, his hair plastered around his head. "I can do that, too."

"Show me, then."

I watched him dive. The seconds slowed as they passed and I let my breath in and out carefully, waiting for him.

Finally he broke the surface, his smile dripping lake water and green slime clenched trophy-like in one hand.

Boone and I swam farther out and began diving again, competing over who could go deepest, while Meg dog-paddled out toward the east side of the cove.

Deep below the surface, I opened my eyes. The water roared and rocked, endless green against my face, full of black particles. I tried to put out my tongue to test their composition, but too much breath escaped. My hands reached through cold water, fussed in black loam, found a plant. Pulled until the lake bottom released it with a sound muffled by the lake's sheer weight. I pushed my feet against this valley of loam and ascended. I reached the surface at the same time Boone did. We looked at each other, waved our green trophies. Turned around to mark the progress of Meg.

Our mouths fell open. Our fists released the green plants. Our mother had disappeared.

I rubbed the water out of my eyes and looked again. "Boone, where is she?"

Out of the corner of my eye I saw the fisherman's black waders lying on the bank. The man himself was in the water, swimming hard in full dress toward the center of the cove, where we saw Meg's head briefly emerge and then disappear again.

We froze for just a moment before we hurled ourselves in the direction of our mother and swam with all our fury. My arms pumped and my legs kicked, my lungs aching for oxygen. When Boone and I stopped, gasping, in the middle of the cove, the man had already beaten us to the spot where Meg had disappeared. He dove underwater, and when he came back up, Meg was wrapped around him, grasping at him, coughing. She clawed at his face, then reached around his head and seized his ponytail as he grimaced.

Boone and I treaded water, unsure of what to do. The man started towing Meg to shore, her head in the crook of his arm, and we followed him. Boone and I waded to the bank as the man was laying her down. She had stopped struggling and lay very still. Her skin had turned a light shade of blue.

"Mother," I said.

Boone tried to kneel down next to her, but the man suddenly lunged at him, pushing him back so hard that he fell backward on the bank. I helped Boone up and we crowded close, watching the man work on her. He pressed on her chest. Water ran out of her mouth. He pressed again. More water. I felt as though my own brain were full of water, and each time he pressed on Meg's chest, pressure would leave my skull and my thoughts would clear briefly. We stood there, watching, until there was no water left in her. She coughed as the man supported her head and neck. The rubber band that held his ponytail had been pulled so far down that his black hair hung forward around his face.

"Ma'am?" he said. "Ma'am?"

By this time Boone and I had sunk to our knees.

"Meg!" we said, just as loudly.

Finally she opened her eyes. She didn't look at us. She looked at him. She smiled vaguely.

"I'm tired," she said.

"I'll bet," said the man. The words came out in an exaggerated Texas drawl: *All bet*. He still had his arms behind her head and neck; my mother rested her head in his lap.

"What happened?" Meg asked.

He arched his eyebrows. "You don't 'member? You was drowning. You grabbed ahold of me out there."

"I did?"

"You got some fight left in you."

The man's voice was a silky thing. Silky as the plants at the bottom of a lake. I didn't like the way he held my mother, or the way he'd pushed Boone down. I didn't like his ratty black ponytail. I hadn't liked him dry and I didn't like him wet. Somehow it wasn't the near-drowning that had spoiled our perfect day but the man himself.

"You saved me," Meg whispered. "You saved me."

"Had a fish on the line," the man said. "Catfish, by the pull of it. Damn thing swam off and took my pole down with it."

"You lost your pole to save me?" Meg said.

The man smiled. "It was my sacrifice."

I would come to hate that word.

Chapter Three

My name is Simon Jester," the man said. He looked up at us. "And what might be your names, kids?"

"Alice," I said reluctantly. I pointed. "And that's Boone."

"Well, Alice and Boone, you two sure swim good. I was watching you before your mama went under. Like a couple of sharks, you are. I wish my boy had been a better swimmer . . ." His voice trailed off.

Meg's breath had regained its deep and steady rhythm, and she slowly extracted herself from the man's arms. She twisted around to him, frowning.

"You have a son?"

"Used to." He wiped a stray hair back from his face. "I used to have a beautiful little boy and a wife, too."

"Not anymore?" Meg asked hopefully.

He looked away, toward the blazing sun. A rut appeared between his eyes. "They both passed on. I'm sorry, ma'am, but I can't talk about it. Some things are still too hurtful."

"I understand," said Meg, but her eyes were bright and her smile was back. I knew that she was struggling not to yip with glee about this dead wife. "You saved me," she said.

"No, ma'am. I didn't save you." He pointed up at the sky. "It was God in heaven."

"Yes," said Meg. "God." In complete agreement. If the man had said, *I didn't save your life, a large green kanga-roo helped drag you to shore,* Meg would have had the same smile on her face.

Boone said, "I believe in God, too."

"Do you, son?" the man said. His tone was curious, almost a snarl. He stood up and shook Boone's hand. "Well, you seem like a nice young man. Sorry 'bout pushing you away. I was just so worried about your mama." The man never took his eyes off Boone as he spoke. It was late in the day, and the shadows were playful enough to mask intentions and disorient signals and moods, but I could have sworn that in that glance I saw contempt and even hatred.

He looked back down at Meg. "And your husband. Is he a religious man?"

"I don't have a husband. He left."

"Well, ma'am, if you don't mind me saying, any man's a fool who'd leave you."

Meg couldn't have looked happier. Part of me wondered if she would suddenly leap back into the water and drown herself again, just to bask a bit longer in this man's attentions.

Simon Jester helped Boone and me get Meg into the boat. Her swimsuit had gathered into the crease of her cheeks, and as she stood up, her hands flew back to correct this embarrassment. She sat down on the middle seat of the boat and swiped at her wet hair. Rubbed under each eye in search of renegade mascara.

"Hey, Meg," said the man. "What's your last name?"

"Fendar."

"You in the phone book?"

Meg gave a strange, high giggle. "Yes," she said. "But our phone is still in my husband's name. Dan Fendar. F-e-n-d-a-r."

The man winked at her. "Someday he'll come crawling back to you on his belly." He smiled. "But maybe someone else will be in his place."

He pushed the boat off the shore.

Boone got the engine started and we glided back to the warm delight of a Saturday afternoon, passing the stretch of glassy green water that, fifteen minutes before, had covered my mother's head. Meg waved at the man on the bank, who was inspecting his string of sunfish again.

"Do you think he'll call?" she asked.

"Bet on it," I said.

Simon Jester called my mother that very afternoon, and she immediately invited him over for dinner. I stared down the table at him, my view obscured, at times, by the red rose he'd brought my mother. It was stuck in an empty Dr Pepper bottle, its bud tightly folded around itself. As tightly as my own arms were folded across my chest.

Simon's hair had been dressed with some kind of oil and gathered back into a tight ponytail. He looked over at me. "My little boy didn't eat much neither," he said. "Barely picked at his food. And he was so stubborn, you couldn't tell him nothing."

His eyes filled with tears. Boone looked grieved. Meg pressed Simon's arm.

"I'm so sorry," she whispered. "About your little boy. And your wife."

"That's the way of God," said Simon. "He gives, and He takes away."

"He does both," said Meg.

"I think He gives more than he takes away," said Boone.

"Is this going to turn into a God rally?" I asked. "Because I'm leaving if it does." Somewhere out in the backyard, the fragments of my sacrificial marble glowed green in early moonlight.

The others ignored me. "Simon," asked my mother, "where do you work?"

He put down his fork and wiped his mouth, bending forward as he did so. He twirled his napkin until it made a twisty thing, and then laid it down on his lap. "I am God's megaphone."

Meg clapped her hands. "That's such a beautiful-sounding job!"

"What does that mean?" I asked.

"Religious-type work," he said. "You see, I used to sell cars. I was the best car salesman on the lot. But you know what they say about car salesmen. A lot of that is true. There was some . . . deceivin' going on. After . . . the tragedy . . . I started thinking about things different. I couldn't lie to people no more about engines and mileage and so forth. So I took to telling people about God instead. Helping people with their troubles. Counseling. I'm part of a church. *Affiliated,* they call it."

"Pay much?" I asked.

"Alice!" my mother said.

Simon smiled. "Not too much," he said. "And I do without a lot. But doing God's work is better than, say, wearing fancy shoes or eating in a fancy restaurant."

"That's beautiful," my brother said.

"God's work," Meg said, entranced.

And so Simon Jester entered the heart of Boone and Meg, while my heart remained resolutely hard. Perhaps because I trusted my father and he had left. Perhaps because I was eleven years old. Perhaps because I'd already been to one yahoo of a counselor and didn't want another sitting at our table. Perhaps because of Simon's greasy hair, or his close-set eyes that squinted in all variations of light. He gave me an unsettling chill, as though I'd swallowed the coldest marble from a set of Chinese checkers.

Boone had no such reaction. He and Simon talked about God, and Boone showed Simon his proudest possession— the butterfly collection.

The Laird twins noticed the new activity in our house. They came over in matching sailor suits, glaring at Numbhead as they passed him. Any creature that could hold a smaller, more helpless creature in his mouth day after day without hurting it did not have their affection. Numbhead spat out his toad gently and began pawing the ground behind it, trying to make it jump. The toad looked stunned as it sat dripping with Numbhead's saliva. I could see Lucinda in the distance, on a checkered quilt, one leg straight out and the other folded beneath her.

The boy eyed our trash can longingly.

"Don't even think about going through our trash, you little rat," I said.

He blinked at me. "There's a man coming over to your house."

"Yeah, so what?"

"Is he your boyfriend?"

"No, stupid. I'm eleven years old."

The girl looked around at their sister. "Lucinda is fifteen. And Mama says she'll never have a boyfriend."

"She got hit by lightning while she was riding Bernie," said her brother solemnly. "That was her horse." He fell to his knees. "I'm the horsie," he said.

The girl climbed on her brother's back. "I'm Lucinda." She looked at me. "Be the lightning bolt."

"I don't want to be the lightning bolt."

"I'll be the lightning bolt," said the boy.

"You can't," said the girl. "You're the horsie."

Meg hummed among the bees. Nectar flowed freely. A glut of nectar, more sweetness than ever allotted her. The bees danced around her head, moved as if to sting her, then stopped themselves. Her pale hands darted among them. She wouldn't wear gloves. "It ruins the feeling," she said. Then she leaned down to my ear and whispered: "Like rubbers." I didn't understand, but Meg laughed and laughed.

One night Simon came over with a small leather bag under his arm.

"What's in there?" I asked.

"Shaving stuff," he said meaningfully. "Toothbrush and toothpaste."

Halfway through dinner, he paused. "Kids," he said. "Me and your mother are falling into love. You know that, don'tcha?"

Boone nodded. I remained silent.

"I'm a God-fearing man," Simon continued. "I believe spending the night means something real special. It might even mean the start of a commitment"—Simon pronounced it this way: *committeement*—"so I wanted to tell y'all a story. A story about Simon Jester. How he came to be the man you see today."

Boone and Meg leaned forward, hanging on his every word. As he told the story, I supplemented his words with my own. In my mind I smoothed out his accent, corrected his grammar, deleted his suspense-killing asides, added profound observances, added dialogue and color, added blond hair when none was specified, added music, variations of light, heartbeats, deep breathing, the creaking of limbs, the splash of the lake against the shore, the sighs of fish, the splayed wing shadows of herons swooping down, the tolling of deep-throated bells. I darkened the water. I lightened the skin of the characters involved to a blown-out alabaster. I made Simon's story my story, too, and when it was over, I sat silent with my family, soaking it in.

Simon Jester, happily married and father to one, is basking in a beautiful day on Lake Shine with his wife and child. He's tired because three crickets were calling to him the night before, from three different rooms in the house, and he could find and silence only two of them. He's rented a boat from the marina and has taken it out on the main channel, past coves of swimmers and forests of pine and a smattering of hardwood, he has steered around the tops of rotted pecan trees left over from the flooding of the lake by the Trinity River Authority. Now he has found a quiet place, a little state park with a smooth sloping bank, and he has tied his boat up to an old cedar dock, and he and his wife and child are sitting a few feet from the shore, having a picnic. Peanut butter and blackberry jam sandwiches. Washed down with orange Kool-Aid. The Kool-Aid, somehow, isn't as good as usual, but the sandwiches are fine. His three-year-old boy wears a powder-blue swimsuit with whales across the seat. The child gets his feet wet, then wades in farther so that the water comes up to his fat little knees.

Bluebird sky, the fishermen call it. No clouds, not even filaments of clouds to tickle the geometry of the perfect round sun. The tree line starts a hundred yards behind them. Here on the bank, the family has no shade.

Come over here and eat your sandwich, Simon calls to his son, but the boy ignores him. Instead he pounces on something he sees in the water: a minnow or a quick-witted sunfish. Simon finishes his own sandwich and calls to his son again, a little hurt that the boy is being so disrespectful, after all of Simon's efforts to plan a perfect day.

Simon's wife says: *Go ahead and eat his sandwich. He doesn't want it, Simon.*

She has on a plastic swimming cap to keep her red hair from spilling out. When she smiles, a gap shows between her teeth (my addition), and her toenails are painted red (me again).

A new breeze rustles the boy's blond hair and then sweeps in to shore, carrying a barely felt static, and Simon feels it and recognizes it, like the smallest buzz of a sciatic nerve, the most subtle pang of a trick knee. The sky has grayed slightly and Simon sees one dark cloud, so far in the distance that he isn't worried. He's having a good day with his family, and nothing could be further from his mind than any danger. He looks at his boy again, then leans forward to give his wife a kiss on her red, red mouth. (Meg frowns, taps her foot on the floor. She can't finish her beets until the woman is dead.)

The wind picks up. The boy turns around and Simon can see his eyes, his blond curls slapping against his face. His slightly puzzled expression. Their picnic blanket rises at one corner, and the terry-cloth robe of Simon's wife opens and shows the pale skin of her legs. Now Simon looks anxiously toward the cloud bearing down on his family, followed by other sudden clouds, equally dark.

Let's go home, he says.

No! his boy screams from the shallows. *No! No! I don't want to go home.* (A brat. I picture the Laird twins recruiting him: *Could you throw a cat down a cistern, son?*)

Simon looks at his son's red face, his open mouth and its row of baby teeth are prominent. The boy screams louder. *NOOOOOO! NOOOOO!*

Simon looks at his watch. (In my mind, the watch is a Seiko. Its second hand moves ominously, a quick little dart and then a dead stop. In the manner of a cockroach.) He can hear the wind rushing through the shallow woods behind him, and the cars beyond that, racing along the road that winds around the lake. The smooth blue water has grown waves and froth. A drop of rain hits Simon on the back of the hand. He looks up and the dark part of the sky is almost upon him, black crushing the passive blue, clouds roiling. More drops fall, and his wife hurriedly packs the picnic.

Should we leave? she asks her husband. *Or wait it out here?*

A faithful wife, deferring to her husband's judgment even as the wind takes her napkin.

His worry is for the boat. If he leaves it tied to the old dock, it might break loose, and he would be liable for any damages. He decides that he will take the boat back to the marina as quickly as possible, before the brunt of the storm hits. He thinks he can make it.

Thunder rolls, and lightning hits a power line on the other side of the lake. The water is being jostled rudely, the waves rising and falling.

Get out of the water! Simon yells to his son, but the boy ignores him. Simon wades out, seizes him around his fat waist and screams at his wife: *Get in the boat!*

And the boy screams *NOOOOO!* His face red, his eyes streaming.

Simon follows his wife to the boat with his son struggling in his arms, unties and pushes off, starts the motor and wrestles with the throttle. The scene turns elemental, foam and spray and wind all around. His boy's blond curls are plastered against his head; water drips down his angry face.

Simon presses down on the accelerator steadily, steering around the stumps of the pecan trees.

Simon's wife has lost her hat and her robe is flapping around her and she is holding on to the boy, whose hair is stinging his face.

Slow down! she calls to Simon.

I can't! Storm's getting worse!

His boy turns to face him and screams at the injustice of it all. Later that scream will haunt Simon because it contains no fear, only the rank anger of a three-year-old denied a good time.

So suddenly this chaos. This summer storm out of nowhere. Black water, clear rain, wind, foam, spray, roaring. The sun has disappeared from the sky.

And there is a stump ahead of Simon. One he doesn't see because of the wind and the rain and his wife yelling in his ear and his son screaming at him.

He feels the impact in his knees and his back, and the wheel is jerked from his hand as he and his family and the boat itself fly into the rainy sky. The process of separation has already begun, each member of the family occupying their own dark wet space and the boat spilling seat cushions and sunglasses and picnic supplies as it crashes back into the water. And Simon seems to spend a long time up in that dark sky, his legs out in front of him, his flip-flops knocked off, some color to his left or maybe a voice or maybe he is all alone at this point, maybe his family has already fallen into the water, his boy so far from the arms of his wife, and both the boy and the woman lost somewhere in the churning water. Are they calling his name?

Simon falls. Racing the rain that falls with him, the world upside down and lit up by lightning, he falls into the lake, it slaps his face darkly and invites in a red color, slimy red like the blood of cut fish, and he is profoundly dizzy in this swirl of red that is really the struggle of his mind to bring itself back to quick thinking, but of course it is too late for quick thinking. He flails in the water, through the rain, looking for his family, for the woman he had met in the parking lot of a supermarket, for the little boy whose kicks Simon had once felt as his wife sat on an ottoman and moved his hand across her stomach. He screams the names of his wife and his son, turning around and around in the water. In these names are contained the entire normalcy of his life. His eating. His shaving. His uneventful sleep. And yet no one answers these names with a returning shout.

The rain has slacked off and he looks around in the water for boats. *Help! Somebody help us! Somebody help us!*

He sees a boat in the distance. Have they seen the accident? They must have, because it seems the boat is coming toward them, but moving slowly through the waves. There is no sign of Simon's wife, but suddenly he sees a blond head bob up from the water.

Simon calls his son's name and begins crawling toward him through the water, but something's wrong with Simon's arms and legs. They spasm, full of agony. He reaches for his son, but the boy is too far away.

Wait. Wait, wait, wait.

The boy's head goes under.

The boat draws nearer. Simon continues his desperate search, writhing in the water. *Wait,* he calls. *Wait, wait, wait!*

The red color drains out of Simon's head and leaves it clear. Empty of triangular waves, of hard rain or fast lightning. Just a transparent liquid space, something that could hold a colony of Sea-Monkeys or keep a patch of lilies afloat. The absence of sound. Of sensation. Of fear. In the clarity of unconsciousness, no emotions float. Anger needs color and so does hysterical grief.

When he wakes up, he is in a hospital. Something is measuring the beats of his heart. A needle comes out of his arm.

Back out on the lake, the water is calm now. The afternoon nearly over. A diver cries on the deck of a sheriff's boat. Two bodies lay covered by tarp. The sheriff wearily says into his radio speaker: *We got 'em both.*

Simon's hospital sheets are white and this counts as a color. And so he falls apart.

A minister comes to the hospital and Simon howls at him like a wolf, pushing up against the restraints on his arms. The minister says: *God gives, and God takes away.*

When they finally send Simon home, he sits on the kitchen floor for a week. Then he goes to bed and lies there day after day. The ceiling fan turns. The daily paper lands. Dogs bark. Neighbors care.

Somehow during the accident, the nail of his index finger was peeled down to the quick—a minor and almost mocking injury—and by the time the nail has grown back far enough that Simon can use it to scratch at the beard crawling down his neck, a condolence letter comes in the mail. It includes a picture of his boy someone took at a family reunion two months before the storm. Those eyes and those blond curls. That girlish smile. The picture both destroys Simon and comforts him. He stares at it for a long time before he decides to live for that bright-eyed boy who was so full of life himself.

And so he lives. He dedicates his life to God, and he never cuts his hair again. In remembrance of his dead family, he lets it grow long.

We all sat there silently when Simon was finished speaking. Boone was crying, and Meg looked as though she'd been struck by a freight train. She put her hand on Simon's arm.

"That's the saddest story I ever heard."

"I'm sorry you had to hear it."

"You poor, poor man."

"Well, now, every man's got a sad story."

"Not that sad," Meg said firmly. "And . . ." Her voice became a whisper. "I know what it's like to lie in bed for weeks and weeks."

"That's right," said Simon tenderly. "You had a tragedy, too. When your husband skedaddled."

"Oh, that was nothing compared to what happened to you."

Simon's voice was so silky-smooth. "It's probably worse for you," he said. "Because I knew my wife still loved me. She didn't abandon me. She got took from me. The loss of your husband was probably worse because it made you feel unloved."

"Yes, unloved," Meg agreed fervently.

"I can't never go back to that state park," said Simon. "I do my fishing from the coves."

"I don't remember hearing about a boat wreck on Lake Shine that summer," I said.

"Alice!" Boone said. "People die on Lake Shine all the time."

I sat there squinting at Simon, my arms folded. It was a tragic story, to be sure, though something didn't seem quite right about it. Not right at all. I could sense Meg and Boone looking at me reproachfully through their tears. But those two were easy prey.

A girl of savage faith has sharper instincts.

Chapter Four

The hydrangeas in the front garden had bloomed a stunning pink when Simon showed up in a denim suit and ankle boots and asked my mother to marry him. King of grand flourishes, Simon had even summoned Numbhead inside the house to sit in the kitchen and hear the big proposal.

"I know that hound dog means a lot to you, Meg," Simon said. "Staying by your side those two months you were crazy and what have you."

Simon got down on one knee at the dinner table and, as I stared at the moles along his hairline, proclaimed his love for my mother. She was the best thing to ever happen to him and (Numbhead, sit!) she was the sexiest woman in the world, a great cook, mother to two great kids (Numbhead, sit!), a great beekeeper and the only person who could possibly begin to replace his (someone throw that fucking dog out of the house!) poor drowned sweetheart.

Simon wiped the sweat from his face as I shoved a heartbroken Numbhead out the kitchen door. "I'm sorry, honey," Simon said to Meg, "about using that bad word. It's just that dog was throwing me off my timing."

"It came out wonderful," Meg sighed.

"I'm not done," Simon said. He looked over at Boone and me, and I saw the same strange look of contempt on his face that he'd worn that day at the lake. *"Others,"* he continued, still looking over at us, "are not pure in their love. They will *betray* me."

"We wouldn't betray you, Simon!" Boone protested.

"Of course not," said Simon. "I was simply looking at you and your sister like you was all *the other people* in the world." He turned his gaze back to my mother and took her hand. "But you, Meg . . . You are the only person in the whole damn world that would never betray me. You and me are like Adam and Eve. In you I put my trust, my heart, my whole body and everything. Do you understand me, Meg? Do you understand how much I trust you?"

"I understand," said Meg solemnly.

"And you love me, right? Above all others?"

"Above all others," said Meg. "Except my children."

Something seemed to freeze in Simon. I looked closely at him and saw a line between his eyes. His face had turned a deep red, and the muscles in his jaws bulged. I imagined his teeth grinding together. Boone and I exchanged glances.

"What did you say, Meg?" Simon asked, his voice tight.

"I said 'except my children.'"

Simon stared at her a minute, the tension building, but then he seemed to gather himself. His jaw relaxed but his eyes were hard. "That's a natural motherlike instinct, Meg. Natural." He took a deep breath. "Would you do me the honor of becoming my wife?"

"I will! I will!" Meg shouted.

Simon pulled Meg down onto the floor with him, the weight of her body pushing him backward, and they kissed fervently as I thought desperately of another man, *any* other man, Meg could have. My father. The blind Fuller Brush salesman. The lead singer of Three Dog Night. Or maybe Mr. Walt, even with those three strikes against him: his bad heart, his resolutely tragic luck, his undying love for his long-dead wife.

As Boone and I tried to sleep that night, we heard Simon and Meg in the next room together. Their bed slid across the floor. The headboard banged. My mother moaned. I tried to cover my ears, but to no avail.

"Ohhh," Meg said through the wall.

Boone rolled his eyes. "Do they have to be so loud?"

"Well, he is God's megaphone."

"Why don't you like him, Alice?"

"Because he's evil."

"How can you say that? I like him. And Meg and Numbhead like him."

"Those two don't count. Numbhead would have licked Charles Manson's face while Meg was shaving her head for him." I fell silent, frustrated at my inability to communicate to Boone exactly what I found so unsettling about Simon. There was something in that man beneath the surface.

Rage. That's what I saw in his eyes, his face, his gestures. And although he had never raised his voice, and his movements were slow and careful, I could not shake the feeling that he was biding his time.

Persely Snow escaped again in early June. Boone's eyes lit up when he read the newspaper. Under the headline— CAN ANY WALLS HOLD HER?—the story unfolded. She had somehow broken the security lock on the service elevator and slipped out a back door. She crawled up a fence topped with barbed wire and escaped through a field in her bare feet, leaving a small swatch torn from her hospital uniform dangling from the fence. (I imagined Persely darting through the field with her blond hair flying behind her, the cows backing up nervously, *Watch your cud, it's the poisoner*).

Farther down on the page were brief interviews of people who had run into Persely the last three times she escaped, together with pictures. The remarks of a woman whose hair was Pentecostal-style and who squinted up from a recliner: "The girl came by and asked for a drink of water. She had her nuthouse clothes on. Weird front teeth and pretty hair. She was kooky as a bat but polite as could be. She asked if I knew who she was and I said, sure, you're Persely Snow. You're famous. She said, I am? And I said, Come on girl, you know you are. She shrugged and drank her water and asked if there was any clothes she could wear. Well, my daughter just went off to college, and she had some old jeans and T-shirts in her closet. A couple pair fit Persely perfect. Plus I got her some huarache sandals for her poor bare feet. Before she left I asked her, Why'd you do it, honey? And she said, Escape? And I said,

No, honey. Why'd you poison your folks? And she said to me—and I won't forget the look on her face—she said, 'We all have our ghosts, Marshal. You hunt your way and I'll hunt mine.'"

"That's from *Hang 'em High*," Boone said.

"Makes perfect sense, then," I said.

"I've got to take out an ad," Boone said.

Later on in the day we heard Simon's car in the driveway. He entered the den eating an apple turnover and wiping the sweat off his face. He sat down in a recliner and put up his feet. Since he'd asked Meg to marry him, he never rang the doorbell anymore.

Boone and I were watching *Marcus Welby, M.D.,* with the volume down low.

"Where's your mother?" he demanded.

"Out selling honey."

"Wanna bring me the paper?"

I sighed and retrieved the paper from the kitchen and dropped it in Simon's lap, glancing again at the headline as I did so: CAN ANY WALLS HOLD HER?

Simon Jester sneered. "So she's out again," he said. "I 'member when that craziness happened." His voice turned serious. "What that girl did is the worst sin of all. What they call an *a-bom-i-nation.* Do you kids understand that?"

"Sure we do, Simon," I muttered, only half listening.

"A double murder," said Simon.

"She just killed one parent," I said. "The other one lived."

"Might as well have killed them both. Once you do something in your heart, it's done. Don't you *understand* that God orders children to serve the mama and the daddy?

And to love the mama and the daddy? And did you know that the Bible says to spare the rod and spoil the brat?"

I had a quick, enjoyable vision of the twins being knocked around with a stick, but there was an edge to Simon's voice, one that I was just beginning to associate with his mood when the weather was hot and the sun beat down. I turned around and looked at him. He was looking back at us with a hostile expression. That line appeared in the flesh between his eyes.

The doorbell rang. Simon didn't move, so I answered it. Two policemen were on the other side. They appraised me coolly, as if trying to decide whether I was old enough to bother intimidating. Meanwhile Simon came up behind me.

"What's the problem, Officers?" His voice silky again.

"Is there a Boone Fendar living here?"

"Why, yes sir, there is. But you must have made some mistake. He's just a kid." Simon motioned the men inside. "That's Boone," he said, pointing.

Boone was still absorbed in the television. I had to pull on the sleeve of his shirt to get him to turn around, and when he did, he leaped to his feet.

"Are you Boone?" asked the officer.

"Yes."

Simon's eyes were spooky things, moving from Boone and then back to me. The brown color in them pulsated, or so it seemed.

One of the officers pulled an envelope out of his shirt pocket and slowly unfolded it. "You been writing Persely Snow, Boone?" the officer asked. He said her name so hatefully that I knew all of her insults about the police had reached his ears.

Simon's mouth dropped open. He stared at Boone.

"Yes, I have," said Boone.

"Why?" asked the officer.

Boone was silent for a moment. He scuffed his feet and I desperately wanted to say something in his defense. "I just wanted her to know," he said, "that God still loves her."

The officer laughed. "God, huh? You know, reading this letter—and all the other ones—it sounds more like *you* love her."

Boone's face turned red.

"And we noticed you always included your home address in the top left-hand corner of the envelope. Hoping for a visit, maybe?"

Boone didn't answer.

"Persely Snow escaped yesterday. Have you seen her?"

"No."

The officer took a step closer to him. "Would you tell us if you had, boy?"

Boone wasn't good at lying, so I lied for him. "Of course he would. He used to be in Boy Scouts."

But the officer was glowering at Boone. "Do you think this girl is some kind of movie star? Do you think it's *funny* what she did to her parents? Do you know what it's like to die of *cyanide* poisoning?"

Simon stepped in smoothly. "Now, Officers. Y'all are looking at a boy who don't have a lot of friends. I think he was just lonely. He's never had a girlfriend, and I think his imagination just plumb ran away from him. That's not a crime, is it?"

"And who might you be?" asked the officer.

"I'm his father," said Simon. "And I'm telling you personally, on my honor, on my Bible, that Persely Snow has never been nowhere around our house."

The officer regarded him a moment. I was about to be privy to the first taste of Simon's persuasive powers, because the look on the officer's face softened.

"She gets letters," he admitted, "from all over the country. But we know that this boy's been writing her for a long time—and all her mail *is* read before she gets it—and that makes him a little more interesting to us. Plus, this house isn't more than thirty miles from the hospital."

"I haven't seen her," Boone said. His voice took on a great sadness. "She's never answered my mail. Not once."

"Well, son," said the officer, "how about getting a more appropriate girlfriend? Someone who can get through a meal without killing someone?"

"Yessiree," Simon said jovially. "He should certainly do that!" He went over to Boone and clapped him on the shoulder, flashing a smile at the officers.

The tall one spoke. "So, Boone, you'll call us if you see her?"

"Of course he will," I said hastily. "I'll make sure he does."

"We all will," said Simon.

The officers left. Behind us, *Marcus Welby, M.D.,* was ending with someone dying and Dr. Welby shaking his head sadly. Simon lifted the drape high and peered into the front yard, watching as the policemen drove away.

He turned, went over to the television and turned it off, stood before a blackness that buzzed like a dying bee.

"You're writing that girl?" Simon whispered. "Are you crazy, too, boy? She giving you ideas? You think it's Christian that she poisoned her own parents? You think *God* will forgive that?" His face had transformed into the most baleful expression I had ever seen.

Boone didn't answer him. He seemed frozen in place, transfixed by Simon's eyes.

"Boone just wants to save her soul," I explained weakly.

"Writing a girl who killed her parents is a betrayal to all parents," Simon said. The look on his face chilled me to the bone. "And every betrayal," he added, "calls for a sacrifice." With that, Simon turned and walked out the door. We went to the window and watched him head toward the backyard.

"What's he doing?" I asked.

Boone's eyes were glassy. I tugged on his arm and finally got him to walk into the kitchen. We looked out the back window.

Simon was building a fire on our burned-out trash pile, using branches and leaves. It took a while to get it going, but soon the flames were shooting up into the sky.

"I don't understand," I said.

Simon walked back to the house. He came in through the back, passing us in the kitchen. We heard him moving around in the back of the house, then he reentered the kitchen with something in his hands.

Boone's butterfly collection.

"What are you doing?" Boone gasped, but Simon ignored him. We followed him outside, calling to him.

"Simon, Simon." Desperation in our voices.

When he reached the fire, he turned around. "Every betrayal," he said again, "calls for a sacrifice."

"Please," I said, "Boone won't write Persely anymore."

Simon broke the glass frame over his knee, scattering the dead butterflies. He leaned over, picked up a monarch by its one remaining wing, and dropped it in the fire.

"No!" Boone rushed forward and Simon pushed him back. "Don't even think of it, boy," he said. By the light of the fire, his features seemed demonic. He sifted through the glass, found something that had once flown high and yellow, and dropped it into flames equally bright. I watched the butterfly curl and blacken.

Boone put his hands over his face.

"How could you do this, Simon?" I said.

"To show you what happens when people go to hell. Like people who kill their own parents." I stood there watching him, because Boone couldn't look and couldn't move, either.

"I'll let you in on a secret, kids," said Simon. A gust of wind caught a swallowtail, made it seem almost alive, then carried it to a second death. "It weren't no accident I was at Lake Shine that day. You see, I was lookin' in the classifieds for a fishing rod and I ran across this sweet little ad. 'To P.S. No walls can hold you, but *God's love can*.' I thought to myself, who's the dumb-ass preacher who thinks God loves Persely Snow? Being a preacher myself, I just had to see. So I showed up at Hollow Cove at noon just to get a look at this dumb-ass. But there weren't no man there. Just a boy. Just you and your stupid sister and your stupid mama who can't swim worth a shit." Sweat dripped down Simon's face. "I didn't know you was *writing* her, too, Boone. You're learning tricks from her, ain'tcha? You made a fool of me. You turned on me, like children do. You betrayed me, like children do. The chil-

dren are always gonna turn on the daddy. Always, always."
Simon leaned forward. "Unless," he whispered, "they
drown first."

Simon turned and walked away. We heard his car start
up in the driveway and roar down the road. Boone's hands
were still over his face. I touched his knuckle.

"Boone, are you okay?"

He made no answer, just stood there, his eyes covered
and his body shaking uncontrollably. I didn't say what I
was thinking—that Boone's classified ad had accomplished its goal. It had attracted a monster.

Persely Snow was caught the next day, in a farmer's
grain silo in Vidor, Texas, wearing a midriff gingham
blouse, cutoffs and desert boots given to her by a teenage
fan. She put up a fight, blackening one officer's eye and
splitting another one's lip. An embarrassed hospital admin-
istration replaced four of the guards and added new locks.
Certain privileges were taken from Persely Snow, and her
room and person were subjected to twice-daily searches.

Meanwhile, the style and color of Persely's blouse became a rage among teenage girls. Mrs. Laird even bought
one for Lucinda. I saw her wearing it as she sat on a lawn
chair in the early morning, a lap robe over her knees.

I begged Boone to let me tell Meg what had happened.
"I'm telling you, Simon is evil."

"No," he said. "He's a man of God. I just made him
mad, that's all."

"Oh, please!"

"And Meg's so happy. Remember when she was sad?
We can't let her go back to being that way. She'll die."

I looked at Boone narrowly. "Maybe we'll die."

"Oh, come on, Alice."

Boone hid all his pictures of Persely in his room, including the one he had clipped from the paper and photocopied. His fear of Simon Jester was obvious. He avoided him when possible, and his eyes twitched when Simon spoke to him. But Boone stubbornly refused to join me in my hatred. "He's had a horrible tragedy," he would say. "Some men don't take that too well."

Unconvinced, full of hatred, I began my war on Simon Jester, the battle to heave him out of my mother's life before the wedding. My mother and father had once gone to a Wayne Newton concert in California and had brought back a feather. I stuck this feather in my hair as a lonely declaration of unrest.

"Come on, Boone," I said, bent on recruiting him for the new army. "You hate him, too." We were rocking on the cypress glider, watching two bees circle each other.

"God says you shouldn't hate."

"You should be mad at God. His megaphone burned your butterflies."

He was silent, staring off into space, and I knew he was thinking of Simon's drowned son. Boone, who saw innocence and light in all children—even in the twins— had been tormented by the story of the little boy playing knee-deep in calm water. I knew this because he'd been having nightmares about it. "There's something good in Simon," he said at last.

"Good? What could be good in him?"

"There must be something. We'll find it."

"I don't want to find it. Why don't you just write your girlfriend? Tell her she can even poison Simon by mail. Return postage guaranteed."

He jerked his legs out straight so the glider reared back like something ready to pounce. "I swear, sometimes you go too far. You really do."

I didn't listen to him. Instead I began to get back at Simon Jester, my desperate campaign filled with a million tiny guerrilla acts. A campaign only an eleven-year-old could run, full of ridiculous hope and stunning helplessness.

I first attacked Simon on the level of magic. Late at night, under moonlight or starlight, Numbhead tripping by my side, I went out into the backyard, through the bee yard to the edge of our property, holding some prized possession that I had just destroyed, ready to throw it to my savage god. An onyx ring shattered by the hammer. An Etch A Sketch broken with that same hammer. My Easy-Bake Oven (which I had outgrown, anyway) reduced to plastic and metal by a handheld ax. I tried to break all the pieces in my Barrel of Monkeys set. They simply bent in rebellious red silence so that I had to hit them repeatedly to bring about their ruin. The antique bisque doll my great-aunt Garnet had given me for my birthday was hardest to part with. But I did, blackening her face with a Bic lighter so that it looked like that of a pioneer woman exposed to harsh conditions.

If someone had come along and shaken that holly bush, they would have seen the evidence of my desperation. Dolls without arms, useless jacks, Lincoln Logs, Play-Doh left out to dry, broken crayons. All my deliberately destroyed possessions. These were the sacrifices I made in the dead of night, to the winding god of fate, to the mass of circumstances that has no conscience or ability to love but responds to spoken commands like a dead frog's leg jerks at a surge of electricity. Boone's God, on the other hand, was fully formed of flesh and grace; He roared out of the Bible to love crazily; He knew the number of the hairs on my head; He counted my cells; He knew my every thought and monitored my beating heart. A diving, twirling God, athletic in His mercy and His rage.

I didn't like this God. He was too indiscriminate, the way He loved both Boone and Simon.

My own god was stripped down to simple command and simple response, the payment and the deed.

Get rid of Simon, I barked to the open moonlight, my teeth bared, my treasures flung into the holly bush, Numbhead sniffing at the air. As my possessions cleared from my room, as the sacrifices grew bigger, so did my requirements. *Kill him,* I said to the moon, and when the moon faded, I repeated to the stars, *Kill him, kill him, kill him.* The use of this magic horrified and strengthened me, and I felt myself grow ever savage beneath my T-shirts, inside my ankle socks and my Keds. I felt beastlike, masculine.

I tried to keep Simon disoriented, destroy little parts of him, tear him down. I rose in the dead of night and unplugged the air conditioner until not just Simon was bathed in sweat, but my mother and brother were sweating as well. I captured a half-dozen fierce-looking bees in a jar and let them loose in Simon's two-tone Chevy. I dabbed mayonnaise on his rearview mirror. I added hair remover to the shampoo he used on his wretched black hair. I hid his socks. I went to the hamper and pulled threads I found on his shirt. I mixed Tabasco sauce into his lemonade. I watered down his cologne until it was as scentless as the water in a steam iron.

And I continued to sacrifice my treasures under the night sky, turning to that holly bush as if it were a father and I could beg it for shelter. Wind came through my shirt, crickets sang in the grass. Numbhead stood by my side, calmer and less beastly and more reasonable than me. Some maniacal go-cart had knocked out of him all dread, all worries, all fear and suspicion, and now he stood by me, grinning at my unseen reluctant god, for Numbhead didn't need him.

My maneuvers were starting to affect my stepfather-to-be. The hair remover ruined a patch of shiny hair just above his ear, so that when he put his hair in a ponytail, a spray of it stuck straight out from his head. One of the bees I'd put in the car stung him. And he'd frowned when he'd tasted the Tabasco-laced lemonade. He peered at me. He was a man for whom things didn't quite fit. His socks had unraveled and he was too hot at night and his hair was looking ratty and his neck itched. When the weather was particularly hot, that line formed between his eyes and he looked at me as though he wanted to kill me for some vague, hot reason.

I was eleven years old. I savored these sad victories. In my mind, Simon would simply find our house unsuitable. Then he would drive away from us forever, and I would ask my bush god to send Meg another man.

Listen, Boone," I said one night, sitting up in bed, "I've been thinking about it a long time, and I think that drowned-family story is a giant crock of shit."

"Come on. Not that again."

"Wait. Listen to me. I finally figured out what doesn't fit. They were having a picnic on Lake Shine, right?"

"Right."

"At that state park by the Baptist camp. Where the trees are set back. What does that mean?"

Boone shrugged.

"It means no shade, Boone. And it was summertime. His wife had on a terry-cloth robe, and remember, the crickets were bothering Simon the night before."

"So?"

"So, Simon is sitting on the shore in the summertime with no shade. And not a cloud in the sky, remember? So he's hot . . ." I crept over to my brother's bed. "Don't you see it?" I whispered. "The kid's playing in the water. Being a brat. He won't come in when Simon calls him. And then he throws a big fit when the storm's coming, because he wants to play longer. And Simon lets the kid have his way. Is that what you think the real Simon would have done, in the heat of the summer, no shade?"

Chapter Five

One afternoon the girl twin looked out her bedroom window and saw me dragging my fingernail scissors down the side of Simon's car. I had grown bolder. Scratches had become long lines stretching toward one another. A latticework of righteous anger.

I heard the phone ring inside the house, but I paid no attention. Simon suddenly stormed out of the house and seized my arm. The scissors went flying as he jerked me around to face him.

"You!" he said. "You're the one!"

I glanced over at the house across the road. The girl twin

still had the phone in one hand and was waving at me from the window.

Simon didn't hesitate. He went into the garage and came out with the very bat our family—the original, peaceful one—had once used in softball. He charged into the house with me hot on his heels, didn't stop until he reached our bedroom. The bat swung. Statues of Indians broke in half. Clouds of plaster of paris drifted toward the ceiling.

"Stop!" I shouted. "Stop! Stop!"

Meg and Boone came running, Numbhead close behind. Boone and Meg stopped in the doorway, but Numbhead squeezed through, convinced a long-ago game of softball was finally renewing itself. He dived at the head of a famous Cheyenne chief that came sailing toward the far corner, missed it, whined.

"Simon!" Meg screamed. "What are you doing? What are you doing?"

Simon paused. The bat dangled from his fingers, and beads of sweat ran down his face. "Your daughter scratched my car. I'm just teaching her a little lesson about loyalty."

I stared at my broken Indians, too precious even to have been sacrificed to my bush god.

Meg's voice turned sluggish and uncertain. "I don't care what she did. You have no right to wreck her things."

"Then I guess you don't want to get married."

She looked up, her mouth open. "Yesssss. Oh yesssssss, I do."

"I think that's what you're saying, Meg. Just let the kids run wild, huh? Just let them treat me any old way?" His eyes filled with tears. "You ain't my friend. You're poison.

Good-bye. Good-bye forever, my beloved." He dropped the bat, brushed past us all and left the house. The three of us went to the front doorway and watched him screech out of the driveway and zoom off down the road, scattering gravel. Numbhead loped after the car a moment, then circled around and flopped down in front of us. He looked from face to face uncertainly. Deep in the recesses of his brain, the tension shimmered through a nest of neurons but lost initiative. Numbhead rolled on his back and yawned. The twins were now standing in their front yard, craning their necks.

Meg looked down the road. She turned around and her voice was lifeless.

"Go to your room, kids," she said. But my brother wouldn't move. He stood still as a statue.

"Come on, Boone," I said gently. "Time to go."

He shook his head. "I can't move."

It took me thirty minutes to get Boone into the hallway. Later this paralysis would manifest itself more frequently.

Meg froze, too, in her own way. She went back to bed and lay under the sheets, as the ceiling fan turned and more bees died outside in the yard. Poor ventilation. Lack of water. Dead queens.

Out of guilt and love, I tried everything to please her. I brought her food on a calico tray and orange juice in a glass with a Krazy Straw. I read to her from *Life* and *Reader's Digest* and *Redbook*.

Sometimes when Meg looked at me her eyes were soft. And sometimes hard. In her glance and in the growling of her empty stomach, I heard her tearful accusation: *You drove him away, dearie, with your smart-aleckiness and*

*your fingernail scissors and your hatred and all the bitter-
ness of your dead Indian friends.*

Boone took out his pictures of Persely Snow and put
them back up on his wall. He wrote her with impunity.
Kindly words about God's love, very formal on the manila
pages. Increasing passion under the stamp.

Mrs. Laird knew something was amiss in our household. With the selective intuition of the chronically
tragic, she could stand in her front yard and look toward
our house, her gaze missing her diabolical twins, her
slumped-over daughter, the button weed that was bullying
her St. Augustine grass, instead finding our family's need
for immediate intervention. Apparently she called the
sliding-scale doctor, because one day I answered the phone
and it was him.

"How's your mother?"

"Bad again."

He said that she was repeating an old, tired pattern. Simon was really her father, and she was trying to gain back
the love her original father had once denied her, because
the people we meet and love are really none other than our
own parents traveling like ghosts in the bodies of—

I hung up on him.

But the doctor had given me an idea.

"Boone," I said one night. "Simon can't come back if
the space is filled."

"What do you mean?"

"Guess what came in the mail today? Another check
from Daddy the Louse."

"So?"

"It's got a return address."

"So?"

"Don't be stupid, Boone."

Boone and I wanted to make the cleanest presentation possible. We washed and combed our hair carefully and put on our best clothes. I wore an old Sunday dress and a grosgrain ribbon that used to belong to my grandmother. Boone put on chinos and a black shirt that showed sweat under the arms.

"Keep your arms down, Boone," I said.

My father lived in town, somewhere, so Boone and I had to ride our bicycles to town, buy a map at the bus station and take three different buses before we found his street.

The woman who answered our knock was the very same woman we'd seen in the emergency room last fall. Her hair had been clipped short and rolled into severe curls. Her lipstick was brighter, and she seemed shorter. When she spoke, her chilly voice vibrated in us.

"What can I do for you?"

I moved forward. "Remember us?"

"Yes."

"We're looking for our father."

Her shirt was untucked a little from her skirt, and her shoes were a color Meg would not have known was stylish. We stood there and watched the door begin to close inch by inch. Behind us, the sun started sinking.

My father came in from the hallway, and I caught sight of him. The pale, thin, graceful sight of him. I was surprised by the rush of blood through my body from my face, then down in a speeding symmetry to my knees and shins and feet. I felt desperate in his presence. Like my mother who had drowned so that she might be saved by a man. I wanted to grab his hand and pull him down the street, through that maze of unpredictable city blocks, to the bus station, to our house, to the baseball diamond in the back whose bases now served as havens for grub worms.

"Kids," said my father. He wore madras shorts and a loose navy tank top. He elbowed past the woman and opened the door wide, stepping forward to place one hand on top of my head and the other on top of Boone's. I couldn't read his expression: a strange half-smile and eyes that barely connected with us, the look of the man who has smelled a far-off fire and it's made him remember something. Or the look of a man who's been stung by a bee and just discovered that it didn't hurt at all. So many possibilities wavered in this expression. Its sallow neutrality confused and angered me.

"How did you find me?" my father asked.

"By your address. It was on the letter you sent."

My father looked at the woman. "Give me a minute, will you?" he said.

The woman disappeared into the house.

"So what's up?" my father asked.

"Not much," I said. "Bees are dropping dead pretty regular."

"Oh?" My father raised his eyebrows. "Are the twins behind it?"

"More like natural causes, I think." I cut to the chase. "Look, we have to tell you something."

"What is it?"

"Meg needs you."

He sighed, put his hands together. The wind moved, and the shadow from a peach-tree branch crossed his face.

"Meg always needs somebody."

"But Daddy, she's dating a creep. A monster. He's strange, Daddy. We think he killed his family."

"Well," said Boone, "Alice does."

My father looked at me. "What makes you think that?"

"He says they drowned on Lake Shine. I don't believe him."

He hesitated a minute. "Alice," he said. "You've always been a little dramatic."

"Daddy, listen," I said. "He's gone now. Come home with us. Meg's lost weight. And she's wearing makeup again. And she bought some nice new clothes. You can come back to her and she won't mind a bit. And we can be together again."

"Please," said Boone. "We miss you."

My father rocked back on his heels, saying nothing for a long time. There was no breeze. A piece of red fruit dropped from an ornamental tree.

"I can't come back. I don't love your mother anymore. I love someone else." He nodded toward the dark hallway. "And we're getting married."

Boone and I went back up the flagstones, past the mailbox smothered by a passion vine, down the narrow pretty street and to the main thoroughfare, where we waited for a bus. We found our bicycles where we'd hidden them. Branches were tangled in the wheels and we didn't even bother to pull them out, but rode home like that.

* * *

Boone and I knelt in the monkey grass in Spencer Katosky's front garden, our spades busy. It was the day after we'd seen our father, and we didn't talk much.

"Thanks for helping me," I said at last. "I'll pay you half of what I get."

"No, that's okay."

"You thinking about Dad?"

"No." He ducked his head and whispered, "Persely" into a cluster of purple lantana.

"Well, they're both just as likely to come visit us," I said. "And let's see . . . they both have their own special way of saying good-bye to their families."

"Please don't make jokes about Persely," said Boone. "I never make jokes about Spencer."

We continued to work in silence, my own thoughts moving from my father to Spencer Katosky. Spencer hadn't come out in the front yard again after that first time, and since school had let out, I'd been pining for the sight of him. His yard and his garden had taken on a mystical quality to me. I felt as though all the flowers contained the clear, briny fluid of Poland's waterways, and if I followed a strand of buttonweed to its source, I would find as its final root all of Poland's sadness, and I would understand the sadness that lived in the heart of Spencer, some vaguely heirloomed grief that he didn't understand. I wanted some of his grief for myself, and often, as I'd knelt there pulling weeds from his yard and trimming the gentle arc of their ligustrum bushes, I imagined him coming out of the door, making his way toward me, standing so close that I could see the fine pale fuzz on his cheeks. I would tell him things. I would say that my father had left, and though I hated him, I had once found one of his half-done crossword puzzles, and the word *sanctuary* he'd penciled in had not fit in the space, and seeing that word so cramped had brought such tears to my eyes that I had to go to my room. I'd tell him about how Simon had come into our lives. I'd tell him I was afraid of Simon's mystery, that he had left and that my mother was back in bed, and that I was afraid of her mystery, too. This thing that kept her weak and helpless.

Spencer would not look at me in disgust as he heard this. Instead he would take my hand—his would be warm—and he would make me understand everything. My body would be next to his. And I would feel him, every quivering organ in him, his unambitious immune system, his spidery veins, his weak heart.

I knew that my brother was still thinking about Persely Snow as he knelt beside me. I wanted to ask him what the feeling of his love was like. Was it like mine? Did it occupy his thoughts day and night? Did the sight of an open blue sky remind him of her? I gave a contemptuous snort, ripped up a patch of clover by the roots and threw it into the trash bag. Probably not an open blue sky, in Persely's case. More likely an open jar of Tang.

The front door opened, and my heart stopped as I caught sight of him. Spencer approached us cautiously. "How are you guys doing?"

I couldn't speak, so Boone answered.

"Almost done."

Spencer didn't even seem to notice me. He was looking at Boone with something like hero worship in his eyes.

Boone had been quite the star on the swim team. "You swimming this summer?" Spencer asked.

"No. Next summer, maybe."

"What other sports do you like?"

Boone shrugged. "I like soccer. And we used to play softball in the backyard, just our family . . ." Boone's voice trailed off and he looked down.

"Softball?" said Spencer. "I love softball. But no one plays in my family. My brother's too little and my dad has asthma." Spencer whirled around and went back in the house, and I thought that was the end of that. But he returned a moment later with a bat, a mitt and a softball. "Wanna play? I mean, I can pitch and you can bat and maybe your sister can field."

I dropped my spade, alive with the prospect of fielding a ball hit by Spencer Katosky. How it would sing into my mitt and lie there, captured . . .

"Sure," said Boone, and so we walked over to the other side of the yard, where there were fewer trees in the way. We determined that Spencer would pitch and Boone and I would take turns fielding and hitting. I took the mitt from Spencer, backed up into the driveway, and waited for one of Boone's pop flies. Spencer wound up and released the ball in a surprisingly graceful fashion—one small step, like my father. Boone swung his bat, but instead of the ball flying high into the air, it shot toward Spencer and dinged off the side of his head. Spencer went down.

"Oh, God," said Boone.

We ran to him. Spencer lay in the thin grass, his eyes half open, his face paler than I had ever seen it.

"You killed him, Boone!"

"No, I didn't. See, he's waking up."

Spencer's eyelids fluttered. The front door burst open and Mrs. Katosky came rushing out. "Spencer!" she shouted. "Spencer, what happened?" She knelt and cradled her son's head in her lap.

"I'm . . . all right." Spencer tried to sit up. "We were just trying to play softball."

Spencer's mother gave us a look that said: *Why don't you just kill my pale Polish son next time, assholes?*

"We're sorry," I said. Before I could stop myself, I had bent down to Spencer and kissed the swollen place on his head where the ball had hit him. It felt warm and hard under my lips. Mrs. Katosky looked at me as though I were crazy, and Spencer rubbed his eyes. Would he remember the kiss when his head cleared?

"Why'd you do that?" Boone asked as we were walking home. "Why'd you kiss him like that?"

"I don't know," I said. "Why'd you try to kill him?"

"I didn't and you know it! It was an accident!"

But my kiss had made me spirited. "You know what that counselor would have said," I teased. "He would have said Spencer reminded you of Daddy when he was throwing that softball, and you hit him because you're secretly angry."

"Be quiet, Alice."

"Come on, I'm kidding! You couldn't hurt a fly!" And I really believed that there was not one speck of violence in my brother. When I look back at that moment, this total absence of doubt surprises me.

When we returned home, we saw the twins standing in the middle of their front yard with Numbhead.

"Hey!" I shouted. "Get away from our dog!"

Numbhead broke away and came running up to us. We bent down to inspect him. "All right," I growled at the twins. "What did you do to him?" I had a quick, horrible vision of Numbhead being sodomized with the pegs from a Lite Brite set.

"We didn't do anything," said the girl. "We gave him a bath."

"Drop a radio in the tub, by any chance?"

"We taught him a trick," said the boy. "Watch this." He pointed at a dragonfly that was hovering over a patch of clover. "Attack!" he ordered. Numbhead pounced at the creature, opening his jaws wide. The dragonfly flew inside, and Numbhead shut his mouth.

"See?" the girl said.

"That's terrible!" Boone said. "Numbhead's never hurt a living thing in his life."

"He licks his balls a lot," said the girl.

Just then, Numbhead opened his mouth and the dragonfly flew out unharmed, trailing a long filament of saliva that broke as the creature flew away.

"Shit!" cried the girl.

"See?" Boone said. "Numbhead is a saint."

"Don't ever try to teach our dog your evil tricks again, you freaks," I said.

And as though invoked by that spoken word—*evil*— Simon came back two days later, barging in like he always did. Meg lay on the couch in the den. She hadn't eaten in so long she could barely raise her head to see who it was. When she did, she covered her face, embarrassed to be seen in a plain state in front of him.

Simon sank down into the chair my body had recently warmed, his expression benign, his hands clasped. Boone and I remained standing.

"So how are y'all?" he asked.

"Pretty good," I said. "Until just about ten seconds ago."

Simon laughed. "Ah, you crazy girl," he said. He looked at my mother. "And how are you, Meg?"

Meg blinked at him. Her bare feet were sticking over the side of the couch. "You haven't called," she said.

"I wanted to," said Simon. "But I was talking to a friend. Do you know the name of that friend?" He paused. "His name is God."

I snorted audibly.

Simon blinked but kept on. "And God told me: 'Simon Jester, you are a horse's ass. Here you got this beautiful woman and these beautiful kids and you had to go and lose your temper. You're a man, and you represent me. Now, you've gotta go and share with your new family the sorrows of your soul and what have you.'"

Simon made God sound like Foghorn Leghorn, but I kept quiet.

Simon reached into his back pocket and took out two pictures, both of them worn around the edges, and held them to the light for us to see. Meg did not get up but craned her neck forward. Boone and I leaned in to steal a look. One picture showed a pretty woman with a beauty mark on her cheek. The other showed the most beautiful boy I had ever seen. Curly blond hair and blue eyes and a sweet, girlish smile.

"This was my wife and child," said Simon Jester. "My family."

"They were both very beautiful," said Meg.

My brother gazed at the picture of the boy. His eyes watered and his lip trembled.

"Ah, yes, they were," said Simon. "'Specially my boy. My sweet little boy." Simon began to cry. The pictures slid from his fingers to the floor, and Simon covered his face and began to shake. "Ohhhhhhh," he sobbed.

"There, there," said Meg, rising off the couch to kneel beside him, placing a hand on his shoulder.

"I loved my boy! I loved him! And he betrayed me!"

"Betrayed you?" Boone murmured.

Meg the Armchair Psychologist looked at her son wisely. "Simon means his son betrayed him by dying."

Simon finally pulled himself together, wiped his eyes and collected the pictures. "They been dead for three years," he said softly. "And it seems like yesterday. Forgive me, my beloved. I can't live without you."

In response, Meg put her head on his lap, her hair so tangled it handicapped his gentle stroking.

And so Simon Jester came back to us, riding into our lives again, on a white horse, its mane dripping with a drowned family's water. And this time there was nothing I could do about it.

Chapter Six

Simon promised my mother that things were going to be different. He was a new man, really. He taped the picture of his dead son to the wall above the kitchen table so that the blond-haired little boy could watch us pass the pepper or pour the tea. His presence up there disturbed me, his eyes sparkling blue, his predrowned smile tickling at my conscience. But my brother quickly fell in love with this poor boy, and he would gaze with sorrowful eyes at the sweet, pretty face.

Meg had sent out wedding invitations to every single person she knew even remotely—including my father and his new wife—and was disappointed to get only a dozen responses. Four of my aunts came in from North Carolina—Mabel, Laura, Jane and my great-aunt Garnet. My mother's sisters were all soft, dimply, opinion-free women like her; they all had married young and had children and had never once thought of doing something noteworthy. But Aunt Garnet had never married and didn't want to. My grandfather came along as well. My mother had rarely spoken of him, but he had a kindly face and a good-natured smile, and Boone and I immediately liked him.

They all crowded into our small clapboard house, filling up the kitchen and crowding the hallways with their luggage. Simon seemed overwhelmed and subdued by this houseful of visitors, and Boone and I felt safe among so many witnesses. When we sat down at the dinner table that night, I shot Simon a smug little glance.

My mother looked beatific in the circle of her sisters, all gathered around the table with their meaty arms touching.

"Simon is God's megaphone," my mother said suddenly.

My aunts nodded, wide-eyed.

"That's nice," said my grandfather agreeably.

Aunt Garnet swiveled her head and peered at Simon.

"What does that mean?" she asked.

"Well, ma'am," said Simon, "it means that the power of the Lord comes through me. You see, I'm a counselor. I help stray sheep get themselves right again. Drunks. Thieves. Bad women. You see, sin is like poison, and I've got the . . . the . . ."

"Antidote," I said.

Simon glared at me.

"I went to a counselor once, a long time ago," said Aunt Garnet. "I had what they call the change of life and was hating the whole world. This counselor, poor man, had some kind of an itchy crotch. He'd be looking straight at me, and his hand would be sneaking over for a quick scratch. He thought I didn't notice. Doctor Crotch, I called him. He might have had crabs."

"Crabs?" I said.

"It's some little critter in your crotch," Aunt Garnet explained. "And when you go to messing with someone, the critters jump from your crotch to theirs."

Simon threw down his fork, cutting off Aunt Garnet's words and fixing her with a withering glare. "I do all kinds of counseling," he said through gritted teeth. "No matter what the problem."

"All counselors are yahoos, if you ask me."

"You don't know what the—" Simon said sharply, then caught himself. He took a deep breath and said, "I wasn't always a counselor. Something very bad happened to me . . ."

I rolled my eyes.

But Aunt Garnet wasn't listening. She was staring at the picture on the wall. "Who's the little girl?"

"That's a little boy," Simon snapped. "My son."

"Where is he?"

"Dead."

"Oh." Aunt Garnet stabbed at her chicken-fried steak. "How?"

Aunt Jane picked up on the tension and tried to change the subject. "Where are you going for your honeymoon?" she asked Meg.

"Corpus Christi," my mother said. "We're going to wade out in the ocean and pick up shells."

"I got caught in an undertow once," said Aunt Laura. "Off the coast of Florida. It sucked at my feet and dragged me out to sea. A nice young man with bad skin saved me."

"Don't talk about drowning," Simon said meaningfully. "It upsets me."

"He's right," Aunt Garnet said. "Let's talk about funny things. Speaking of honeymoons, I've got a good story."

I sat back and smiled.

"Back in Carolina," said Aunt Garnet, "this older couple lived down the street. They'd been saving for a second honeymoon for years. Know how they saved for it? Every time they made whoopee, they put a dollar in a big pickle jar. After thirty years, they were gonna have enough to go to France on a big ship. Well, they had enough money in just twelve years. And the husband got suspicious. Turned out the wife was making whoopee with the neighbor man, and she was throwing in a dollar every time she hopped in bed with him, too!"

Aunt Garnet hooted with laughter, and I watched the dark place where her side tooth had been.

Simon threw down his napkin. The barest crease of a line had formed between his eyes. "That is the most disgusting, un-Christian story I ever heard!"

Aunt Garnet stopped laughing. "Oh," she said. "I'm sorry."

Under the table I touched her hand.

"Just remember, ma'am, that you are in God's house, in front of kids who are trying to learn to be good," said Simon.

"Please forgive me," said Aunt Garnet. "I am deeply sorry."

Simon took a deep breath. "I receive your apology," he said grandly.

Under the table, Aunt Garnet took my hand and traced letters on my open palm. A-S-S-H-O-L-E.

I wanted her to stay forever.

* * *

The lack of people at the wedding made the service seem even more depressing. Besides the family and my father, who brought his new wife, only Mrs. Laird showed up. Later, at the reception, Aunt Garnet sat between Boone and me as we watched Simon and Meg dance to music from the Supremes blaring scratchily from a turntable.

"Where's his family?" Aunt Garnet asked me as Simon twisted and turned on the dance floor in a tuxedo whose flared pant legs almost brushed the floor. "I mean, doesn't he even have brothers or sisters? Cousins?"

I shrugged. "He came out of thin air."

"Like litter thrown from a car. I don't like the looks of him. He's got a face like a rat."

Simon glared at us from the dance floor as though he knew we were talking about him. A shiver ran through me.

On the other side of the dance floor, my real father spun around the floor with his wife. Halfway through one spin, the two of them stopped dancing and began to argue over something. His wife pulled him off the dance floor and into a corner, where they continued to fight.

"I was surprised when Meg married Dan," said Aunt Garnet. "He was so nice. It seemed like a miracle. He might have been a flake, but at least he wasn't a creep."

My grandfather glided out to the dance floor with Aunt Laura and began to do the Charleston. "I wish Meg would marry someone more like Grandpa," I said idly.

Aunt Garnet looked at me. "She just did, honey. She just did."

"What are you talking about? Grandpa's great."

Aunt Garnet didn't answer me.

I was about to tell her the whole story of Simon, how he threw evil fits and sacrificed our prize possessions and told rambling tales of his mysteriously dead family, but he had stopped dancing and now motioned me toward him. Reluctantly I arose and went over to him. He led me over to the punch bowl and turned to face me.

"What do you think you're doing, Smart Girl?"

"Just talking to Aunt Garnet."

"Just talking to *Aunt Garnet*," he mimicked nastily. "Telling her wild stories about me?"

"No."

"Let me tell you something." He poured himself some punch out of a big ladle. "Maybe I lost my temper a couple times. So did Jesus with the money changers. There are just some secrets a family's got to keep. Know what I mean?" He was still pouring. The punch spilled over the top of the cup, running down his hand.

I stared at the spilled punch. "I know what you mean."

"You better, Smart Girl." He set down the ladle. The punch had slid off the table and was dripping down steadily, making the sound of a woodpecker against the top of Simon's shoe. "Because I know something about you. As much as you love those damn Indians, you love your Aunt Garnet more. And wouldn't it be sad to lose someone you love, like I did?"

I went back over to Aunt Garnet and sat down beside her. I wasn't sure what Simon was threatening, but now my only thought was to keep Aunt Garnet out of danger until she left the house.

"What did the creepo want?" Aunt Garnet asked.

I touched her hand protectively. "Nothing. He said I don't look like I'm having fun."

She laughed. "Well, who could, when some big rat's just married into your family?"

On the morning of my relatives' departure, I went outside and found my grandfather and my brother sitting on the steps of the back porch, playing with Numbhead. My grandfather seemed especially fond of the dog. The night before we'd caught the old man sneaking him a piece of his steak.

"Poor dog," Grandpa said. "Kinda stupid, isn't he?"

"Not totally," I said. "He knows one trick."

"What's that?"

I pointed to a butterfly hovering around a mandevilla bloom. "Numbhead," I commanded, pointing. "Attack!"

Numbhead obeyed, dutifully snapping his mouth shut around the butterfly but leaving his cheeks puffed out a little, extra air for the delicate wings. After a few moments, he opened his mouth and the butterfly flew away, a movement of yellow rising out of the rank breath of a hound and up into the sky.

Grandpa laughed and clapped. "I'll be damned!"

"Numbhead has never hurt a living creature," Boone said. "Not even a flea, as far as I know."

"And I tried everything," I said, "to make him crave the taste of twin."

"He may know one trick," Grandpa said, "but he's still stupid." He looked around and noticed a large red wasp hovering near a fallen branch. "Numbhead!" he commanded, pointing. "Attack, attack!"

"No!" I shouted, horrified.

"Attack, attack!" my grandfather shouted.

Numbhead pounced upon the wasp without a second thought, suddenly letting out a huge wounded yelp as the venom found his tongue.

"Numbhead!" cried Boone. We chased the hurt dog around the yard until we caught him, then forced his mouth open. A long black stinger was stuck in his tongue.

Grandpa was laughing and laughing.

"Boone," I shouted, "get the tweezers!"

We pulled out the stinger, but Numbhead's tongue was swelling up. Boone and I carried him two blocks to the house of a veterinarian who worked out of his garage. He gave Numbhead a shot, and within a few minutes, Numbhead was breathing easier.

"Your dog's allergic to wasp stings," said the veterinarian. "You were lucky I lived nearby."

Grandpa was still shaking his head when we returned to the house.

"What a stupid dog!" he said.

When it was time for our relatives to leave, I hugged each of my aunts and ducked under my grandfather's outstretched arms. Before Aunt Garnet climbed in the rental car, she whispered to me: "If God's nut job turns out to be the creep he looks like, you and Boone come on and live with your old aunt Garnet."

I felt a sudden relief at the thought of this new escape route—one that would be cut off later.

Simon put his hands on his hips and watched them drive away. "Thank God they're gone. Especially that crazy old bat."

"She's my favorite," I said.

"What a friggin' surprise."

Simon spent the rest of the day moving his things into our house. One of the items was a small gray safe, which he put in the sewing room.

"What's in that safe?" I asked.

"Money. Lots of it. In cold cash."

"Where did you get it?"

He looked hard at me. "If you must know, it's the life-insurance money from my wife's untimely going away. Ten thousand big ones."

"You're kidding!"

"Don't give me that wide-eyed look. You people aren't ever gonna touch any of it. It's mine, fair and square."

Meg's face had changed.

Her expression lost all its tension, her eyes their hooded, haunted look. Color flooded back into her face: redder lips, bluer eyes, pinker skin. Her eyelids fluttered. Her smile stunned. Back into her face and her entire body had crept the presence of a man. The ring on her finger proved it. Boone and I caught her at least a half-dozen times a day holding the false jewel up to the light.

Simon bought Meg roses once a week. Called her his princess and his darling. Made love to her at least once every other day, from what Boone and I could hear in the next room.

At dinner Simon threw out the same Bible verses, one after another, strung together in an endless stream. He spoke of God's wrath, His intolerance for drunks and sluts and loud rock music, His condemnation of any form of betrayal. Betrayal shimmered in Simon's monologues. Samson and Delilah. The brothers of Joseph. Peter, shamed by the third crow of the admonishing cock. And Judas, world's champion turncoat, who kissed Jesus in the garden.

"You know who is the only person in the world who would never betray you?" Simon asked. He didn't wait for an answer. "God. God is the only one. But each of us would turn around and betray God at the drop of a hat. Shit, we nailed His boy's hands to a cross! You see, God planted the temptation to betray Him in every human being, starting with the Garden of Eden and the snake and whatnot. God made temptation even though it woulda been easier for Him if He hadn't. Ain't God wonderful?"

I pictured Simon in his counselor's office, some wrecked jury-rigged extension of some wrecked jury-rigged church, where the pastors were insane enough to unleash Simon and his philosophy upon the saddest in their flock. Did the poor sad people who came to Simon put up with such gibberish? Did they scream and run for their lives? Or did they simply accept the fact that God sometimes favors the maniac, that God Himself is drawn to that passion, that single-mindedness, that berserk but always entertaining devotion?

My dinner was getting cold. Meg always made us put down our forks when Simon started preaching. As a sign of respect, she said. Sadly I watched the steam from the yellow squash wither and die.

Simon looked up at the picture on the wall. The blond-haired boy.

"God lost His temper with me a couple of times," Simon whispered. "For my own good, I guess."

* * *

The hiatus from Simon's strange anger gave Boone the courage to continue writing Persely Snow in secret. Because of the increasing standards of security in the asylum, she had not been able to escape again, and I imagined her prowling through the halls restlessly, pulling at her yellow hair while her eyes rolled around in her head.

I asked Boone: "What if she writes you back and Simon finds the letter?"

He shrugged. "I get the mail every day, not him. Besides, look how much better he is. Especially those times he goes into the sewing room to count his money. He's always in a great mood when he walks out again."

Boone did have a point. As much as I hated Simon Jester, his temper seemed to have left him. In its place was that silky voice we'd heard in the early days of his courtship with Meg. He used it when he rambled about God and when he murmured into Meg's ear, his arms around her waist.

One warm afternoon after school, Boone rushed into the house, throwing Simon's mail on the table and then grabbing my shoulders.

"Where's Simon?" he whispered urgently into my ear.

"On the phone."

"Good. Where's Meg?"

"At the bank."

"Good. Come with me."

I followed him out to the backyard, through the beeyard and to the edge of the property. He sat down behind the holly bush, his left knee almost touching the battered red arm of a plastic monkey that peeked out from beneath the bush—evidence of pagan rituals. I sat down next to him.

He took a letter out of his pocket and handed it to me. I looked at the address: Boone Fendr 1123 Crver St.

"So?" I said. "Who's it from?"

He smiled. "Can't you tell?"

"No."

"It's from Persely Snow. She doesn't like the letter *A*. That's what she said in an interview."

"That's from Persely?" I peered anxiously around the holly bush. "This is bad, Boone. Simon hates that girl. If he catches you with this letter—"

"He won't."

"God help you if he does."

He tore the envelope open, his hands shaking. "I can't read it," he said. "I'm too nervous. You read it."

I unfolded it and read aloud as he shifted nervously in front of me.

Der Boone:
Is tht your nme, Boone? tht's got to be the stupidest nme in the world. The best nme in the world is Cooper. Cooper didn't tke shit from no one. Cooper sid I guess my life isn't worth two kisses. tht's true for my life too. Thnk you for writing me those letters the police think we know ech other he he! Your e sissy boy. I'd poison you in two seconds. You probably got e smll pecker Stop your dmn tlking about God this and GOd tht. There isn't GOd. He would hve stopped it when they put Jesus on the cross.

You re stupid.
Keep writing!
Persely Snow

I folded the letter back up and put it in the envelope. Boone sat down on the ground, breathing deeply, staring at his palms, a habit he had picked up, through blood or through rote, from his absent father.

"Did you hear that?" he whipsered. "She said to keep writing!"

"Are you crazy? This isn't a friendly letter."

"That's because she was afraid the people at the hospital would read it." He took the envelope from me and stared at his address.

"Wait a minute! The address is slanted! She left me a message under the stamp!"

He put his tongue on the stamp and waited impatiently for his saliva to moisten it. We sat there together, the sun on our backs. Finally Boone took his mouth away from the envelope and peeled back the stamp with his thumbnail. I leaned over his shoulder. The letters were so tiny I had to squint.

I know your stupid stmp trick you stupid moron.

Boone took this in, rocking back and forth.

"Why would she say that to me? About being small . . . you know where?"

"I don't know, Boone. The same reason she poisoned her parents. Because she's crazy."

Boone looked hurt. "Do you think I have a small . . . ?"

"I don't know. I've never seen it. And I don't want to."

"Then how do I know if it's the right size or not?"

I thought a minute. "If the twins would want to torture it to death, it's probably too small."

"Alice, you're horrible." He got up and did a little dance, pausing after a few minutes to grab me around the waist and swing me around in a delirious circle. "Persely Snow wrote me!" he sang. "She wrote me she wrote me she wrote me!"

We wanted to share the good news with Meg, but by our own hesitancy, we realized that we no longer completely trusted her. And besides, she had other things on her mind. Winter was coming, and her bees were dying at an alarming rate. The supers had been so light that Meg had made only two hundred dollars from the sale of the honey. Some of the colonies stank—the smell of disease.

"Foulbrood," Meg said sadly.

She had to kill off four of the infected colonies. Weeping, she put a spoonful of calcium cyanide into the hive entrances and ran away to cry while her bees died in the poison gas.

Boone and I made a small white cross and put it up at the site.

"The Tomb of the Unknown Bee," I said.

My brother shook his head. "Meg sure is unlucky."

Chapter Seven

Meg had been hovering all day in the beeyard. Simon didn't like this hovering. It took attention away from him. He had asked for chocolate mousse for dessert that night, and Meg had scoured her recipe books and tried her hand at it. Now we ate it silently out of fluted custard glasses. Sweat ran down her face as she stirred her mousse.

"Really good mousse has Grand Marnier in it," said Meg. "But I didn't have time to get any."

Simon didn't answer her. He was swirling his mousse.

"There's all different kinds of ways to make mousse," Meg continued.

I looked at her. She had an anxious expression on her face.

"Do you like it?" she asked Simon.

He shrugged.

"It's very good, Meg," I said. "I tasted it. It's got a real metropolitan taste."

"What's that mean?" asked Simon. "Metropolitan?"

"You know," I said. "Like the big city."

"You think you're real smart using those big words, don't you?" His voice had an ugly tone.

"I just like big words," I said. And then I saw it. The line I hadn't seen in weeks, forming between his eyes. I caught my breath as though I'd seen a snake. I looked into the dark eyes on either side of that line and felt the old terror.

"You know a few more words than your mama," said Simon.

Meg looked up at him, blinking. She laughed, openly nervous now. "I'm not very good at big words."

"You're not very good at nothing, are you, honey?"

She looked surprised. "Simon, that's not true. I'm working in the beeyard and helping you, too. I'm balancing two careers."

"Two careers? You slop together a few jars of honey every year, you deposit my checks, and those are your two careers? Are you out of your stupid mind?"

Meg looked at her plate.

"Let me ask you something, Meg. I've been wondering about this for a long, long time." He looked at me, then back at her. "You've gotta have the smartest girl in the world, Meg. I can tell from her smart mouth. That smartness musta come from somewhere." He leaned over the table.

"What . . . I'm . . . saying . . . Meg . . . is . . . half of you is in this girl. So you got to be smart in some way, right?"

Boone and I exchanged looks. The air pressure around the table had dropped, so low the tea almost sank in the glass. Nimbus clouds gathered. Lightning flashed.

I looked at my sad mother, and my anger took away some of my fear. "She's plenty smart," I said defiantly.

"Truth is," said Simon, "I married the stupidest woman in Texas. A woman too stupid to swim. Too stupid to keep bees alive. Too stupid to get pregnant."

These last words sank in the quickest. So that was it.

"We haven't been trying for very long," Meg said meekly.

"Not very long? Have I ever used a rubber, Meg? Even back in May, when you first hopped in bed with me like a slut? After two weeks?" He counted on his fingers. "May, June, July, August, September, part of October. That's over five months! You got a poisoned womb, Meg?"

"Maybe we just haven't been lucky."

"Luck ain't got nothing to do with it." Simon licked his custard glass clean and set it down. "That's all I've ever asked you for, Meg. A child of my own. You see"—he looked over at us—"these kids aren't mine. There's not a bit of me in them. Nothing matches about us. They got no reason to love me or to be loyal to me."

"But they are loyal to you!" Meg protested. "They do love you!"

He looked at us again. "Oh, sure. Taking love lessons through the mail from friggin' *Persely Snow*." He looked back at Meg. "Best get working on that new baby, *dear*."

* * *

That fall the subject of pregnancy became a giant spider creeping through Simon's head. Every night we heard him with Meg, not the feverish lovemaking that marked their early courtship but a grim assault. He had lost his child under the waves, and now he entered Meg as though her body had stolen the boy and needed punishment for the deception. Some nights Simon took Meg in the kitchen or on the sofa in the den. Anywhere in the house, finding her and pushing her down wherever she stood.

"Don't they know we can hear everything?" Boone whispered. He shivered. "Yesterday I saw it, too."

"Simon doesn't care."

I would wait until the house grew quiet and then steal outside to the backyard, where my sacrifices began again. My old Barbie doll, my silver ring, my favorite socks, my Lincoln Logs, bright marbles and a see-through belt with Mickey Mouse faces in between the holes. Night after night I whispered in the dark: *Make him go away! Make him love someone else!*

My lazy god ate my possessions and then gave me the finger.

One night, as I stood alone before the holly bush, my hand still open and the confetti from a ruined jigsaw puzzle still falling through the moonlit air, I saw the holly bush move. My breath caught. Distinctly, it shook again. I felt a thrill of hope and terror at the thought of my pagan god finally awakened by the noise of desperate sacrifice. Then I heard a moan.

I approached the bush carefully, moving around it until I saw two bare feet sticking out behind it. I craned my neck and then I saw them. My mother was on the ground with her knees in the air, and the bare body of Simon Jester was sandwiched neatly between those knees. Each time he

moved against her, she moaned again. Neither of them noticed me as I stood there watching them. I had heard but
not ever seen the act of sex, and it stunned me with its violence. Like a pagan ritual, coarse and strange and desperate. Simon came down on her again. The wind had carried
one of my jigsaw-puzzle pieces away from the bush, and
now it balanced on his spine. I crept away, my stomach
hurting. The god of the holly bush had spoken. It would
provide me no answers, it would give me no relief, and
most of all it welcomed monsters.

Meg's period came a week later. I found her out
among her bees, crying. Secretly I was torn. I knew a
baby would calm Simon down some, but I didn't want to
see any child of his brought into the world. "Don't worry,
Meg," I said. "You'll have a baby."

Meg wiped her eyes. "I don't understand what's the
matter! You and Boone happened right away. We didn't
even have to try."

"Maybe it's him," I said.

"Don't be ridiculous, Alice. He had a child, too."

"I've heard," I said.

She looked up at me, her eyes red. "I have to get pregnant. I have to."

Boone still summoned up his courage to write Persely
every week in the darkness of our bedroom, squinting
over his love's labor. Sometimes he turned over the letters
to me, anxious to make sure he had achieved the correct

mixture of Christian love and delirious adoration that he sought.

"If Simon ever walks in on us, you're dead," I warned him. "And so am I."

"I'm careful."

"If you were really careful, you'd stop writing her. She doesn't care about you. She sent you that one letter saying you were stupid and that you had a small pecker, and she hasn't written you since."

Boone pushed his glasses up on his face. His eyes twitched. The glasses moved. "She needs to know that someone out there hasn't given up on her," he said.

And this was the trait in my brother that distinguished him so. This reservoir of mercy, this love for all people: the victims and the abusers. The hurt and the ones who hurt. Murderers, children, grasshoppers, monsters, the minnows that dangled from fishing hooks. While my mother's love was wrapped in clingy material, Boone's flowed outward. It had its currents. It made a rushing sound and covered everyone, even Simon.

"There is good in Simon," Boone insisted one night as we heard Simon yelling at Meg through the walls about the baby again. "He's not truly evil. No one is."

"You're right," I said. "And you know what the world really needs? Another little Simon." We listened a few more minutes. "Maybe Simon's shooting blanks," I said.

"What does that mean?"

"I don't know. I heard it on TV."

The next morning Meg waited until Simon went to town, then put on her best dress, her pearls and her red sling-back shoes.

"Do I match?" she asked me.

"I think so," I said, looking wonderingly at her. "Where are you going?"

She shrugged. A few minutes later I heard her in her bedroom, dialing the phone. I crawled toward the open doorway, straining my ears, while Boone looked on disapprovingly.

"Please," Meg was whispering, "I need to see you. I've been thinking about you. And I know you're thinking about me."

Silence.

"Thank you. I'll see you soon."

I darted away from the room just as she walked out with an old shirtwaist dress under one arm. She picked up her clutch purse from the table by the front door, unsnapped it and inspected the contents as if they each came with a tiny instruction about how to proceed through the day. Finally she closed the purse and walked outside, Boone and me trailing behind. Meg threw the old dress in the backseat of the station wagon and turned to look at us.

"If Simon wants to know," she said, "tell him I had to get eggs."

I waited until she drove away before I began dancing, trampling the grass, my hands stretching toward the sun.

"What are you in such a good mood for?" Boone asked.

"Meg is going to meet Daddy! Maybe that means they'll get together."

"She's married now," he said disapprovingly.

"And to such a great guy. Besides, you saw Daddy and his wife at the wedding. They're not getting along."

I sat down on the porch, happy as a clam, so convinced was I of my mother's seductive powers. True, I hated my father, the wan distracted softball-lobbing memory of him, but I had some mercy and I could forgive him. Deep down, his abandonment of us had killed me, but I could be un-killed in time.

And so I rejoiced. The plan already in motion. A few months of sulking, gradual forgiveness, and then my father and me together again, driving into town.

Boone looked doubtful for a few minutes and then got in the spirit of things, too. We sat there together and planned our new life as he played with a yo-yo and I threw pebbles at the trash pile.

Simon came back around three in the afternoon. I greeted him warmly, for I truly believed that I wouldn't have to talk to him very much longer.

"What are you grinning at, little girl?"

"Nothing."

"Where's your mother?"

"In town. At the store."

"Thought she just went yesterday."

"Forgot the eggs."

"She's as dumb as that dumb dog."

My mother returned late that afternoon. She had removed her pearls, scrubbed her face clean of makeup, taken off her nice dress and changed to the shirtwaist. And she had remembered the eggs. She looked as if she'd returned from any usual day. Her ordinariness a shield.

I marveled at her composure as she kissed Simon on the cheek. The kiss of Judas, I imagined, prelude to abrupt betrayal. It wasn't until she was out in the beeyard that Boone and I had a chance to talk to her.

"So, Meg," I said. "I know where you were."

"You met Dad in town, didn't you?" Boone said.

"I don't know what you're talking about."

"Come on, Meg, you tell us everything," I said.

She shrugged.

"So," I insisted, "when are you and Daddy getting back together?"

She looked at me. "Never." I couldn't quite identify the look on her face. Not disappointed. Not happy. A grim peacefulness. The weariness of a woman who's accomplished some task that now bored her. "I have to take a shower," she said.

I turned away and walked in a straight line to the edge of the yard, past the border of holly bushes, into the next yard. I heard Boone calling, but I just kept walking, feeling the last of the elation leave me. I passed in front of my neighbor's clothesline and wiped my eyes on a billowing sheet, then continued through the backyard and into the yard of the next house over. The neighbors were accustomed to children wandering through their yards, and none of them approached me. Some of them waved, but I didn't wave back.

I couldn't believe it. I had been so sure my father was coming back, that after all these months, he felt remorse at his conduct and his silly woman. That it would be my father at the head of our table once again. That Simon would peel the picture of his dead son from our wall and go, and his scent and his crazy notions and his curious threats would leave, pushed out by a gentler father with a distracted nature and an easy way of throwing a softball. I walked so far, through so many neighbors' yards, that when I came back, night had long fallen and my family was already asleep.

That night I dreamed that I saw my mother in the backyard, walking toward the holly bush, her eyes glassy under the moonlight. She carried something broken in her arms that looked like a battered doll. Meg threw the doll in a slow-motion arc toward the holly bush, and it flew through the air, its eyes open and staring.

The doll had my brother's face.

Chapter Eight

Something new was growing in Meg. I imagined it taking shape: the skin and the ears, the chaos of the forming brain, the gills and later the lungs. The urge to bully and destroy. The fear of betrayal. The line between the eyes. The nascent pocket of belief that could be filled with Christianity or hatred or both.

Meg had come home one day and handed the blood test to Simon, her eyes shining and her skin already radiant with the promised life.

"You're . . . pregnant?" Simon breathed.

Meg smiled.

Simon danced around and whooped, hugged my mother and spun her around and around. Kissed her face and her neck until I felt nausea stir within me.

New life had taken hold in her, but more of her bees were dying. She tried to feed them sugar water and keep their hives well ventilated, and yet they died in gouts. Predators were moving in. Wax moths, roaches, mice, and a skunk that ate them despite their stings and spat out their remains in wet balls before disappearing in the morning light.

Meg moaned softly.

"It's all right it's all right it's all right," Simon whispered in her ear. "You don't need to be a beekeeper, anyway. Your job is to grow that kid inside your belly." He looked over at us. "My own child is coming. My own. And this time I'm gonna raise him right." He looked at her piercingly. "It *is* my child, ain't it?"

"Simon!"

He smiled. "Just joking, honey."

The next day, when I went to check the mail, I found a letter whose random handwriting was ominously familiar. It was addressed to Boone, and the writing on the envelope was slanted toward the stamp.

Boone put his hands behind his back when I tried to hand him the letter. "You read it," he said. "I'm too nervous."

We were out behind the row of ligustrum bushes that separated our yard from the neighbors', safely hidden from Simon Jester. The twins were in their front driveway, creeping up on ants with their genocidal magnifying glass.

I opened the letter and read:

Der Boone,

You sure don't give up, smll pecker boy. Your stepfther sounds like n sshole. Like my fther. The story about his fmily sounds like he mde it up. Don't be such e chickenshit. Investigte. Sniff eround. But you won't do it, will you? Becuse you don't relly wnt to know. Becuse you re chickenshit!

When you tke the devil into your mouth you re doomed. You know wht movie tht's from, right?

The truth will set you free!

Love,

Persely

P.S. You sid your little sister just turned twelve? Hppy birthdy chickenshit!

Boone lay back with a groan of ecstasy. "She said 'love.'"

"That's encouraging."

"Alice, look under the stamp."

I put my tongue to the stamp, hoping it wasn't sprayed with poison, and peeled it back carefully. Underneath were the words: *Piss on your stepfther. It's esier thn you think.*

I squinted and read it again.

Poison your stepfther. It's esier thn you think.

"Well," I said. "She's getting better every day."

"Read me the letter again," he said.

I read it again. This time I could feel my face turning red.

"I am not chickenshit!" I said.

"Persely was just kidding," he said quickly. "We can't go snooping around."

"Are you just going to sit there and let the woman you love call you a coward?"

"She didn't mean it. Besides, how do we check on his story?"

"If it really happened, it would be in the newspaper."

"Where are we going to find a newspaper that old?"

"Come on, Boone. Everyone knows the library keeps them in the basement." I jumped up and walked around in a tight circle, agitated. "Persely can go to hell. I'm not afraid of Simon Jester."

Boone's tic was worse behind his glasses. He stood up and touched my arm. His fingers were ice-cold. "I'm afraid of him, Alice. I have bad dreams about him. Sometimes I wake up in the middle of the night and I can't move my arms or my legs."

But I had made up my mind. "Persely's right about one thing, Boone. The truth will set us free."

Chapter Nine

Boone and I sat together in the last available seat on the bus. All around us were loud people, out to shop or eat in the cafés that lined the main street of town. I touched Boone's hand.

"It won't take long to check his story out," I said. "And then we'll know for sure."

"I don't want to know for sure."

"Well, I do. Simon met Meg early last summer, and he said his boy had drowned three years before. That's the summer of sixty-eight. We'll start there."

The county library had been standing for most of the

century, and its large gray steps had chips in them that had never been repaired. The doors swung on rusty hinges; the librarians were old and cranky. One of them directed us to the archives room in the basement.

"There it is," she said nonchalantly, swinging a blue-veined arm toward a shelf crammed with papers. "That's the year you want."

"All those?" Boone asked.

She smiled wryly. "Takes a lot of paper to explain the world, son." She disappeared, leaving us standing there, breathing the musty smell.

Boone looked at the shelf. "Alice," he said. "How are we going to look at all these papers?"

"We don't have to look at all of them. Just May through September. If there was a drowning on Lake Shine, there would be an article about it."

Boone and I spent the entire day cross-legged on the cold tiles of the library floor, our fingers growing dark with newspaper print. In the late-August editions were head-lines of Persely Snow's trial, and Boone began to read those articles intently.

"If you don't hurry it up," I said sharply, "we'll never get done."

"Sorry."

By the end of the afternoon, we had learned about all of Lake Shine's summer tragedies. A Mexican man went swimming drunk with his blue jeans on; three days later, the sheriff's office found his body floating near the dam. A businessman went fishing with his partner and returned without him. He told the authorities his partner had fallen overboard and never surfaced. Three days later, divers found the business partner. He was wrapped in rope, weighed down with an anchor, and had two bullet holes in his head.

Lightning struck a family picnicking at the park. It killed no one but left third-degree burns on the father's legs.

Three men racing their bass boat at dusk ran into a pier. One was decapitated.

Two young children went swimming and were entangled in an illegal trotline. Both children drowned.

And that was one summer's news on Lake Shine, a body of water whose specialties range from channel catfish to sudden and senseless tragedy.

We found not one word about a boy and his mother drowning in a freak boating accident after a picnic. I looked over at Boone. "I told you. Simon's story is a lie. Just like all his other stories."

"Maybe we missed one of the articles."

"Then let's go over them again."

"No!"

The tone of his voice startled me. "Why not?"

"Because Simon's son drowned, and that is that!"

"He didn't drown, and you know it!"

"No, I don't!" Boone threw down the newspaper and sprang to his feet. "I don't want to know anymore, Alice! I want to believe Simon and so I will!"

"Fine!" I threw down my own paper. Boone's dogged belief in Simon only reminded me of his dogged belief in God. And I scorned both sets of faith, for I felt they were based on ignorance and fear. I got up and waved my hand dismissively at Boone. "Let's just go, then!"

Boone touched my shoulder. "Please, Alice," he whispered. "Let's just believe him. And not question him. Because I'm afraid of him."

His lips were trembling. My anger turned to sympathy. "All right," I said at last. "We won't rock the boat. We'll just stay very, very quiet until we turn eighteen. That's not so far away."

And so Boone and I made our pact. And I truly think we could have lived that way, lying low and asking no questions.

And perhaps we could have, were it not for Persely Snow.

Chapter Ten

Boone and I sat outside on the grass with Lucinda Laird. For seven years now, ever since the Lairds moved in, Boone had made regular pilgrimages across the road to tell Lucinda about God.

"She's got brain damage," I'd said time and time again. "She doesn't understand what you say."

"You never know," Boone replied.

Later, after the twins were born, I had come around to Boone's opinion. "Maybe you're right," I told Boone. "That family needs all the God you can give them."

Now I watched as Boone held Lucinda's hand and told her all about how God loved girls like her, and how God had a horse waiting for her in heaven, gently broken by soft white angels. A horse of silver, with chocolate hooves. As he described this angelic horse, it became clear that he was inserting attributes of Persely Snow. The golden mane. The turned-in front teeth. The untamed spirit.

I heard a rustling sound and looked toward our house. The boy twin was hovering near our trash can, looking suspicious. I craned my neck. From the trash can itself, I could see the legs of the girl twin sticking out, clad in white leotards.

"Hey, you brats!" I yelled. "Get out of our trash!"

The boy pulled out his sister and they both disappeared into our backyard, giggling.

Boone was still talking. His horse had sprouted wings and was hovering above rivers of molten gold. Lucinda's lids opened a crack so that I could make out a sparkling dash of color. Green. I imagined her nine years old again, her eyes full and bright, her horse underneath her, possibilities stretching before her and lightning in the distance.

Boone stroked the teenager's hair as if she were a little girl. "And no rope can hold that beautiful horse," he whispered.

The Laird twins had come back from behind our house and were marching across the street toward us. As they approached, I could see bits of Hamburger Helper in the girl's hair, mustard on her leotards.

"We know a secret," the girl announced.

Boone looked at them and then went back to whispering to Lucinda.

"What could you know that's important?" I asked. "You're just a couple of brats."

The twins smiled. One of them unfolded an envelope and waved it tauntingly.

My heart stopped.

"Boone," I said, trying to keep my voice calm. "What did you do with that envelope from Persely? The one with that charming message written under the stamp?"

He looked over at the twins. "I saved it, of course. I save everything from her."

"Are you sure about that?"

"I think so. I've just been so distracted lately . . ."

"Did you accidentally throw it in the trash?"

"I . . . maybe."

"Okay, we're dead."

The twins were backing up and smiling.

I smiled at them, waving. From between my teeth I hissed, "I'm going to charge them. You go to the left and cut them off."

The twins turned and ran. We tore after them. Numbhead came dashing from behind the house to join the game. The twins put on a burst of speed and reached the front door just before Boone did. Boone grabbed at them and stumbled. I caught hold of the girl, but she slipped away and the twins darted inside our house.

We stood outside the door, afraid to go in.

"Let's get out of here," I said. "Let's run away."

Boone's teeth were chattering. "I can't move. I'm serious, Alice."

I pulled at him, but he wouldn't budge, so we stood there as the minutes passed. Finally the door opened.

"I need to talk to you," said Simon. I saw the line between his eyes.

When I managed to get my brother through the door, I saw the twins sitting on the sofa, eating caramels.

Simon had the envelope in his hand. "The twins found

something real interesting in the trash, Boone. It has your name and address on it." He held the envelope to the light so Boone could see his name: *Boone Fendr.*

"I read the papers, too," said Simon. "And I know that Persely Snow don't use the letter *a*."

Boone's face had turned white.

"And here's the most interesting part of the whole she-bang," Simon continued, pointing to the area where the stamp had been. "The letters were so damn tiny I couldn't read them, but the twins happened to have a magnifying glass with them." He held the magnifying glass up to the light with a flourish and continued. "In this here corner it says: 'Poison your stepfather.'"

"She was just kidding," I said.

"Shit yeah," said Simon. "Ask her folks."

He looked at the twins. "You can go now. Go take care of Lucinda. She's out there all by her lonesome."

When the twins were gone, I said, "Simon, that was just a letter she sent Boone out of the blue. He hasn't written her since way before the wedding. He thinks Persely's nothing but trouble. Honest."

"Honest? I think you're lying through your teeth." And with that, he stormed down the hallway and burst into our room.

"Wait, Simon!" I rushed into the room behind him. "Hold on a second!"

But Simon had gone mad. He pulled books off the shelves, ripped the sheets off the beds, scattered the contents of Boone's chest of drawers on the floor.

Tears ran down Boone's face and his body trembled. "I'm going to be sick," he whispered.

In the back of Boone's closet, Simon found what he was

looking for, a big manila envelope that had all of his treasures: newspaper clippings, a page cut from *TV Guide* that advertised a special on Persely, a brochure from East Texas State Hospital, all the classified ads and Persely's first letter to Boone. Everything but the photocopied picture of Persely and her second letter to Boone, which I had hidden for him.

"So," said Simon, turning to Boone, "you don't give a damn about her, do you?"

Boone, white as a ghost, didn't answer.

But Simon was nodding. "Now I see. I was right from that very first day, when I knew you would turn on me, Boone. And Alice, you're in on this, too, ain't you? Two traitors. Judas and Delilah."

I couldn't help looking into Simon's eyes and finding the craziness there, the rage and the fear. Somehow we fit into Simon's history, which was more dangerous than his present or his future, because we could not undo it, we could not shake him and say *Simon, we are different people.*

I pulled on Boone's arm again, but he remained frozen in place, staring into Simon's eyes with a hypnotized expression.

"Yes," Simon murmured. "Children will put the ax in your back. Might take them years, but they'll get you when you least expect it. So you know what you gotta do? Gotta beat them to the punch."

He smiled.

"'Poison your stepfather.'"

He looked piercingly at Boone.

"Gotta beat them to the punch."

* * *

In the days that followed, Boone and I tried to stay out of Simon's way as much as possible, walking around the neighborhood or hanging around the park. Anything not to be in his presence.

The last of Meg's bees died soon afterward, and the bee-yard was quiet. Meg wept at the thought of the annihilation of her colonies, but now she had a new career—her pregnancy. She sat in the backyard all day, in the cypress glider, talking to the child growing within her.

Simon's child. His flesh and blood. One he would raise up right this time, as he put it.

One week after Simon discovered Boone's secret, I went into the sewing room to find some thread. I noticed some new books on the shelves, rows and rows of them.

Books on poison.

Chapter Eleven

Old and new. Thick and thin. Scientific and breathlessly sensational. Photos and text and anecdotes involving tea slyly served. My blood went cold as I finally understood why Simon hadn't reacted at first. Dizzily I turned the pages, looking at charts and graphs, chemical compounds, rates of fatality, symptoms and the common household items that held this terror. I set the last poison book on the shelf and walked into the den, where Meg sat knitting a pair of baby booties. The wind was blowing hard outside, and the branch of a dogwood tree scraped its near-bursting buds against the window by my mother's head.

"Meg," I said, my voice shaking, "Simon is collecting books on poison."

She held the booties up to the light. One was small, one big. Shoes for a freak of nature, a curse from God.

"I must have not followed the pattern right," she mumbled.

"Did you hear what I just said?"

"Of course, dear." Meg was still eyeing the booties sadly. "Where were the books?"

"In the sewing room."

"Hmmm. Well, don't go in there anymore."

"Does he ever talk to you about poisons?"

"Sometimes, lately. It's a hobby."

"But why?"

She shrugged.

"Meg, I think Simon wants to kill us."

She burst into a brief giggle. "Don't be silly, Alice. Simon's never been so happy. He's going to have a baby."

"That's right. His own baby."

"He thinks of you as his own children."

"He does not."

"Well, he should," she said. She went back to her knitting, and I knew that appealing to my mother was hopeless.

When Boone came in, I grabbed his hand and pulled him into the sewing room and we went through the books. Arsenic, digitalis, laudanum, strychnine, carbon disulfide, toxaphene. Winding through the body. Slowing the pulse, stiffening the muscles, accosting pure oxygen and dragging it back to some indefinable lair.

"Oh, God," said Boone. "Look what hemlock does to you."

"I already read that part."

"I can't move." Boone's face was pale.

"Just calm down. We have to think."

We heard a car turn into the driveway. "Let's get out of here," I whispered. Sweat ran down my body.

"I can't move."

"You have to!" I grabbed his arm and tried to pull him.

The front door opened.

I pulled harder. Finally Boone took a step. I got behind him and pushed him out of the room.

I could hear Simon murmuring to Meg: "You're beautiful. You're beautiful."

It was hard not to hate Meg for being so blind to Simon's plans and motivations. That almost comical denial in her, that river unfoamed by any intuition. I hadn't noticed this quality in her when she'd been married to my father, but then again she hadn't really needed it.

And we ourselves did have our doubts. Were we being paranoid? Was Simon simply trying to scare us?

We couldn't be sure. The night I discovered the books, I told Boone that we needed to spend all our free time learning about those deadly chemicals.

He groaned. "What good would that do?"

"It will help us keep from being poisoned. Do you remember the part about cyanide smelling like almonds? That's good to know."

"But Alice. Just learning about that stuff makes me sick."

"Do you want to die?"

He did not, and neither did I. And so, over the next few

weeks, Boone and I secretly read all the books in the sewing room and became experts on poison. We learned that arsenic gave milk an orange tint, that thallium was tasteless and odorless, that ammonia could be neutralized with diluted lemon juice, that barium made a green flame when lit on a platinum wire, that fluoride salts tasted soapy and could be mixed into an omelette with deadly results.

As the weather turned warmer and the azaleas bloomed outside, we quizzed each other. Benzene's boiling point was rather low. The presence of chloral hydrate left a pear scent on human breath. There was no antidote to sodium fluoracetate, and the heavy breathing caused by napthalene poisoning sounded like the snores of a restless night. A lethal dose of antimony: one to two tenths of a gram.

As we gained knowledge, we became aware that the world around us was a vast reservoir of poison. It could be found in the mothballs in the hall closet, in liniments, in furniture finisher, in our mother's permanent-wave solution, in nutmeg, ant bait, dental cement, firecrackers, silver polish, fertilizer, cattle dip. It lived beneath sinks, in medicine cabinets, in old sheds and new cars. It dripped down the inside of abandoned buildings; it shimmered on the tongues of small, foolish children who would never learn to do a somersault or play Marco Polo in a swimming pool.

Flowers were blooming in the springtime air, but nature itself had become deadly, buttercups sitting on toxic roots, running with toxic sap. Lycorine in daffodils, saponine in periwinkle, solanine in bull nettles and Texas thistles, cyanide in elderberries. Sweet-pea pods caused paralysis, as did rhododendrons. Lily of the valley exported its poison into the water in the vase that held it. And a single leaf from an oleander plant—whose lavender blooms I once admired—could kill a person. Poison, we discovered, made the world go 'round. It was part of the great compromise of the earth in which sparrows lived but so did spiders. Murderers and cotton candy. Blowfish and chocolate éclairs. Take away the poison and life would grind to a halt; we'd stand there stupidly, impotent but safe.

Poison was so easily obtained, so easily put into action. It served the grudges of sages and morons and Simon Jester. Boone and I began to pick at our food, which hurt Meg's feelings. We worked out a system of blinks, warning each other about food that we'd seen Simon fool with or hover around.

Simon himself began to speak about poison almost conversationally. "Did you know," he said one night, "that if bees suck up that—what you call it . . . nectar?—from a yellow jessamine flower, then the honey turns to poison?"

"That's interesting, dear," said Meg.

"And did you know," Simon continued, glancing over at us, "that this poison called car-bear-ill can come through your skin and get you? And that one of them nighttime berries can kill you dead as a duck?"

Carbaryl. Nightshade berries. We'd done our homework. Simon saw our visible distress and smiled.

Boone and I began to eat in smaller portions, for we saw poison everywhere. In the salt and pepper. In the sugar. In the ice cubes. In the sweet potatoes and the fruit salad. Even tap water smelled of almonds.

"Boone," I whispered in the dark. "Remember how Simon said his boy would have betrayed him if he hadn't drowned first? Well, what if that kid didn't drown? What if Simon poisoned him?"

Boone was quiet for a minute on the other side of the

room. "But what about Simon's wife? Why would he poison her?"

"Maybe she got in the way."

At school, Boone and I wolfed down our lunches and went for seconds and thirds. But still we began to lose weight. "Maybe we could hire the twins as poison tasters," I told Boone, but my own joke came cold out of my mouth, as if the humor itself were a wan pale thing, slowly sickened by doctored muffins. We moved through the halls silently. Our time with Simon and its gradual escalation of horror had left us feeling that the world could not touch our house with its rules, that our lives depended on us alone, that no one was going to protect us. I saw Spencer in the halls. Did he notice the look in my eyes, the shiver in my spine, the cowering spasm in my bloodstream that had once been my appetite? And would he grieve for me if I died? Would he stand on one side of my coffin with my father on the other side, and would they look at each other with a sad understanding?

Deep down, Boone and I held out the hope that we were being overly cautious. Deep down, we believed that we knew Simon's limits, how far he would go. We were wrong, of course. As wrong as the children who sat among their colored blocks with poison shimmering on their tongues.

One day Numbhead disappeared, which wasn't like him at all, for he was far too stupid to find his way even to the end of the street. We checked the crack between the foundation and the sidewalk and found the toad calm and dry. It had recently begun to put on a lot of weight, perhaps to make it harder for Numbhead to pry it out of its hiding place.

"Fat toad accounted for," I said. "Numbhead must not have gone far if he didn't take his frog." My eyes narrowed and I looked across the street. "Unless . . . he was kidnapped by the forces of evil and he's tied down to a table somewhere."

The twins looked bewildered when we confronted them. "We didn't do nothing to the shit dog, fuck-ass," the girl said.

"You better not have. You've already caused enough trouble for us."

"Your dog has a horse in his ass," said the boy.

"I think we're done here, Alice," my brother said.

"Don't leave town, brats," I said.

Boone and I looked all over the neighborhood, calling out Numbhead's name over and over.

"Think, Boone, where would a really stupid dog go?"

"He's not as stupid as you think."

"Yes, I think his habit of yelping when he sees his own pee is just his way of hiding his genius."

Boone sighed, put his hands on his hips and looked to his right and his left. "There's only one more thing to do," he said. "Let's go door-to-door and just start asking."

"No, maybe a better idea would be to get a picture of Numbhead and make flyers out of it. 'Have you seen this ugly stupid dog peeing and yelping? Boy is he precious to us. Reward offered.'"

But as it turned out, our own absent father solved the mystery. He called that night. When Meg got off the phone with him, she said: "It's the strangest thing."

Simon looked up from the kitchen table. "What?"

"Dan said that he looked out the window tonight and Numbhead was standing in front of the living room window, staring in. He scared Dan's wife half to death. Anyway, Simon, don't worry about it. The kids and I will go pick him up."

"Right, Meg," said Simon. "Like I'm really going to turn you loose at night to go see your ex-husband. I'll go get that dog."

"Don't hurt him!" I said before I could stop myself.

"Oh, shut up. I'm not gonna hurt some stupid dog. Give me the address."

Meg wrote it down for him and he stomped out the door.

"Isn't it a miracle," said Boone, "that Numbhead found Daddy's house?"

"He's like Lassie!" Meg chimed in.

"Oh, please," I said. "Don't insult the memory of Lassie."

Boone took my arm and led me into the living room so he could speak to me alone. His eyes were shining. "Don't you know what this means? Numbhead knows we're in trouble so he's asking Dad for help the only way he knows how. Maybe Numbhead is our savior."

"Please don't compare Numbhead to Jesus again. Jesus doesn't press His big wet nose against people's windows at night."

"The world is full of mysteries," Boone said. "And God helps us in strange ways."

When Simon pulled into the driveway and let Numbhead out of the car, the old dog immediately ran to the shelter of Meg's arms. Meg stroked his neck. "Did Numbhead have an exciting night? Did you, my pretty boy?"

"Stop coddling that stupid dog," said Simon.

"It's just so strange," she said, "how Numbhead found his way over there."

"Yes, ain't it?" said Simon. "You'd almost think that dog had been there before, wouldn't you? Maybe in the backseat of your car, Meg, one of them days you told me you were going to the store."

Perspiration was running down Simon's cheeks. Under the floodlight his face seemed even more menacing. I could smell his sweat.

"Now, don't be silly, Simon!" Meg insisted. "Dan is married to someone else and I love you!"

"Do you love me? Or you love all that money I got in the safe? Is that what you love? Is that what you're loyal to?"

"No, Simon!"

"And is that child growing inside you mine?"

"Of course it's yours, honey."

Simon walked up to my mother and stared into her eyes for several long moments. Boone and I edged over to each other until our arms were touching. Now that Simon looked like he was finally going to hit our mother, I was horrified by the prospect. But how could we stop it?

Finally he stepped away from her. When he spoke again, his voice was calmer. "I'm going to teach that dog a lesson about running away." He went into the garage and returned with a section of rope.

"What are you going to do with that?" Meg asked.

Simon nodded toward the tree in the middle of the front yard. "Gonna tie him to yonder oak tree for a couple of days."

Boone and I let out our breath, relieved that Numbhead

wasn't going to be beaten or God knows what. Simon bent down and began to thread the end of the rope through the metal loop in Numbhead's collar.

My mother went berserk.

She lunged at Simon and knocked him off balance. The end of the rope slid to the ground. And now it was my mother's turn to look crazy in the floodlight.

"No! No, Simon Jester! You will not tie that dog to a tree! Get away from him with that rope!" She bared her teeth.

"What's got into you, woman?" asked Simon, bewildered. He looked over at us as if asking for an explanation. We could only shake our heads. He turned back to her. "You're telling me no, Meg?"

Something seemed to have possessed my mother. I had never seen that look on her face. "I'm telling you no," she snarled.

Simon walked into the house.

"Meg . . ." I said, but she had backed away from us, out of the floodlight, so that we could hear only her breathing.

That night I could barely sleep, I was so angry with her. I could not believe she had let Simon frighten and threaten us and then she had fought like a tiger to keep him from tying a stupid dog to a stupid tree. And it certainly wasn't like Simon to take it all lying down. He was sure to extract his revenge—most likely on Boone and me.

"Can you believe it?" I whispered to Boone across the room.

Boone stayed quiet for a moment. "I don't understand it myself."

We had no way of understanding her reaction at the

time. We were children, and so we lay there on opposite
sides of the room, an angry girl and a boy who had already
forgiven his mother for whatever it was she had done.

Simon returned from work that next afternoon in a
hostile mood. We could tell he'd been thinking about
Meg's defiance the night before.

"How was work, honey?" Meg asked, meek now.

Simon glared at her. "Work was work. Lots of stray
sheep. Sheep need teaching. Sheep need to learn lessons."

"Well, I'll bet you helped them. Anyway, I'm making
your favorite dinner tonight—"

"No," he said, still glowering. "I'll make dinner."

I felt a chill at the sound of his words. He was going to
get us back.

"I'll help you, honey," my mother volunteered.

"No! Everyone stay out of the kitchen."

Boone and I paced around nervously as Simon rattled
pots and pans.

"What are we going to do?" my brother whispered.

"Just pretend to eat," I whispered back.

When Simon called us to dinner, we edged over to the
table and took our seats. He had made us Hamburger
Helper and a green salad on the side, with ranch dressing.
We stared down into our food. Antimony, acrylamide, eth-
ylene chlorohydrin, malathion, parathion, strychnine, diel-
drin. A billion different possibilities whirling through our
minds. In our terrified imaginations, powders mixed with
fluids, symptoms plotted against one another, cures took to
their beds. We remembered the victims. Socrates,
Rasputin, Romeo. Six teenagers with a sudden urge for

wild mushrooms on a camping trip in California. Boone and I stirred the food around our plates and leaned forward to take discreet little sniffs.

My mother looked troubled but ate her food.

Simon paused and looked at Boone and me. "What's the matter? Why aren't you eating?"

It was hard to meet his eyes. "We're not that hungry, Simon," I said as nicely as I could.

"It's good," Meg said.

"I don't care if you're hungry or not," said Simon. "I made it and you're going to eat it."

Boone was trembling. "I can't. I can't eat it," he whispered.

"Yes, you can."

Boone took a forkful of Hamburger Helper and tried to guide it to his mouth. I wanted to stop him but felt suddenly paralyzed myself. Just before the food touched his lips, my arm came to life and I knocked the fork out of his hands. It flew across the room and hit the oven. Pieces of hamburger clung to the oven window.

"Damn it!" Simon shouted. He lunged for Boone, seized him by the back of the head and slowly began to force his head down into his plate. I pounded on Simon's back, but he ignored me.

"Please," said Meg. "Let's not fight. Let's all just eat in peace."

Suddenly Simon released Boone. "That's okay, boy," he said, and began to pace around the kitchen floor. His smooth voice was back, though the line between his eyes hadn't faded. "If your sister hadn't stopped you, I would have. Because you know what? You shouldn't have to eat food you don't wanna eat. I worked so hard to prepare something for you, something special, but if you want to insult me, hey, it's a free friggin' country."

"I'm sure they didn't mean to insult you, honey," said Meg.

Simon grabbed our plates. "You are just two ungrateful kids. And you've ruined dinner." He hustled the plates to the screen door, opening it with his pinkie finger. "I guess that idiot dog is the only one around here with any manners. He'll eat it."

Boone and I sighed in relief, trying to steady our breathing and our beating hearts. Suddenly our eyes met. We jumped from the table and ran out of the kitchen.

"No, no!" we shouted, bursting into the backyard. "Don't give that to Numbhead!"

But it was too late. Numbhead was already licking one of the plates clean.

Simon looked at us with disdain. "You kids are . . . what's that word? That word where you think everyone's out to get you?"

We had dropped to our knees and were anxiously inspecting Numbhead.

"Aren't you going to tell me the word, Smart Girl?" Simon taunted.

Numbhead grinned up at us, basking in the attention and the thrill of hamburger meat after his long, cold regime of dry dog food. We ran our hands over his body as if poison could be tracked like a flea. Numbhead stretched out his long neck and groaned with pleasure.

Simon stared at us a moment. "I'm gonna have total loyalty," he said, and he went inside.

Boone and I sat back on our haunches and stared at our dog.

"How's he look?" Boone asked anxiously.

"Stupid."

"That's good, isn't it?"

"I guess."

"He's slobbering a little. That could mean cadmium poisoning."

"He's slobbered every day of his slobbery life. Besides, cadmium makes you throw up."

Numbhead wagged his tail and licked my face.

"Do you smell anything on his breath?" asked Boone.

I felt helpless, so I said: "Let's see. What kind of poison would make his breath smell like he's been licking his balls?"

"Don't be funny. His eyes are rolling a little."

"His eyes have been rolling around ever since that go-cart hit him." Numbhead put his head in my lap and I scratched him behind the ears. "Maybe Simon's right," I said. "Maybe we are paranoid."

The next morning we found Numbhead with his head between his paws, his eyes open and fixed. His sweet stupidity so cold.

Chapter Twelve

The fat, dry toad in Boone's hands brought the mourners to four. We buried Numbhead near the Tomb of the Unknown Bee, out by the holly bush and my impotent god, in whose presence I was now a heretic.

The sacred weed from Spencer Katosky's yard was in full bloom now. I pulled it and laid it across our dog's new grave.

"Chew on it in heaven, Numbhead," I whispered.

"There will be other weeds," said Boone, "but there will never be another Numbhead."

The cross we'd fashioned out of plywood and inscribed with Magic Marker: OUR FRIEND NUMBHEAD.

Meg stood with us over Numbhead's grave, sobbing. "Poor old thing," she managed. "His big old heart just finally gave out. Probably from walking all that way to Dan's house."

I glared at her. "Don't you see what Simon did? He poisoned him."

She cried some more and then calmed down and said: "I know you're sad, Alice. But that's just crazy talk. Numbhead was an old dog."

"Everything around Simon dies," I said darkly. "Bees. Dogs. Children."

Terrified, Boone and I inspected ourselves for symptoms. The burning sensation in the mouth and throat that could mean monkshood poisoning. Dilation of the pupils (belladonna). Lines in the fingernails (arsenic). Abnormal reflexes and tremors (thallium). Bluish-black discoloration of the skin (silver nitrate). A tingling in the nose (sodium fluoracetate). Blurred or double vision (atropine, benzene, foxglove, nicotine or the venom of a beaked sea snake). One morning Boone discovered he had drooled on his pillow, and this made him refuse to go to school—convinced that Simon had poisoned him with malathion, which causes excessive salivation.

At night we lay awake, the ceiling fan ominous and our bodies itching with imaginary symptoms. In that dreamy passion brought on by constant fear, we swooned for our separate loves. Boone's Persely. My Spencer. Life had become more precious to us, and also the people that we lived for. And so Boone closed his eyes and held Persely in his arms, and I held Spencer Katosky in mine, or at least I lay near enough to touch the side of his pale face. *I've been poisoned, Spencer. May the world be good to you. May softballs miss your head. May chlorinated water be gentle to your eyes. Kiss me, Spencer. Kiss me as my heart fails. Kiss me as arsenic collects in my fingernails and hair. My pale boy. Who will pull your weeds? I loved you, I loved you, I loved you.*

Boone still had his faith. He prayed at night, sometimes in a whisper so loud that I could hear the names of those he prayed for. Meg. Alice. Lucinda and the twins. Mr. Walt. Aunt Garnet. Persely. And Simon.

I glared at him through the darkness. "It's bad enough praying for the evil twins, but do you have to pray for Simon, too?"

Boone let out his breath as fragments of his interrupted prayer rode the draft of the fan. "You're supposed to pray for everyone, Alice."

One night I had another nightmare about my brother. In this dream, Boone was sitting at the kitchen table, his half-finished plate before him. He stared at me, unblinking, his breathing shallow. I knelt down beside him and took his hand.

"Boone," I said. "I love you."

I saw the light leave his eyes.

"Oh my God," I whispered. "He's dead."

"My baby!" Meg shrieked. But her hand was on her swelling stomach.

I turned my head and saw Simon standing there. He said: "Close his friggin' eyes."

Chapter Thirteen

Once there lived a girl who loved to ride her horse across the green fields, but one day the lightning found her and took everything away from her. And the girl's mind went dark, dark as the rich wine cushions in a Catholic church, and lightning never strikes the same place twice because that place—or person, or girl on a horse—is never the same. One day in blooming, buzzing May, Lucinda Laird crossed our street and entered our house. And the lightning followed her and shot through our lives with a snow-white pulse: *zzzzzzzzz*.

* * *

Mrs. Laird had come over the week before and asked Simon and Meg if Lucinda could stay with our family while Mrs. Laird took the twins to Corpus Christi for a little vacation.

"The twins have never seen the beach," she explained. *(The alarm went out from sand flea to hermit crab: Magnifying glass! Magnifying glass! And the seagulls exploded from ingested Alka-Seltzer. And the authorities broke into a sand castle and found horror there, horror.)*

"No problem," Simon said. "God tells us we gotta love others, so it isn't no problem at all for us to watch over little Lucinda." He gazed out across the lawn, over at the girl. "Although she's not so little anymore," he added softly.

On Tuesday, Mrs. Laird led Lucinda over. She'd packed a suitcase for her daughter.

"I hope she won't be too much trouble," she said, handing the suitcase to Meg.

Meg beamed. "She'll be fine."

Lucinda's hair was neatly combed and her eyes were open to the same degree they always were, shining as though releasing deteriorated lightning. Her mother had polished her shoes bright black. Her smile came and went. She was very pretty, really, if one could judge her so.

"She can have my bed," said Boone.

Mrs. Laird shook her head. "You're such a sweet boy. But keep your bed. Lucinda likes to sleep on couches. She prefers them, really."

"How can you tell?" I asked.

"Because I'm her mother."

Boone was thrilled to have Lucinda in the house. He

was the perfect baby-sitter, reading her stories, brushing her hair. At night, at the dinner table, Meg had to cut her food and feed her. Soon Boone and I discovered an added benefit—Lucinda never ate very much, leaving half a plate of food for us to scavenge after Simon left the room.

Simon himself regarded Lucinda with fascination. "God," he said one night. "She's got fish-and-chips for a brain, but she's . . . real *developed,* don'tcha think?"

Something about the way he looked at her sent a chill down my spine.

"Don't you think it's creepy how Simon was looking at Lucinda?" I asked Boone later.

"I didn't notice."

Meg's laughter suddenly came through our bedroom wall. She was noticeably pregnant now, and Simon's delight with her had grown.

"How can they be so loud?" Boone asked. "They've got a guest in the house."

I pictured Lucinda waking up in the den in unfamiliar darkness, and I wondered if the loud whinnies from Meg's room reminded Lucinda of her horse. If, somewhere in her mind, her old friend was running through a green field. I felt vaguely afraid for Lucinda but couldn't quite figure out why. Perhaps that was one reason Meg's laughter annoyed me on this night more than the others.

"I can't stand this," I said. I got out of bed and turned the window unit on, drowning out the sounds coming from the next room.

After a few minutes wc finally fell asleep.

I woke up in the middle of the night to the whoosh of the

air conditioner and to Boone's steady breathing. And to
fingernails scraping against glass.

I turned my head to that last sound.

I gasped.

Persely Snow was at our window.

Chapter Fourteen

***

I rubbed my eyes and looked again. She was still there, a girl whose distinctive appearance had been sewn into me by repeated glances at newspaper clippings. It was as though all the poison in my consciousness had taken bodily shape and formed that icon of poison herself. The hair stood up on the back of my neck. She saw me looking at her and scratched on the window again. *Let me in,* she mouthed, jabbing her finger at the window lock. I shook my head and she bared her teeth at me.

Across the room, my brother was asleep. "Boone," I hissed. "Boone, Boone!" I was trembling violently.

"What?" he mumbled.

"Persely Snow is at our window!"

He sat up in bed and rubbed his eyes. "Very funny, Alice."

"I'm not kidding. Look, look!"

He fumbled for his glasses, put them on and looked. "God," he whispered. "Am I dreaming?"

Persely motioned him over to her.

"Don't let her in, Boone," I begged. "She's crazy."

He ignored me. He leaped out of bed, opened the casement window, reached for her hand and helped her climb inside the room. When she was safely inside, Boone let go of her and backed away, taking her in. The wild blond hair. The big, slightly turned-in teeth. The light olive smock and pants that must have been the uniform of East Texas State Hospital.

"You came," he whispered.

"Acourse I caaame," she snarled in an exaggerated Texas drawl. "You quit writin' them stupid letters and I was bored."

"Shhhh," he cautioned gently. "Keep your voice low."

She flopped down into a chair by Boone's desk and crossed her arms. Boone moved back, and he and I stared at the famous teenager, still in shock that she could be sitting in our room. Her body had the imperious and defensive posture of one used to infamy. I could sense a slight anger in her. Some grudge that took shape as the vaguest aura. She met my gaze challengingly, and I looked away, feeling small and somehow insulted and yet noticing that the terror in our house seemed a little more balanced now, with the addition of this new monster. Did Simon know she was in our room? With a demon's razor-sharp senses, could he hear her heart beating, smell the starch in her clothes or the lemon scent of institutional shampoo?

Persely looked around our room, taking in every detail that showed in the moonlight coming through the window. Her gaze fell on Boone's swim-team trophies, and she rose from her chair to inspect them. "Swim-team hero, eh?" she said.

"Boone can swim like a fish," I said.

She looked him over. "I had you pictured different, Small Pecker Boy."

Her insulting words and the jut of her lips made me dislike her immediately. "Don't call my brother that."

She looked over at me with one eyebrow cocked. "Who's the brat?"

"My sister," Boone said. "Remember? I mentioned her in the letters."

"Oh, yeah. The Indian freak who ain't never kissed a boy."

"Boone!" I gasped. "How could you?"

"I'm sorry, Alice," he said miserably.

"I've kissed a boy!" I said.

"Kissing some boy your brother just clocked on the head don't count," Persely said.

I glared at my brother.

Persely's bare feet made no sound as she continued to pace around our room. Her hair was tangled, and her pants were loose and dirty in the knees. "What a dump," she said.

"At least we don't have straps on the beds," I said.

Persely tossed her head. "Hmmph. Ain't no straps on my bed. I could get out of them, anyway. And I can pick any lock there is. I'm what you call an *escape artist*. Don't you read the papers?"

"I read the comics. Stories about maniacs bore me."

"Shut your sister up," Persely ordered Boone.

"She doesn't mean anything by it," he said patiently. "She just has a sharp wit."

"Or a smart ass," said Persely. She went over to Boone and jabbed his chest. "Got a cigarette?"

"I don't smoke."

"Why the hell not?"

"Shhhhh," I whispered. "Our stepfather will hear you and then we'll be in big trouble."

"For what?"

"Harboring someone who's guilty of patricide."

Persely snorted at me contemptuously. "You swallow a dictionary, runt?" She sat down at the end of Boone's bed. "From the letters, your stepdaddy sounds like a real shit-head," she said to Boone, ignoring me. "Except you don't give me any good *details*."

"He's not very nice, I'm afraid," said Boone.

"Not very nice? That the best you can do? How about he's a bastard? A son of a bitch? A mo-ther-fuck-er?" She said the swear words lovingly, as though she enjoyed the feel of them piercing her drawl like skewers through a poisoned wiener.

Boone knitted his hands together and stared at the floor.

"Boone doesn't use those words," I said. "He's very religious."

Persely rolled her eyes. "You don't think I know that? All them damn letters about God and Jesus and forgiveness and flowers and bunnies and peace and love and ain't God *somethin' else, whoopee*!" She began to clap lightly, singing in a lilting tone: "What a friend we have in Jeeeesus, laaaa la la la la la laaaa!"

"Shhhh!" I warned.

Boone looked devastated.

"You know," said Persely. "One time the judge said to Cooper, 'For the love of God, son!' And you know what Cooper said? He said, 'God has nothing to do with it.'"

"Don't insult God," I told her in a low, angry voice. "It upsets Boone. He got in trouble for you, you know. My stepfather went crazy when he found your envelope."

"What envelope?"

"The one with the message under the stamp. You know. 'Poison your stepfather.'"

Persely shrugged. "Shoulda done what I said." She turned to Boone. "This asshole got any cigarettes?"

"He's been trying to quit because he's got a new baby coming. But I think he left half a pack in the sewing room on the safe."

"What safe?" asked Persely, perking up.

"It's where he keeps his money," Boone said. "I'll go and get the cigarettes."

"Be very quiet," I warned. "If Simon hears you and comes in here, we're all dead." I looked at Persely. "Unless you've got any poison with you."

Persely drew in her breath sharply but didn't answer me.

Boone opened the door and disappeared, leaving me in the room with her. We sat staring each other down.

"Cute outfit," I said.

"That's my nuthouse uniform, smarty. It's hard to stop and change clothes with every homo cop in Texas on your ass."

"Listen. I want you to know something before my brother comes back. He loves you."

She snorted. "So do a lot of other boys. From all 'cross the country. They write me and send pictures. One of 'em sent me ten dollars."

"Well, Boone is special."

She shrugged and turned to look out the window. "I bet the whole country's after me. I'm gonna be in all the papers tomorrow. I'll make the front page. And the headline will be somethin' cool . . ." She looked back at me as she swept her hand from right to left. "PERSELY SNOW ON THE LOOSE AGAIN! You'll never know what that feels like, runt."

"I'm never going to be a headline, I admit. But maybe someday I'll have a quiet little article about curing cancer or winning a Nobel prize. Doing something good for someone. *Helping* the world."

"No ma'am," said Persely. "You gonna have a quiet little article about how you're forty years old and no one will hump you 'cause you're a *smart girl*." She said the last two words with glee and malice.

"You're crazy."

She stopped smiling. "That's what the judge said to Cooper. He said—"

"Oh, just shut up about Cooper! I saw that movie, too. He isn't anything like you! He didn't kill anyone in cold blood. And he brushed his hair."

"Cooper was about justice and I'm about justice, too. Maybe you'd understand if you didn't have your big nose in an Indian book night and day. Cooper could've kicked Sitting Bull's homo ass."

I was in a room with a crazy murderer, there was a monster snoring in the next room, and yet my blood was boiling over. I climbed off my bed and walked right up to her, looking straight into her eyes.

"At least Sitting Bull's mother died of old age. He didn't poison her."

Persely lunged off the bed and grabbed my throat, so tightly I could feel the blood squeak off its course. We remained in that clinch, Persely's eyes wild and staring into mine, her pupils enormous and all the color drained from her face, leaving her skin ghostly pale in the moonlight. Weakly I tried to pull her hands off me, desperate for oxygen, desperate to shout for help and desperate to remain silent.

The door opened and Persely let me go. Boone had finally returned with the cigarettes. I fell to my knees, holding my throat and sucking air.

"What's the matter with you?" Boone asked me.

I glared at Persely. "Nothing," I croaked. I sat down cross-legged, still taking deep breaths.

Persely picked up a pillow, took off the pillowcase and handed it to Boone. "Put this under the door," she said. "That way smoke won't get out."

Boone did as he was told. Persely lit up a cigarette and we both sat watching her. She handled the cigarette in the overly confident way of someone too young to be so experienced at it. After a few moments she began blowing smoke rings, her lips jutting out and her eyes squinted. Boone looked as though he'd like to dive through those smoke rings right into Persely's arms.

"Every time I get caught," said Persely, "the doctor at the hospital takes my cigarettes away. Then the nurses tie me to the bed and fill me with so many drugs I don't know who I am. It's punishment."

Boone looked horrified. "That's terrible!"

"That's life, homo."

"But they're supposed to be *helping* you."

"Ain't no help, Boone. Nowhere in the world." Her

voice had lost some of its sassy confidence. "Anyway, it
don't matter. They untie me after awhile, then I bide my
time and I break out again."

"How do you do it?" Boone asked.

"You mean escape?" She shrugged and leaned down to
pick up one of Boone's sneakers, tapping her cigarette
ashes into it as she spoke. "Well, the last time, they'd put
locks on the door to my room so that I couldn't open it, but
it was movie night on Sunday, and I sat near the back and
snuck out and went down the hallway to the laundry room.
The back door there had a pretty easy lock. I took off.
Climbed the fence. That fence is a joke."

"What made you come and find me?" asked Boone.

She inhaled deeply, then leaned back and exhaled toward the ceiling. "I don't know," she said. "Your letters
bored me to death. 'Cept the part about your asshole stepdaddy. He at least has got some get-up-and-go."

"He's really quite strange," said Boone.

"You should have done what I said to do."

"Poison him?"

"You bet."

Boone shook his head. "I can't do that. I think everyone
in the world is God's child. God doesn't want you to go
and kill his children . . . I mean, not that I'm judging what
you did."

Persely ground out the cigarette against the wall.
"Good," she said. "Because you don't know what you're
talking about."

Boone sat down next to her and spoke tentatively. "I
want to help you, Persely."

"Help me what?"

"Forgive yourself."

Persely stared at him a moment, and in the darkness I thought I noticed a Cooperesque squint. "Cooper had a scar all the way around his neck. It came from being hanged for the wrong crime. I got hanged for the wrong crime. And I got 'em back. I don't lose no sleep at all. Justice is my province, Marshal."

Boone looked stricken.

"You don't have a conscience," I said.

"And do you, creep?"

"Yes."

"And where's it got you? Sniffing your damn food every day?"

"It's better than being where you are."

"Shhh!" said Boone. "Don't be rude, Alice."

"That's all right, Boone," said Persely. "She don't know nothing 'cept about kissing knocked-out boys. Now, Boone, you got to do me a favor."

"Anything," he said eagerly.

"You ain't that much bigger than me. I need a pair of your jeans. And a T-shirt."

"Boone's not going to give you his clothes," I protested.

But Boone was already rummaging through his closet.

"Here," he said.

She stood up and pulled off her pants, then lifted her smock over her head and threw it in the corner in one smooth motion. Boone and I sat staring at her pale breasts, dumbfounded, as she stood in her panties watching our reaction with amusement.

She nodded at me. "I'd ask if you had a bra, but I figure that's a long shot, huh?"

"I've got a training bra!" I said hotly.

Persely turned to Boone. "These don't mean nothing to me. Want to touch 'em?"

Boone looked stunned. He dragged his eyes away from the points of her breasts and stared at the shape of an old swimming trophy on the dark wall.

"Well, go on," said Persely. "Touch 'em." Her voice had a curious flat quality.

He shook his head.

"What's the matter, Boone? Aren't you fourteen now, for God's sake?"

"Yes, but . . . stuff like that is meant to be special."

"Only justice is special, boy."

Boone looked tortured.

"Leave my brother alone," I ordered.

She waved her hand dismissively at Boone. "I knew you were a homo." She put on the jeans and T-shirt. "Not bad," she said, turning around a little.

"Wait a minute," I interrupted. "What if the police catch you in Boone's clothes and trace them back here? Boone will be a dead duck."

"How smart you think the police are, dimwit? You think a pair of blue jeans has got a person's name in them?"

"Fine. Take his clothes. It's been a pleasure meeting you. Good-bye."

"No!" said Boone. "Persely, don't leave!"

She looked at both of us and smiled, obviously enjoying the rift she was causing. "But, Boone, your little sister told me to beat it. I guess it's time to say so long."

"Please stay. Please, Persely," he said desperately. "I'll do anything."

"All right, all right. Since you look so pathetic. Give me another cigarette."

Boone handed her another cigarette and then flicked the lighter for her. Pure ecstasy showed on his face as she bent toward the flame.

"I want to help you," he said.

"I already told you, I don't go for that God stuff."

"I mean, I want to help keep you safe. I don't want you to go back to that horrible hospital where they do bad things to you."

She took a few puffs. "Really? You'll help me?"

"I'd do *anything* for you, Persely."

"Boone," I said, "you're such a sap."

Persely poked Boone on the arm. "Okay. We'll need a plan."

"You can't stay here," I said quickly.

Boone shot me a look.

"Miss Training Bra is right," Persely said. "I'd last about two minutes here."

As if in response to Persely's last remarks, we heard the door to Meg and Simon's room open.

"Quick, Persely!" Boone whispered. "Get in the closet!" She darted inside, and Boone closed the door just as our own door burst open and Simon entered the room. He flicked the lights on. "What the hell's going on here?" he demanded. "Who was just rummaging around the house?"

"Me," Boone said. "I got up to get a drink of water."

Simon wrinkled his nose. "It smells like cigarettes in here." He kicked the pillowcase away from the doorway, then bent down and picked the cigarette butt off the floor. "Who's been smoking in here?"

Boone gulped. "I have."

I stared at him. His first lie.

"Bullshit," said Simon. "You'd never smoke."

"He's quite the chimney," I said.

"You shut up, Smart Girl." Simon found the rest of the pack and drew out a cigarette, handing one to Boone.

"Let's see you smoke," he said.

Boone shot a terrified glance at me. I gulped, hoping he had watched Simon smoke enough to appreciate the technique. Boone fumbled with the match, and managed to light the cigarette. He drew on it deeply, taking the smoke in his lungs and looking at Simon with near defiance. He exhaled the smoke smoothly.

"Well," said Simon. "I guess you do smoke. I read in the paper that your pal Persely smokes, too. Menthol. You still keeping up with her, Boone? Your pen pal? The one who told you to poison me?"

Boone's eyes had turned red and begun to water. "No," he managed.

"Well, that's good, boy. 'Cause she may not last too long. I hear some people got plans for her the next time she escapes."

"What do you mean?" Boone asked, but instead of answering him, Simon grabbed him around the throat. Boone gagged. The cigarette slid out from between his fingers.

I rushed at Simon, intent on protecting Boone. Simon let him go just before I reached them. Boone fell to his knees, gasping.

"Not another step, Smart Girl," Simon said. He looked down at Boone. "Don't ever snitch my cigarettes again," said Simon. "Or you might find a surprise in the filter."

Boone coughed violently from the cigarette smoke and the pressure of Simon's fingers. He grabbed his throat as I had grabbed mine minutes before.

"Are you all right, Boone?" I whispered.

He nodded and kept coughing.

I opened the closet door. "You can come out now, Psycho."

She was trembling all over.

"That's Simon," I said. "Isn't he great?"

"I have to leave here," Persely said.

Boone had recovered himself somewhat. "I'm sorry he scared you. Really, I'm all right."

"I have to get out of here. Good-bye, Boone."

"Wait!" he said desperately. "When will I see you again?"

"Never."

"No! I want to help you."

"I ain't coming back here." She crossed the room and slid out the window in a motion so swift that I barely saw it happen. Just before she disappeared she told Boone: "You probably got enough poison in this house to kill him ten times over."

Boone leaned out the window and whispered, "Wait! Wait! Come here!" Persely must have stopped and turned around, because Boone remained in that position for several moments, murmuring something I couldn't hear. Finally he pulled his head back into the room and closed the window gently.

"What did you tell her?" I asked.

"To meet us tomorrow night," said Boone. "In the park."

Persely's horrible suggestion still hung in the air, but my

brother was shivering with delight, a big smile on his face, his body turned half toward the window.

One hour since his first meeting with Persely, and already these tiny sins of cigarettes and lies.

Chapter Fifteen

I didn't sleep that night, and not just because my brother was lying on his bed and humming to himself. I knew terrible things were coming. I'd had the premonition when I saw Lucinda led across the street to our house, and now, with the addition of Persely, my dread was complete. Some kind of tension was gathering in the house, in the world, too huge for me to understand. And so I lay awake and watched the moonlight on the walls. Crickets were chirping outside and warm air came in the window, moving through the crack in patches, in the same way that I imagined visions from the daylit world moved into the green slits of Lucinda's eyes. I looked out the window that

Persely had used to enter our house. That glamorously feral teenage poisoner still seemed to be in the room. She had electrified things around her, objects and even walls. Across the room my brother baked in that charge. My thoughts kept returning to her. I hated her and I hated my fascination with her. Wild though she was, and so prone to escape, she nevertheless had a pinned-down quality, as though she wasn't really free at all.

I knew, even then, that my brother's relationship with her would only lead to grief. And though I knew it would do no good, I turned to him in the darkness and said: "Don't meet her in the park tomorrow night. Just forget about her."

He didn't answer me for a long time. He turned his head and gazed over at the window whose pane had been sanctified just hours earlier by Persely's clawing fingernails. The sky was beginning to lighten. "No," he said at last. "I can't do that."

The next morning I ran to get the paper before Simon, afraid that news of Persely's latest escape would set off another paranoid tirade and another room inspection. I shook the dew off the dramas of the world and scanned the headlines. A car wreck, a celebrity divorce, a chemical spill on the 59 Freeway. No mention of a crazy girl. Perhaps the news hadn't caught up with Persely yet. I breathed a sigh of relief.

All that morning Boone sat with Lucinda Laird on a quilt out in the front yard, telling her stories about the angel horse, and how this horse had visited a lonely boy in the middle of the night. The sun was high when Simon came out on the front lawn. He hadn't been going in to work lately, and I wondered if he'd been fired, if perhaps one of the senior ministers at the church had put his ear to Simon's door and heard his crazy talk.

"What are you kids doing?" he asked, walking over to us.

"I'm telling Lucinda about God," said Boone.

"What do you know about God?" Simon asked. "I know who your God is, boy. The God of stab-you-in-the-back. Now get gone. I'm the Bible expert, not you."

Lucinda stared ahead at nothing through half-open eyes. Her breathing did not change, or her expression, as the angel by her side was replaced by a monster. Such was the devastation to her mind.

"Hello, Lucinda," Simon purred. "You're looking good today. You've really grown into a nice young woman." A stray hair fell into her face, and Simon very tenderly pushed it behind her ear.

"Let me tell you about the kiss in the garden," Simon told her. "When Jesus was betrayed."

I didn't like the look on his face, or the way he leaned in to her, or the way he said *kiss*.

"We don't mind watching her, Simon," I said. "I know you're probably busy."

He glared at me. "What are you still doing standing there?"

Before I could answer, a large van came into view, rumbling down the road to our house, gravel making its presence known against the metal underside. On the side panel in a flowing cursive type it said: PERTIER'S FLOWERS. The van pulled into our driveway and a teenage boy climbed out with a vase of yellow roses.

Simon stood up. "Who are those for?" he demanded.

The boy looked at his pad. "Meg Fendar. She here?"

"Her name's not Meg Fendar. It's Meg Jester!" Simon sputtered.

The boy was unmoved. His braces seemed to give him pain, and he scuffed his foot against the short grass. "She here?"

"Give them to me. I'm her husband." The line had formed down between Simon's eyes. He took the vase and set it on the front porch as the boy drove away. He removed the card and sat down to open it.

"Simon," I said. "That's not for you."

He ignored me, ripping open the envelope and holding the card up to the light. "'Thinking of you,'" he read. He turned the card over. "There's no name." He looked at us. "Who would send your mother roses?"

Boone and I didn't answer. I felt my heart thumping mildly in the summer heat. Daddy? *Daddy*. You've come back for us. All is forgiven.

Simon stood up and opened the front door. "Sweetie," he called. "Do you mind coming out on the porch?"

Meg appeared, still in her nightgown and house slippers. Lately her pregnancy had begun to make her listless. "Oh! What pretty roses!"

"They're for you."

"For me?"

"The card says: 'Thinking of you.'"

Meg straightened her robe as if the roses could see her. "Who are they from?"

"That's what I want to know, Meg."

She looked at Simon uneasily. "I have no idea, honey," she said at last.

"I have no idea, honey," Simon mimicked nastily. He

picked up the vase and threw it as hard as he could. We watched it arc into the road without spilling its roses, then shatter. Lucinda jerked. Out in the road, a small flood of water spread out among the scattered roses and broken glass and humped patches of tar.

Simon's face had turned red and his hands were poised in the air, ready to twirl around in that peculiar way that meant he was about to go insane. "Who have you been seeing, Meg? Tell me!"

Meg blinked. "Simon, honey. I would never cheat on you." She nodded at us. "Ask the kids."

That's it, Meg. Turn to us for protection. Like you've protected us. But I said: "She'd never cheat on you, Simon." Boone nodded frantically in confirmation.

Simon pointed at her stomach. "That ain't my baby. That ain't my flesh and blood!"

"Of course it is!"

"You don't understand! This is one kid I'm gonna raise to be loyal! And how can a kid be loyal when it ain't even mine? It's hard enough to train one that *is* your kid!"

Standing there, gazing at my mother's extended belly, my heart full of fear, I remembered that day last fall when Meg went into town to meet some unknown person, in her best sling-back shoes, in a cloud of mystery.

Simon's hands were twirling around and around in the air, like two softballs hit glancingly. "You whore. How dare you betray me! I turn my back for one second and you scamper into the sack with God knows who."

Meg ran her hands through her hair and then over her belly, looking at me pleadingly for a moment before turning back to Simon. "It's your baby, Simon. It's yours."

"Let me ask you something, you stupid whore," Simon

whispered. "How can I bring back my drowned boy if you're carrying the son of another man? How am I supposed to *start over*?"

"I swear to you, Simon—"

"You better, Meg. You better swear. 'Cause woe to you, woman, if you've betrayed me." He turned and went into the house, leaving the three of us standing there motionless and Lucinda, ignored, sitting patiently on the quilt.

"Meg," I said. "Who were those roses from?"

Her face was drained of color and her lie came out softly. "I don't know. I just don't know."

I had to admit that there was the smallest relief in me that Simon was angry at Meg rather than at us. But the larger part of me felt no safer for it, because anyone could see that something was coming unraveled in Simon, some dark thing.

But perhaps my real daddy was coming back. Perhaps he was circling in, determined not to just win Meg back but to save us all, lifting weights to grow his muscles, taking boxing lessons, aiming a gun at a target, earmuffs on and an instructor shouting orders. Perhaps he was calling the police or the evening news. Or maybe he was stooped in a distant graveyard, digging up two bodies—an adult and a child—to turn over to a lab. And was that my father's boy growing in my mother's womb?

Simon sulked in his room all day and wouldn't come to the dinner table. Boone and I ate like wolves, then split the food left on Lucinda's plate. That night Meg was afraid to go into the room with Simon. She spread a blanket out on the den floor next to Lucinda's couch instead. Boone and I retired to our room, where we argued in sibilant whispers about Boone's need to see Persely Snow. We finally agreed (or rather Boone insisted and I finally relented) that sneaking out of a house whose tensions were reaching the fever point, in search of a teenage maniac whose presence in our lives would only add to those tensions, was something we needed to do.

Boone had brought a flashlight and a can of Vienna sausages and a small box of saltines for Persely. We skulked along the side streets, listening for sounds of footsteps and news crews and sirens. When we reached the park, Boone switched on the flashlight and directed the beam toward the hardwoods that separated the park from an electric power facility. He had told Persely to wait for us in the shelter of this coppice.

We climbed the fence and moved through the woods, kicking ancient leaves, some so dead they didn't even crackle but coated the bottoms of our shoes.

"Persely," he whispered. "Persely?"

Silence.

We stood there and listened to the night birds call. Suddenly, Persely Snow leaped into the beam of the flashlight.

My heart stopped.

"See? You can't sneak up on Persely Snow. Persely is at home in the woods." Her voice was confident again. She was no longer pale and shivering, but restored to her obnoxious self. "What did you bring me?" She tore the paper bag out of Boone's hands and eagerly pulled out the food. "Vee-anna sausages!" she cried. "I haven't had Vee-anna sausages in years!" She wolfed it down, drank the fluid in the can and tore open the saltines.

"What have you been doing all day?" I asked.

"Hiding out, dimwit." She swallowed the last of the food. "I am patient. I lay low." Her expression grew suddenly somber. "Your crazy stepdaddy didn't follow you here, did he?"

"Of course not," said Boone.

"Why?" I asked. "You scared?"

"Me? I'm not scared of nothing. It's just that, you know, some of the stuff he was saying about me last night . . . about people out to get me . . ." Her voice fell and she seemed to go into a trance for a moment, her pupils very large despite the direct beam of Boone's flashlight. She shook her head slowly, looked at me and finished her thought. Her voice trembled slightly. "You ever hear of the Snow Hunters?"

"No," I said, but Boone nodded.

"What are the Snow Hunters?" I asked.

I heard Boone's foot scuffing against the ground, and he spoke solemnly. "They're a group of people—"

"Young rednecks," said Persely.

"Who want to—"

"Hunt me down," Persely finished for him.

I didn't understand. Were they some kind of citizens' group, a bunch of do-gooders dedicated to bringing criminals to justice? "They want to turn you in?" I asked Persely.

She laughed harshly. "Boone," she said. "Tell your sister what's what."

"Ah . . ." said Boone. "They've got CBs and they ride around in trucks together. One of them's got a police scanner to find out the latest Persely sightings. They want to . . . they want to . . ."

"Catch me and throw me down and fuck me," Persely finished for him again. "It's like a sport. Once they had me trapped in a warehouse, and they were circling around like wolves. I broke out a back window and scraped my shoulder to hell. But they didn't get no Persely."

"Persely," I gasped. "That's horrible."

"Ah, that's fame, honey. By the way, are all the people on TV talking about me?"

"Not a one," I said.

"Really?" She looked disappointed. She sat down and leaned her long back against a tree. Boone and I sat down, too. Boone switched off his flashlight, darkening our space in the woods. "I know what it is," Persely said finally. "The hospital's trying to keep a lid on it. They're embarrassed 'cause they're all a bunch of horse's asses that keep letting me give 'em the slip." She held up her hands, fingers spread, pushing them close to my face so I could count. "This is numero seven."

"Where do you usually hide?" asked Boone. "I mean, when you escape?"

"Most anywhere. Warehouses, silos, woods, parks, nice people's houses, sometimes in the backs of stores. Two nights I slept down at an old pier off of Lake Shine."

"Lake Shine?" Boone said. "That's right! You used to swim down there."

"No, I did not swim down there. I used to live 'round there. But I can't swim a stroke."

"But I read it in the newspaper," Boone said. "You were the captain of the swim team in seventh grade."

"You probably also read that I set my bed on fire in the hospital. Bullshit. I don't know where they get this crap. You bring me cigarettes, Boone?"

"Are you kidding?" Boone answered. "Do you think I'm going to try stealing them from Simon again?"

"You could have bought me some."

"It's just that I've never bought cigarettes before," said Boone. "It makes me feel a little . . . guilty."

"What's guilty, Boone? Is it buying cigarettes? Or is the town singing 'Amazing Grace' while they're hanging two boys for rustling cattle when those boys ain't never been in trouble before? Cooper saw it all from Miss Rachel's window, and he would have cried if he could of."

"God," I said. "Why don't you shut up about that stupid movie?"

"Let's not fight," said Boone. "We have to get home soon."

"How is your bastard stepdaddy, anyway?" Persely asked. The tone in her voice had changed slightly.

"Crazy," I said. "Now he's got it in his head that our mother's baby isn't his."

"Well, maybe it ain't."

For some reason I felt the need to lean forward until I could make out Persely's features and share my wild hope. "I'm thinking it's our real father's baby. The last I saw, he wasn't liking his marriage too much, so I figure he might be coming back."

When Persely spoke, her voice was strangely sympathetic. "Poor kid," she murmured. "The world just ain't that way." She fell silent, and we let the conversation die, listening to the new breeze and to the crickets.

"Poison him, Boone," she added suddenly. "And poison her, too, for being so weak. For caring more about him than her own kids."

My brother shifted his position. The crackle of old leaves and the mulchy whisper of pine straw. "Don't talk like that. Please. It's not right."

"He deserves it, don't he? And don't she?"

"It's not up to us to judge."

"And who's supposed to judge?"

"God."

"There ain't no friggin' God. There's nothing in the world but the way things are already gonna turn out. You gotta be God yourself, and sometimes even that don't help."

Boone turned his flashlight on again, putting his hand over it so that the light came through his red fingers. He didn't speak for a long time, but simply stared down into the light as though God himself lingered in that tiny bulb, just under Boone's fingers, and was instructing him in tiny chirps. "There is a God," Boone finally said. "And He's your friend."

In response Persely jumped to her feet, moving backward so that almost all of her was lost in the intersecting shades of a barely starlit night. Boone pointed the flashlight, and its tepid yellow beam found her face. A different face, wild and ferocious.

"Why didn't He answer me, then?" Persely shouted. "Didn't I ask Him right? When I was thirteen and I said, please God, don't let me . . ." Her voice trailed off.

"Persely, what's the matter? What are you talking about?" My brother stood up and she moved away from him, backing up into a cluster of vines and branches and then sliding sideways behind a tree. The flashlight beam hugged the old tree. We could see just a little of her T-shirt.

"Forget it," she said.

Persely must have been right about the hospital covering up her escape, for the rest of the week passed and the media was silent. There were no articles on Persely Snow, no news coverage. No one spoke about her in the halls at school. No one knew that Persely was active again, on the loose, shinier than the electricity whose plant bordered her woods, freer than the birds that stood upon their half-finished nests and eyed her golden hair.

More important, Simon didn't know it, although his mood could not have been darker after the incident with the roses. "Tell me, Meg," he said. "I just want the truth. Is that baby mine?"

"Of course it is, Simon," said Meg.

"You lying bitch! May God strike you dead!"

"Simon," said Meg desperately. "Tell me how I can prove it to you."

Simon walked up to Meg and put his arms around her, drawing her close. "Let me cut you open and pull it out," he whispered. "And check the color of its eyes."

The more he pushed Meg away, the nicer he was to Lucinda. So nice and so absorbed that he seemed to have forgotten about Boone and me. He sat with her on the quilt, told her Bible stories, held her hand. Brushed her blond hair out of her face while Lucinda, insensate, let her back slump into an arc.

I watched them with a growing apprehension.

When we visited Persely, we found her increasingly restless. "What do you want me to do?" she asked one night. "Stay in these stupid woods forever? No ma'am! I'd rather jump the fence to the power plant and fry myself."

"No one knows you're on the loose," said my brother. "The last thing I want is Simon finding out. Or the Snow Hunters."

"But how long do I stay here?"

"Until we figure something else out."

"This sucks," said Persely, crossing her arms. "My public needs me."

"Don't worry, Persely," said my brother tenderly. "I'll take care of you." Boone had smuggled her over some soap and a bucketful of water the night before, and all the way home he'd remained glassy-eyed, no doubt fighting the urge to imagine her bathing naked in the woods.

We all sat down in a semicircle. Boone had finally been brave enough to buy her a carton of Virginia Slims, and now she took a long drag of her cigarette.

"Mmmmenthol," she said blissfully. Then: "You know what's wrong with y'all?"

I didn't answer, but Boone had to say, "What?"

"You're both chickenshit. Just like your mother. You won't fight back."

"We're just kids."

"We're just kids," Persely said, her voice so full of mockery that I wanted to slap her. "I was thirteen years old when I showed my parents what-for."

It was about to begin again: another sermon from Persely on resistance, on justice, on getting even, on the complete and total lack of God in the world—themes she'd been repeating to us for almost a week now.

"You sound like you're proud of what you did," I said.

"I am proud of it." Persely's cigarette smoke spiraled up and away.

I leaned forward. "Well, then, let me ask you something, Persely. What the hell did your parents do that was so bad they deserved to die for it?"

I heard Boone catch his breath. Persely stared at me, puffing out her cheeks, then released another cloud of smoke. "Plenty," she said. "If you knew what they done, you wouldn't blame me."

"Alice," said Boone. "Leave her alone. If she doesn't want to talk about it, she doesn't have to."

"I can see wanting to kill one parent, maybe," I persisted. "But how can both parents deserve it?"

Persely stubbed out her cigarette against the side of a tree, and we heard the small crackle of the loose bark. "Boone," she said. "Your sister's bugging me."

"I was just curious," I said defensively.

"Come over here, Boone," said Persely in a weak, tired voice. "Sit by me. I'm freezing."

Boone moved over next to Persely. Even in the dim starlight, I could see that she was shivering, though the night was warm.

"Put your arm around me, Boone."

"Like this?"

"Yes."

After a few moments Boone put his other arm around her.

"Stop talking about God," she said. "It makes me cold."

My brother was falling under Persely's spell so completely that it frightened me. Already I felt Boone leaving me. We were no longer a team. He and Persely were a team. I was just the little sister.

"You don't have to go with me every time," Boone told

me as he slid open the casement window and I prepared to tag along.

But I did want to go, because I didn't want to be left out of anything my brother did. And because try as I might, Persely Snow fascinated me. Her rough manner. Her bitter laugh and her brooding silences. The way she smoked cigarettes. And the stories she told—so frank and yet so shrouded in a deeper mystery. She was hiding something, and her secret moved me.

"What are you going to do about her, really?" I asked Boone one night as we lay in our room waiting for the rest of the house to fall asleep. "How do you think you're going to date a girl that no one is supposed to see? And how are you going to take five acres of woods to your prom?"

Boone shrugged.

"And here's something else to think about, Boone. You're supposed to be such a religious person. Do you think it's right to help Persely? She's a murderer. And she's not sorry. And for all we know, she could kill someone else."

"I've thought about that," he said hesitantly, "but you see, if I can just talk to her awhile, and tell her about God, I'm sure that I could help her."

"Help her what?"

"You know. Find peace."

"Find peace or fall in love with you?"

Boone looked uncomfortable. Naked. "It will all work itself out," he said finally.

I had noticed a slight change in him. He still showed a mortal fear of Simon, still ate his food with great care, still inspected himself for signs of poisoning, but now a stream of defiance was beginning to run through his body. And he was looking at Simon with his eyes a bit narrowed.

Once I caught Boone in the kitchen, staring at the picture of the smiling boy.

"What did you do to him, Simon?" Boone whispered.

Chapter Sixteen

I stood at the kitchen sink, washing the dishes. Boone had gone to the store with Meg. Simon sat outside on the front lawn with Lucinda. The television blared through the kitchen wall. Suddenly I heard something that made me drop a soapy skillet and rush into the living room. A newsman was talking. In the box at the upper right-hand corner of the screen, I saw a picture of Persely Snow. "... in the fall of 1968 was found not guilty of patricide by reason of insanity. Hospital officials can give no explanation for her latest escape, although the psychiatrist on staff released this statement: 'Persely Snow is a criminal of an extremely high intelligence. If there were a thousand Persely

Snows in the Texas mental health system, we would bank-
rupt ourselves trying to keep all of them incarcerated.'"

I went to the window to check on Simon. He was still
with Lucinda.

The newsman continued: "News of Persely Snow's escape broke today when the girl was spotted in the Mont-
gomery County area." The picture cut to a reporter
standing outside a small peach house next to an excited-
looking woman. A group of people was clustered behind
them, holding up signs that said RUN, PERSELY! and PERSELY
SNOW FAN CLUB.

The reporter said, "Mrs. Thomas Greely of 122 Pine Avenue got quite a surprise this morning, didn't you, Mrs.
Greely?"

She nodded. The people cheered behind her.

"Can you tell us what happened?"

"She came knocking on my door 'round about eight-
thirty," Mrs. Greely said in a breathy voice. "She needed to
brush her hair, but she looked like a movie star otherwise. I
invited her in and I made her some scrambled eggs."

"What did she say?"

"She said she's been gone from that nuthouse for a
while, but they were too embarrassed to tell anyone. She
said that the Texas police were the stupidest in the world,
and maybe if they'd stop making out with each other in
donut shops, then they could find her."

The people behind the woman cheered again. The reporter looked a little disconcerted. "Did she say anything
else?"

"Yes," said Mrs. Greely and began tearing up. "She said
she wouldn't be taken alive this time." The woman looked
straight into the camera. "Persely, honey, we'll adopt you!"

The news report moved on to a story about a cheerleader from a local high school who had fallen, drunk, out of a party boat into the still waters of Lake Shine. Her body had not yet been recovered.

I clicked off the television.

When Boone came through the door with a bag of groceries, I hustled him into the back room. "You'll never guess," I said.

"What?"

"Your big-mouthed girlfriend is on the news!"

"Oh, no." He sank down on the bed and put his head in his hands.

"It's worse, Boone. She visited someone on Pine Street. That's only half a mile from here. And she taunted the police. Always a smart thing."

Boone looked at me in sudden terror. "Does Simon know?"

"Not yet."

"What are we going to do?"

"We're going to stay right here and never talk to her again."

"No, seriously."

"I am serious! She's caused us nothing but trouble."

"I don't care," said Boone, more firmly than I was used to. "I've got to find her and hide her somewhere better."

Simon sat at the head of the table and picked at his food. He had not heard the news reports but was in a foul mood anyway, and the distant sirens were making him jumpy. Ever since Meg had received the roses, Simon's suspicions had periodically flared.

"What the hell is going on tonight?" he demanded.

"Maybe there's a fire somewhere," Meg said lamely.

"Maybe it's at your ex-husband's house. You slut."

"Simon, please. Not in front of Lucinda."

Over the past few nights, Simon had moved down the table in increments until he was right next to Lucinda, his right elbow crowding her left breast. He touched her hand, then reached across the table to grab the sugar bowl. He threw back his head and let the sugar flow into his mouth.

"So, Meg," he said, crunching. "Don't think I'm a man, do you?" His eyes were shining.

"Of course you're a man, honey."

"Didn't think I was up for the job, did you? Had to hunt down someone else? Dan, probably. Or maybe the Fuller Brush man. Is that what's going on, Meg? Were you fucking the blind Fuller Brush man while his guide dog stared at you?"

"No, no," Meg said. Tears had begun to run down her face. She leaned over to cut Lucinda's pork chop.

"I was wrong about you, Meg," Simon said. "Wrong as hell. I thought you were loyal to me. That I could *trust* you. Did you know that you were the only person I trusted in the *world*?"

A piece of pork chop dribbled out of Lucinda's mouth. Simon turned to stare at her. Reached over and touched her hand. Looked at her intently. Finished his thought: "Maybe you need to learn a lesson about *loyalty,* Meg."

Chapter Seventeen

By midnight all was quiet, save for the occasional siren blaring in the distance. Boone and I paced around our room in tight little circles, trying to decide what to do. His elbow hit mine as our paths converged. He stopped pacing and looked at me. "What do you think Simon meant by those things he was saying? He couldn't possibly be interested in Lucinda."

"I don't know, Boone. Simon's crazy. He might be trying to get back at Meg."

"By messing with some girl with brain damage?"

"Who else would have him?"

We resumed our frantic circling.

"I've got to go find Persely," said Boone. "The cops are after her now. What if they've got her? What if the Snow Hunters have her?"

"We've got to protect Lucinda, too."

Boone groaned. "How do we do both things at once?" He dropped onto the bed, took off his glasses and wiped them clean, an activity that always cleared his mind. "This is what I'll do," he said finally. "I think Lucinda's okay for right now. I looked in Simon and Meg's room when I was on my way back from the bathroom, and they're both sound asleep. I'll go find Persely, move her somewhere safe, then get back here in a couple hours."

"If you insist." Reluctantly I added, "I'll stay here."

"No! I need your brain."

And so we checked on Lucinda one last time, returned to our room and slipped out the back window. On the way to the park we saw people out in their lawn chairs, or sitting in the street under the halogen streetlamps, drinking wine. Laughing. A carnival atmosphere. A famous murderer had been spotted in their neighborhood and made their lives interesting again. We kept walking, two ordinary children who didn't collect so much as a glance.

Police cars whizzed by us, and trucks full of young men blared country music.

"Hicks," I muttered.

The park was deserted for now. We found Persely sitting on the lowest branch of an oak tree in a little clearing, smoking a cigarette.

"Hello, idiot," I said angrily.

"Hello, yourself."

"You just couldn't keep away from your fans, could you?"

Persely jumped down from the tree and swept her hair out of her face. The wind was making the sound of a fat boy cannonballing into the deep end of a pool. "I didn't break out of that nuthatch just to pee in the woods forever. And I was tired of eating those Vee-anna sausages and those damn crackers. I got a real breakfast this morning."

"You shouldn't have done what you did," my brother said soberly. "Now everyone's after you, and when my stepfather hears you've escaped, he's going to go even crazier."

"I heard the cops pass by today, blasting their homo sirens," Persely said calmly. She took another long drag from her cigarette and exhaled slowly, the smoke captured by the wind and borne away to corrupt thc lungs of the singing crickets. "Persely's back and better than ever."

"Crazier than ever," I said.

My insult only seemed to lift Persely's spirits further. "You know what I did at the hearing? You know, way back when? I acted real polite and normal. But I tried not to blink. And every now and then I licked my arm like this . . ." She swiped her tongue around the inside of her wrist. "That's all it took. And when I saw the shrink they hired, I told him I did it 'cause my mama and my daddy had too many As in their names. He fell for it, stupid jackass. Of course, I really hate that letter. Always have."

"Just to think up that stuff," I said, "you've got to be a little bit nuts."

She folded her arms across her chest. "I'm gettin' tired of you."

"Likewise."

"Stop it," said Boone. "Both of you."

Persely and I glared at each other through the pollen motes in the air.

"Let's make a plan," said Boone. "Sooner or later the cops will make a sweep through here."

"That nice lady from this morning would hide me," said Persely.

"First of all," I said, "the cops already know you've been there once. They've probably got the place all staked out. And secondly, you hadn't cleared the front driveway this morning before that woman was on the phone with the newspapers."

Persely shrugged. "Where, then?"

I paced back and forth, my feet sinking into loam as I thought of an answer, squinting each time the crickets chirped. "There's an old Coca-Cola bottling plant in the old town square. Next to the railroad tracks."

"Yeah, I know the place," said Boone. "It's two or three miles from here, at least. We could ride our bikes there. Persely could ride on my handlebars. Like you used to do."

"Good idea. And Persely could sing the national anthem and pass out free Tang. No. We're going to have to dart over there like rats. Away from the streets as much as possible."

Persely threw away her cigarette and hitched up her jeans. "Why are you doing all this for me, anyhow?"

"We want to protect you," said Boone.

"You do?" Her face wore an expression that I couldn't quite discern in the darkness, but her voice was soft, child-like. She walked up to Boone and touched his shoulder. "You'd protect me, Boone?"

"With my life."

They just stood there silently, Persely's hand on Boone's shoulder and Boone motionless in that dark clearing, the wind pulling on their hair. At last I said, "Let's get going, then."

* * *

The three of us crouched together beneath a huge yaupon bush by the side of Oland Avenue, waiting for the cars to pass before we dared cross over. Boone breathed noisily from the long, hard run from the park; sweat ran down his face. Persely, however, seemed exhilarated by the exertion and the danger, and smiled at odd moments. I felt dizzy from the pollen and sick with anger at Persely. Were it not for her, we'd be at home guarding a helpless girl, as we should have been.

"Now!" said Persely, and we ran across the avenue, keeping low. A truck came barreling around the bend and caught us briefly in the headlights just before we reached the curb and threw ourselves over an azalea hedge whose blooms had died in early May.

We lay together, our breath whistling, sounds of cars passing.

"Do you think the person in the truck saw us?" Persely asked.

I peered over the hedge. "I don't know. He didn't stop. Let's just keep going."

We followed the azalea hedge to the next intersection and slipped across another street, then ran through the parking lot of a builder's-supply store and took the back alley to a raised berm. We climbed up to the railroad tracks and walked silently along them. On one side of us lay the warehouse district; on the other side, a steep declivity that ended in another street. We heard the cars passing by but could not be seen ourselves.

"Hurry," Boone told Persely.

"Why? No one can see us now."

"We don't have all night. We have to get back to Lucinda."

"The retard?"

"She's not retarded. Brain-damaged."

"What's the difference?"

"I don't know."

"Why do you need to get back to her?"

"Long story."

The moon overhead. Stars scattered here and there. The cross-ties of the railroad presented a reasonable path for us to follow.

"Ever rode on a train?" asked Persely.

My brother shook his head.

"I have," she said. "Once, when I escaped, I got halfway to Kansas City on a train before they got me. That's where I'll go someday. Kansas City."

A stitch had grown in my side and I pushed two fingers into it, trying to ease the pain. "Don't forget to write."

After an hour we reached the intersection of the railroad tracks and the main street of Old Town. We walked down the broken sidewalk, passing deserted stores whose best commerce had come and gone forty years before, our bodies hugging the buildings so close that we brushed away dust and left the windows looking wounded. The moon threw a heavy white circle down on our shoulders and we picked up our pace. Suddenly two beams of light cut the moon's glow and bounced off the store window in front of us. A truck was coming.

"Just act natural," Boone hissed.

The truck slowed and then passed. We heard the brakes squeal.

"Run!" said Boone and the three of us raced one another

to the corner and darted down a dark street strewn with litter. The truck followed us. Persely was behind me, Boone
just ahead of me. His hand flew out and the beam from a
headlight struck it as we ran faster, our arms and legs
churning, our breath hurting in our lungs. The truck had
stopped and two men were running behind us. We found an
alley, dodging wine bottles, and veered left into another
side street before plunging once again into an alley. My
heart was pounding, the stitch in my side contracting with
an agonizing pain. Boone threw himself behind a Dumpster and pulled me down with him. He was breathing so
hard he couldn't speak for several moments. Finally he
gasped, "Where . . . is . . . Persely?"

As if in answer, we heard a grunt and the sound of
bottles hitting one another. I looked around the Dumpster
and saw Persely down on the ground. A man was on top of
her, trying to pin down her arms. Her hand flew up and
knocked his cowboy hat off of him. He slapped her and
tore at her clothes.

"Oh my God, Boone!" I cried. "Someone's got her. We
have to help her!"

But Boone had that glassy look in his eyes I had seen so
many times. "I . . . can't move."

"Try!"

"Persely." His voice was full of horror. I tried to pull on
my brother's arm, but it was useless. Persely moaned, and
as much as I hated her, I could not remain behind that
Dumpster. I inched out from behind my shelter and began
creeping back down the alley. The other man was nowhere
in sight, but Persely and her attacker were still struggling.
Their movements had a surreal quality, as though I could
stand there until the sun came up and be able to make a

slow, sad, safe decision on how to proceed. The man was trying to unfasten Persely's jeans and didn't see me coming. I picked up a wine bottle, a gallon jug that dripped on my shoes as I carried it, and quietly approached them. When I was in range, I bared my teeth. And swung that jug with all my strength.

A sickening thump. The man said nothing but clutched his head and drew his breath so deeply into his lungs that I knew I'd hurt him badly.

Persely gave a single wild buck, and the man teetered and lost his balance and fell over. She scrambled to her feet and the two of us ran back down the alley. Boone had regained some strength in his legs and was dragging himself toward us. We grabbed his arms and pulled him back to a side street. By the time we reached the next block he'd recovered completely, and the three of us sprinted to the bottling plant, ducking behind a half-fallen brick wall, panting.

After our breath steadied, I said: "Were those Snow Hunters?"

Persely didn't answer me. She sat down and we joined her.

"You're all right, Persely, aren't you?" I asked. "That man didn't—"

Persely pushed the hair out of her face, leaning her head back against the brick wall. "No," she mumbled. She looked over at Boone. "Where were you?"

Boone took his glasses off. "Behind the Dumpster."

"Why didn't you help?"

"I wanted to, Persely . . . but I couldn't. I'm so sorry. Sometimes I get scared and then I just get paralyzed."

"It's true," I said, sensing Persely's anger and Boone's desperation. "Maybe it's a medical thing."

Persely crossed her arms and rested her head against the brick wall again. In profile she seemed a much younger girl. Her silence unnerved me, for it contained no serenity, no resolution, only a torment avidly at work. I wondered what she was thinking, what she was remembering. Was it the Snow Hunter's breath, a sheriff's tight handcuffs, the inside of a grain silo, the grass of the cow pasture that bordered the state hospital, her parents falling in slow motion onto a linoleum floor? Or something else, something that I could not know?

"Persely can't stay at this plant," I said. "It's not safe. Where can we go now?"

"We'll think of a place," Boone assured Persely.

"Wait a minute," I whispered. "I have the perfect place. I don't know why I didn't think of it before." I reached across Persely's lap and touched Boone on the arm. "Never Island. On Lake Shine."

"Why would I want to go there?" Persely asked in a flat, tired voice.

"Because there's a clearing in the middle of the island that no one knows about," said Boone. "My sister and I used to go out there all the time. In the rainy season it's about knee-deep in water, but it's been dry. It would be a good place to hide."

"I don't like lakes," said Persely.

"Do you like the Snow Hunters?" I asked.

Boone touched Persely's arm. "Please. Stay there, at least until we can find a better place for you. I'll bring you food and supplies."

Persely let out her breath with a long sigh. She scratched the tip of her nose and raked her fingers through the sides of her hair. "Okay. Let's go."

"Wait a minute," I said. "How are we possibly going to walk all the way to Lake Shine? It's five or six miles away."

Persely raised her head above the wall and ducked back down. "There's a truck over yonder," she said.

"So? We don't have the keys."

"Who needs keys?" For a moment she appeared to be her old spirited self before her face darkened again. "Follow me," she said quietly.

When we reached the old truck, Persely threw a quick glance down the street, then tried the front door. It swung open. She climbed inside and inspected the steering wheel.

"No wheel-lock," she announced.

"What are you doing, Persely?" I asked.

"We're going to take this truck."

"You mean steal it?"

"You got a pocketknife, Boone?"

Boone dutifully turned it over. I moved closer, rising on my toes to watch Persely reach under the dash and pull out a mass of brightly colored wires, three of which she cut carefully, concentrating, her teeth pressing on her lower lip. She arranged the wires into some magical configuration, and the truck roared to life.

"Climb in," she ordered.

"Don't argue with her," Boone whispered in my ear. "Just get in."

Boone and I ran around to the other side and climbed in the truck. Persely pulled on the headlights and threw the truck into reverse. As it lurched backward and then braked, I lost my balance and slammed my head against the dash.

"Oh!" I groaned. Boone put his arms around me and pulled me close to him. Persely put the truck in drive, stomped her foot on the accelerator and jumped the curb. She slammed on the brakes. Reverse. Forward. Neutral. Forward. Slam. Reverse. Boone's arms tightened around me as Persely finally made it down the street.

"That was subtle," I said.

"Where did you learn to hot-wire a car?" Boone asked. She didn't answer.

"Why did you just turn left, Persely?" I demanded. "You're supposed to turn right. Left is back to Old Town."

Persely stepped on the accelerator and we careened through a red light and beyond.

"Did you hear what I said?" I asked nervously, but she was in her own space now, in some kind of grim trance, and as Boone and I shouted at her to *turn around, go back, what are you doing, Persely do you hear us,* she simply made the turns she wanted to, until once again the truck was hurtling down a familiar alley. A man was lurching along, holding his wounded head. It was the Snow Hunter I'd hit with the wine bottle. And suddenly I knew what Persely meant to do.

"Persely, no!" I screamed.

"You can't do that! You can't!" Boone shouted.

I tried to grab the wheel, but Persely shoved me against my brother with surprising strength. I closed my eyes and braced for the impact.

It didn't come.

I looked back. The Snow Hunter apparently had found the strength to hurl himself out of the way and was pressed against the side of the building that bordered the alley.

There once came a point in my life with Simon when I

looked at him and knew he was capable of things far beyond what I'd expected, and that the limitations I'd put on him were weak, pathetic things. It was with this same realization that I now looked at Persely.

She hit the gas. I heard a dog's lonely howl. And we headed for Lake Shine.

Poisoners apparently did not make for the best drivers. Persely jumped curbs and ran stop signs and careened down the street like the maniac she was. I could not believe every policeman in the state of Texas wasn't roaring after us. Following our frightened instructions, Persely finally got us to the old abandoned highway that led to Lake Shine. We fell silent. The headlights illuminated the cracks in the road. I looked out past ditches full of thistle and studied the sleeping cows.

Persely ran onto the shoulder, crossed the road and drove on the wrong side.

"You're not in England, Persely," I said. "Unfortunately."

"You try it." She managed to steady the wheel, then punched the gas so hard that I lurched forward again.

Boone had said barely a word since our encounter with the Snow Hunter. As we glided down the highway, I heard him sniff. I put my fingers to his face and touched his tears.

We rode in silence.

Persely finally said: "You've got some balls, girl. You fought for me."

I didn't know what to say. Persely took her hand from the steering wheel and patted my leg awkwardly. "You ain't so bad. You're like me. A tiger. A warrior. A marshal for justice. Not a sheep." I knew this last remark was directed at Boone.

"I'm sorry, Persely," he said miserably. "I'm sorry, I'm sorry."

I said, "It's not too much farther to the lake. We've got to hide this truck."

"Fine," said Persely. "I have an idea." The headlights caught a tiny dirt road that led to the cow pasture. Persely slowed and turned. "Boone, go open that gate."

"But that just leads to the cow pasture."

"And what does every cow pasture got?"

"Cows?"

"Open the gate."

Boone got out of the truck and did as he was told. Persley turned to me. "You get out, too," she said.

Boone and I stood together in medium heat, under a medium moon, and watched Persely gun the truck around the cow pasture. Cows woke up and galloped away from her, flicking their tails and craning their necks.

Boone crossed his arms. "What's she doing?"

"Let's see. She knows she needs to be really quiet and not attract any attention, so she's going to run down as many cows as she can and then make a bonfire out of their dead bodies and dance around it naked."

We could barely see the truck lights. We heard a splash and ran toward the sound.

Persely was standing by a large pond, watching the truck begin to sink. She lit a cigarette.

"Why did you do that?" I gasped.

"I'm hiding it."

"But that was someone's truck!"

She shrugged and squinted at me. "And those are some-one's cows and you are someone's kid. Life is sure not fair."

We walked the rest of the way to Lake Shine through the pasture, moving around agitated cows and then the ones still asleep. Mr. Wall's dock was quiet. Boone untied the boat, climbed in, and pulled on the throttle until the motor started. Persely grabbed my shoulder, uninvited, to balance herself as she climbed in. We settled ourselves and then we were off, with only a moon to guide us.

"Did you say you two used to swim here?" Persely asked me.

"Yeah. But you have to be careful. People drown here. Some cheerleader drowned last weekend, in fact. Half the time the divers can't even find their bodies."

"Why not?"

"Lake's too deep. But once, during a drought, the water level dropped so far down that they found a guy still in his wet suit. He'd drowned eleven years before."

Persely gazed out at the black smooth water. I leaned forward and told her: "Boone's on your side, Persely."

"Ain't no sides," she whispered. "Just outside and in-side. And there ain't no . . . inside."

We were all silent the rest of the way. When we neared the shoreline of Never Island, I looked over and saw that Persely was asleep. Boone cut the motor and glided through the cattails, which, under moonlight, were show-ing green through their gray beards. All was quiet, just the waves splashing up against the shore and the deeper, wider sounds of currents moving through the fat green lake. Boone jumped out and tied off on a scrubby-looking tree. I followed him, water moving up my pant legs, and we waded to shore together. We climbed up the bank, then sat down and watched Persely sleep on her seat by the bow of the boat.

"Should we wake her up?" I asked.

"Not yet. I just want to look at her a minute."

"We need to get back to Lucinda."

"Yes," he murmured. "Lucinda. As if having me around is any protection."

The boat rocked in the waves and Persely's eyes stayed closed.

Boone pushed his glasses back on his nose. "I can't believe that you don't even love her and you're the one that saved her."

"I didn't think. I just did it. You will, too, Boone, next time."

Boone stood up and went back down the bank. He waded out to the boat and collected Persely in his arms. Impressed, I watched him climb the steep bank without dropping her or even waking her up.

"She's exhausted," he whispered, and set her down next to me.

Persely stirred. "Where are we?" she murmured.

"On the island."

Boone helped her to her feet, and the three of us went into a forest that immediately darkened around us. We crept forward blindly, the pine straw brushing our faces and every little movement around us causing our breath to catch. Persely tripped once, but Boone caught her before she fell.

After ten minutes we reached the downward slope that ended in the center of the island. We left the shelter of the trees, the moonlight fell on our shoulders, and we saw the clearing.

"You call this a clearing?" Persely asked, waving her hand toward the brambles and briars, the high grass and the scatterings of waist-high tallow trees. She took a few more steps and stumbled. "I can't walk no further. The briars are hurting me."

"I'm sorry," said Boone. "It's grown up since we've been here. I'll have to borrow Mr. Walt's machete and hack us out a clearing."

He took his shirt off and spread it out on top of the briars and weeds.

"Try this," he said.

"Ow," said Persely when she sat down on it. "The briars cut through."

"I'm sorry," said Boone.

"You and your stupid ideas." But Persely's voice was fading.

"We have to go now," I said. "We've got to guard Lucinda Laird."

"Guard her?" Persely asked sleepily. "Why do you need to guard some retard girl?"

"Because we think maybe our stepfather likes her," I said. "I know it sounds crazy, but we think he might like her—you know—in a weird way."

Persely Snow jumped to her feet, all her weariness suddenly gone, her teeth bared and her eyes wide open. "Then get the fuck back there!" she shouted. "How could you leave that girl? How could you leave her? Get back there! Get back there!"

"We're going right now, Persely," said Boone. "Don't worry. We'll protect her."

She turned on Boone and unleashed a savage fury. "No, not you! You're not gonna do *shit*, because you're a fucking *chickenshit* who just stands there and doesn't do nothing! You and your little friend God!" She whirled around to face me. "*You* do it! You protect her, Alice. You fight for her, Alice!"

My brother didn't speak on the way back to the dock, and when I tried to talk to him, he turned his head. I could tell by his posture that what Persely said had undone him. After he tied the boat to the dock, he kicked the bow suddenly.

"What's the matter?"

He kicked the bow again. "I'm the matter!" He jabbed at his own bare chest. "I couldn't protect her back then— whatever happened with her parents. And I couldn't protect her tonight! I'm useless!"

"But—"

"I just stand back and let things happen to people, and I don't do *shit* about it!"

His first swear word. Silently I added this last sin to the others. His first cigarette. His first lie. His first grand theft auto. His first hiding of a famous murderess on a calm fat lake under the golden moonlight. Boone's face had turned a mottled red, and I could not stand by and watch him unravel just as we were returning home to a nightmare. I remembered my dreams about him dying, and my voice shook when I said, "Let's go. We've got to get back to Lucinda."

"What for?" he asked fiercely. "When have I ever helped stop anything?"

"Let's go."

Boone looked around. "Go where? We don't have a truck anymore, remember? And we don't have our bicycles."

"We'll have to walk, then."

"Are you kidding? It's miles from here! We'll never make it back by dawn."

"We have no choice." We started down the road, our pace brisk and our minds clouded by the events of the night. Boone was still angry with himself. He muttered in the dark. The cows were sleeping in the fields and the air was pleasant, ruined only by the motes of drama rising up from our lives.

"Walk faster," I said. Just then I heard the sound of tires on the old broken road. I turned around and looked into headlights.

"Run!" said Boone.

"Why? No one's after us. We're just a couple of kids trying to get home." I stuck my thumb out. The truck slowed down, and a man in a cowboy hat rolled down his window. He was young—eighteen or nineteen—and had a friendly, smooth face and a wide smile. Dust was rising from his tires, and I breathed in a bland cloud of it.

"Damn!" the young man said. "What are y'all doing out in the middle a' nowhere this time of night?"

"My bicycle threw a chain way back there," Boone said. (Lie number two.) "We were just trying to get home from my uncle's house."

"Your uncle lets you run around at night?"

"He doesn't care," I said. "He's got a new woman."

"Well, where are you headed?"

"Carver Street. We live in the neighborhood by the electric plant."

"Oh yeah. I know 'zactly where that is. That ain't so far. Why don't you kids hop in and I'll give you a ride?"

Boone hesitated, but I said, "Sure." Hitchhiking seemed like child's play after stealing a truck.

The man unlocked his passenger door, and Boone and I climbed in. I moved over to the middle seat and Boone locked his door. The truck's interior stank of stale beer and the spicy menthol of Skoal.

The man took out a dip and offered it to us. We shook our heads and he laughed. "What am I thinking? Y'all ain't but kids."

His name was Leonard, and he whistled as he drove. Moths hit his windshield, leaving a sick green color. "Sun's gonna come up soon," he remarked. "Been a long night, and I got to go to work in the morning."

"What do you do for a living?" I asked.

"I work on an oil rig in the Gulf. I fly out in a helicopter for two weeks, then come back for two weeks and raise some hell." He took his right hand off the steering wheel and showed it to me proudly. "I still got all my fingers, though. Lotsa roughnecks lose 'em out on the rig floor."

Boone remained quiet, but I was having a good time with this young man, and I realized how much I missed friendly conversation about nothing at all.

"We're really glad you happened along," I said.

"It was just—what's it called?—coincidence," said Leonard. "I never go down this old highway."

"Where were you going?"

"Oh, I was just on my way back."

"From what?"

He smiled at me as though we were sharing a secret. His teeth were stained and an eyetooth was missing. "Hunting," he said.

I caught my breath. "Hunting what?" I asked. I could hear Boone gulping beside me.

The man laughed. "I would tell you, but you're both too young to understand. Let's just say I belong to a club and the critter we hunt ain't like no other critter." He took his CB off its mounting and handed it over to me. "See this? This is very important. Couldn't track this critter without it."

Boone groaned loudly.

"What the hell is the matter with your brother?"

"My uncle cooked some fish that had been sitting out."

"Jesus God. You all right there, buddy?"

"Pull over," Boone whispered.

The man slammed on the brakes and Boone got out of the truck. He fell on his knees and threw up.

Leonard looked over me and watched him. "Poor little fellow," he said. "What kind of fish?"

"Catfish."

"Aw hell, no wonder he's sick. Everyone knows catfish eat the shit of other fish."

When we arrived at our street, we had Leonard let us off at the corner. Boone climbed out hastily. But before I followed him, I leaned over to Leonard and said: "You know what my daddy does?"

"What?"

"He's a doctor at East Texas State Hospital."

"Oh yeah?"

"And there's something I ought to tell you." I lowered my voice to a whisper. "If Persely Snow is the critter you're hunting, you should know she has crabs."

*   *   *

When we slid through the casement window, it was nearly dawn. Boone hadn't spoken the rest of the way home. He flopped on his bed and was quiet in the dark.

"I'm going to check on Lucinda," I said.

She was fast asleep, her breath coming out in a half-snore, some of her hair sticking to her face and some of it moving in the current of the ceiling fan. After I straightened her covers, I returned to our room. "Everything's fine," I told my brother, whose own breathing seemed slightly strangled.

"Let's go sleep by her couch in the living room," he said at last. "Just to be sure."

Boone and I dragged our blankets into the living room and lay down. I wondered if Lucinda was dreaming of her galloping horse, if her brain had any sunlight left for a pasture.

I knew Boone was still thinking about Persely's hot words and her wild eyes. His island maiden. His hurt and haunted murderess.

Lucinda's mother was coming back home at noon.

Chapter Eighteen

"What the hell are you two doing?"

I heard Simon's ugly voice and opened my eyes. Light poured through the living room window and he stood over us, holding a newspaper under his arm. Lucinda stirred in her sleep.

I rubbed my eyes. "It was Lucinda's last night, and we thought we'd keep her company."

Simon kicked Boone. "Get up, both of you. I'm going out. I'll be back in an hour." He paused, dropping the newspaper on Boone's stomach.

"Your pal Persely's escaped again, boy," he said. "Thought you'd want to know." I looked at the headline in the paper: ANOTHER SNOW JOB PULLED ON EAST TEXAS STATE HOSPITAL.

Simon followed my eyes. "She comes around here and I'll kill her. I'll kill all of you." He slammed out the door and drove away.

Boone and I went into the kitchen, where Meg was fixing breakfast. I touched her shoulder and she jumped. Simon's disbelief in her loyalty had made her nervous lately, and bashful about her large stomach. Now she saw that it was only me and recovered herself. "Hello. How are my two angels doing?"

"Just fine," I said. "Just another boring summer day."

I looked at the bacon sizzling in the frying pan. "Did you cook everything yourself?" I asked her.

"Why, of course."

"Was Simon around any of the food?"

"No." She gave a strange little laugh. "You kids," she said. "Your crazy imaginations."

"Tell that to Numbhead."

The phone rang.

Meg picked it up. "Hello?" She listened, and I saw an expression of worry and fear cross her face. "You're not supposed to call here," she said. She listened some more. "No, I can't come see you. I'm sorry you're not feeling well, but I can't come. Please. No, I do. I can't. Listen, *go back to your wife*. Good-bye." She hung up the phone and stood staring at it a moment, drawing her robe close around her.

I narrowed my eyes. "Who was that, Meg?"

"No one."

"Daddy?"

"Humph," she said. "There's no such thing as Daddy anymore."

"Is Daddy sick? Has he left his wife?"

But all expression had left my mother's face, every speck of the intrigue she'd caused. I would see that same expression years later, on new religious converts and men on the cusp of sexual climax. Meg went back to the bacon.

After breakfast I helped Meg bathe Lucinda and then we put on her dress, the pretty yellow one she'd worn the first day her mother had dropped her off. Meg brushed out her hair and put a ribbon in it. "I wish you'd been less of a tomboy, Alice," she sighed. "I never got to put ribbons in your hair."

"You'll get your chance at my funeral."

"Don't be sassy."

Boone and I took Lucinda out on the lawn and set her down on her quilt. The slits of her eyes turned bright green in the morning light. Boone took her hand and I could see that his was shaking. "What time is it?" he whispered.

"Nine-thirty."

"Two and a half hours to go." He turned and looked anxiously up the road. "Maybe Mrs. Laird will come home early."

"Who knows," I said. "She might be peeling out of Corpus Christi right now with the twins in the backseat and an angry mob waving clubs." I gazed over at a magnolia tree in the Lairds' yard. Those white flowers, bigger than a flower should ever be. In Texas, land of wild proportions. Very mean stepfathers. Extra-rattly snakes. Profoundly crazy girlfriends. Dangerously deep lakes. Rodeo bulls with oversize testicles. Horribly brain-damaged neighbors. Passive mothers. Terrified brothers. Dead dead dogs. Even the bees could not be bees. They had to make their own tragedy, dying in gouts and from every available cause, like Mr. Walt's children. Just once I wanted a moderate day, in a sweet-tempered village by a calm blue sea.

Boone began another story of the horse. This time the horse was on a beautiful island full of red flowers and tall trees that shielded the horse from its enemies (Boone licked his lips and looked down the road). And the horse galloped around the island, and a little boy visited. And it was the little boy's job to protect the horse from harm . . .

"Horse," said Lucinda.

Boone and I stared at her. She smiled.

"Oh my God," said Boone. "Say it again, Lucinda!"

But Lucinda had apparently come back to life only to deliver the strengthening miracle. A gift from Boone's God to bolster his wavering faith. Perhaps something he could remember in the coming week, when the world as he knew it would end.

Lucinda went back to her dark pasture and didn't speak again.

Stunned, we simply sat with her—no more stories, just waiting—until Simon drove up.

Boone looked at me. "Alice, I'd rather die than be a coward."

"You're not a coward. And I won't let you die."

Simon got out of his car and slammed the door. I could still see the scratches in the paint I'd made with my mother's fingernail scissors, evidence of a lonely war that had come to an abrupt end. "What are you two idiots doing?" said Simon. "Planning how you're gonna build an extra wing in the house for Persely Snow?" He pointed his finger at Boone and said, "Bang! Bang!" He looked at Lucinda. "Your mama's coming home today, ain't she?" he asked, as though he expected an answer from her.

"Any minute," I said.

He looked at me with disdain. "At noon, Smart Girl," he said. "Now quit your sitting around. There's yard work to be done."

"We'll do it this afternoon," said Boone.

"No, you won't. You'll do it now. Mow the damn lawn and sweep the damn driveway and edge around the damn patio."

Meg came out of the house in a baggy dress and espadrilles. She looked as though she'd deliberately messed up her hair. There was no makeup on her face.

"Where you going looking like hell?" Simon demanded.

"To the store," Meg said.

"To meet your lover?" Simon peered at her. "Of course, you look too bad today for any man to want you. So you must be going to the store. Unless you're going to see someone who's used to you looking like hell. Maybe an ex-husband."

Meg edged away from him, toward the station wagon.

"Watch yourself!" Simon called after her. "Persely Snow's on the loose! She might poison the champagne you drink with Dan before you fuck him! The whole friggin' world is gone crazy with betrayal! People need to learn a lesson!"

Meg gunned her car down the road.

Simon ran after her like a madman. "Hey! Pick me up a real son while you're over there!"

When he lurched back over to us, he seemed on fire, so mad were his eyes. I couldn't tell whether it was the news of Persely's escape or his doubts about my mother that had electrified him so.

The sun had begun to warm up. The morning glories were closing.

Simon stood over us, breathing deeply, trembling. "I'll watch Lucinda," he said, taking her hand and pulling her to her feet. "Now y'all get to the damn yard work. This damn yard looks like there's nothing but white trash living here." He helped Lucinda into the house, slowly, one arm around her waist.

Boone clutched his stomach as he stood up. "What should we do?"

I looked at the house. "Fire up the lawn mower so he'll think we're working. Then we'll sneak over and look in through the side window." I pointed to a window whose sill was covered with Virginia creeper.

"All right. But I don't even want him in the same room with her." He started the lawn mower and we crept up to the side of the house, staying down low to the ground, crouching beneath the window and raising our heads very slowly to peer into the living room.

Simon was kneeling in front of the girl, holding her hand and looking into her barely open eyes. His lips weren't moving, and the expression on his face was unreadable. We watched him for several minutes, but he didn't move.

"Creepy," said Boone.

"He's not hurting her," I said, but the back of my neck was prickling. "Let's mow the lawn before we get in trouble."

I swept the driveway while Boone started on the lawn. Every now and then I paused to shake a trash bag open and help Boone empty the grass catcher. Our faces were soon streaked with pollen and sweat and bits of grass. "Let's check on Lucinda again," Boone said.

Once again we crouched at the window and peered inside the dim living room.

My breath caught.

Simon was stroking the girl's cheek. She looked away from him, and he cupped her chin and turned her to face him. He resumed stroking her cheek. Her throat. The tip of her nose. Lucinda slumped.

"What's he doing?" I asked.

I saw the familiar glassy look come into Boone's eyes. I looked down and his knees were locking.

Simon leaned forward and very slowly kissed the girl on the lips.

"No!" said Boone, but Simon didn't hear. He kissed her again. He stood up and pulled the girl up with him. She sagged against his arms, and he half carried, half walked her from the room.

Boone gasped. "No!" he said again, and as if responding to a secret password, his knees unlocked and he was free. We ran around the house and charged through the living room and down the hallway.

Simon had paused at the doorway to his bedroom, where he was having trouble getting Lucinda to pick up her feet. Boone darted in front of him, blocking the doorway. "Don't come in here, Simon!"

"What are you gonna do about it?"

"Plenty."

"Get out of my way." Simon let go of the girl's arms and she dropped to her knees.

"I said get out of my way," Simon said again.

Boone's entire body shook, but he held his ground. "You leave that girl alone. You nasty man."

Simon pushed Boone into the bedroom, hard, knocking him down. I entered the fracas, trying to jump on Simon's back. He shook me off and I fell on the floor next to Boone. Simon picked up Boone by the throat.

"Leave him alone, Simon!" I jumped up and butted him like a goat, but Simon's grip was tightening, and my brother's face had taken on the gray color of the strings on a used mop.

Suddenly Simon released him. A moment or two passed before I realized that Boone's pocketknife was sticking out of Simon's arm. Simon turned around and looked at me, amazed. A geyser of blood spurted out in all directions. I felt it against my face, and when I looked at Boone, I saw that blood had sprayed his face as well. A wide streak of it had splashed across his shirt.

Simon didn't say a word. He seemed absolutely astonished to see the knife in his arm and his blood shooting out. He walked past me, stepping over Lucinda, and disappeared into the kitchen. We heard him gasping in pain— three short breaths as if he were pulling the knife out with a series of tugs.

I took Boone's hand and Lucinda's—both of them had the same look in their eyes—and led them slowly out to the front lawn, where we all collapsed under the bare shade of a mimosa tree to wait for Mrs. Laird. Boone's mouth hung open; he didn't blink. Beads of Simon's blood were drying on his face. He began speaking in a distracted whisper, not like a dialogue at all but more a train of thought. *I did it, I did it . . . God said, but Persely said . . . tiger or sheep . . .*

Justice is my province, Marshal . . . Guard the horse, the horse . . .

I pulled the garden hose over to my brother and washed his face. He continued to mumble as I rinsed off my own face and Lucinda's right hand, which had somehow collected some of Simon's blood as well. I felt proud of Boone but somewhat frightened by how far he'd gone, even to protect Lucinda. Perhaps my fear came not from his actions but from who he was and how foreign those actions were to him. And somehow I was also annoyed that Persely had been the one to goad my brother into violence. And, of course, on top of all these emotions was the terror of wondering what was going to come next, now that Simon—betrayed, stabbed, murderous—was flinging blood around the kitchen.

Mrs. Laird came back right at noon. She opened the car door and the twins tumbled out, no cuter for their tans. One of them clenched a cone-shaped shell.

Mrs. Laird hugged Lucinda in delight, then fell silent as she caught a glimpse of Boone's bloody shirt.

"I'll go get Lucinda's things for you," I told Mrs. Laird.

"Just bring them over later, if you'd like," she said uneasily, still looking at the blood.

This was the conveniently magic moment when Mrs. Laird was supposed to say: "Kids, is there some kind of trouble going on? Is your brother in love with a murderess? Is your stepfather a maniac? Did he just try to sleep with my daughter and is he, right this very moment, rampaging through that house flinging blood around a kitchen that happens to have enough poisons under the sink to kill you dead a hundred times?" But Texas is not a place of conveniently magic moments. Instead it offers cactuses and steers and rattlesnake roundups and chicken-fried steaks and the Alamo.

Mrs. Laird did not ask and I did not tell, because I had no faith in grown-ups, in the staggering messes they made of their own lives.

"So Lucinda was no trouble?" Mrs. Laird asked.

"None at all," I said. "She said *horse*."

Mrs. Laird stared at me. "Are you serious?" she gasped. "How did she say it?"

I said: "Like this: 'ho-orse.'"

Boone blinked. "Ho-orse."

The girl twin held up the shell. "There's a crab inside here," she announced. "But he's dead." I could see one limp black leg hanging out of the shell.

Soon after Mrs. Laird and her children went back into their house, Simon appeared in the front doorway, a large cheesecloth wrapped around his arm. The cloth was soaked in blood and dripping steadily. I don't remember if Simon spoke the words or just mouthed them before he went back into the house. *Judas and Delilah.*

"Let's go, Boone," I said. "We're going to run away. Right now."

He stared at me.

"Come on."

He shrugged and rocked back and forth, and I realized we were not going anywhere until he could recover himself. The two of us just sat there under the mimosa tree, watching birds hop around on the telephone wires and listening to the twins argue about the best place in the road to set their dead crab before the next car came along. Blood had dried in the shape of a baseball pennant across my brother's shirt, and I could not tell what he was thinking now as he gently pulled apart a mimosa blossom and looked up into the clouds.

I noticed something fat and gray hopping across the road toward the Lairds' yard. I squinted. It was Numbhead's orphan toad. The twins had eyed it as prey for a long time now, and Numbhead was no longer around to protect it.

The twins noticed the toad just as it touched their lawn. The boy pounced on it and held it up triumphantly.

Before I could speak, Boone suddenly came to life, jumping to his feet and crossing the street.

"Give me that toad," he said.

"No, shit-face," said the boy. "He was in our yard. He crossed the line."

"You'll kill him. Give him to me."

"He crossed the—"

"I HAVE CROSSED THE LINE! I HAVE CROSSED THE LINE! GIVE HIM TO ME!"

I had never heard my brother scream at anyone, much less in that tone. He sounded more like a wolf than a boy. The twins looked stricken. The boy dropped the toad and started to cry.

Boone picked up Numbhead's bereaved little creature and rejoined me under the mimosa tree, his expression blank and his eyes glassy. "Guard the horse," he mumbled.

He was still in his trancelike frame of mind when Meg came back an hour later. She got out of the car and went inside the house, and her and Simon's great reconciliation was born. I left Boone for a moment, crept into the house and lingered by the kitchen doorway so I could listen to them.

Simon was crying. Great weeping, terrible sobbing, as he'd done when he first brought over the picture of his dead family. Meg was soothing him. "What happened, Simon? How did you hurt your arm?"

"Those kids," Simon sobbed, "are all against me."

"Oh, Simon . . ."

"Tell me something, Meg. I gotta know. Tell me the baby's mine."

"It's yours, honey."

"Swear on my dead boy's grave."

"I swear."

I heard them kissing and sighing together. I imagined his blood rubbing off on Meg's billowy dress.

And that was that. The jig was up. That was the day Meg spent the afternoon on the cypress glider, rocking. That was the evening Simon pushed Boone's face down into a spicy little goulash called Chicken Meg. That was the night Meg came into our room after Boone and I had fallen off the bed and lay tangled in a heap, leaned down to us and whispered that single word: *Run.*

Boone and I extracted ourselves from each other and Meg helped us to our feet. I went to the closet and found my overnight bag.

"No," said Meg. "Don't pack. Go now."

She was crying even as she slid open the bedroom window. I was starting to crawl through it when suddenly Boone grabbed my hand and jerked me back. He pulled me out of the bedroom and down the hall. We entered the kitchen, hand and hand. Without breaking his stride, Boone pulled the little boy's picture off the wall and stuffed it into his back pocket, and we ran out the kitchen door and into the backyard. We grabbed our bicycles and ran along beside them before hopping on.

As we rode down the street, I looked back to the house

and saw my mother, her face pressed to the glass of the kitchen window, watching us leave.

Boone and I pedaled furiously down the side of the old highway, the wind blowing pine needles and old leaves, the ditches full of bending thistle, the cows staring, the crickets leaning on their spooky notes.

"You think he followed us?" I panted.

"I don't know."

Headlights. I shouted a warning to Boone, and as one, we jumped off our bicycles and ran through the ditches, sliding through the barbed wire into the cow pastures and throwing ourselves down on earthy-smelling grass, our hearts beating furiously, our chests heaving. The car slowed, then gathered speed and disappeared.

We stood up and brushed ourselves off as the cows looked at us impassively.

"Wasn't him," said Boone. "That was a station wagon."

"You don't think Meg ever told him about Never Island, do you?" I asked anxiously.

"I hope not."

Just then I noticed something I hadn't before. Boone had shoved something partway down the front of his pants. "What's that?" I asked, pointing.

He looked down. "Oh," he mumbled. "Just this." He pulled it out and showed it to me by the light of the moon. It was a white Adidas T-shirt with a huge bloodstain across the chest.

I felt a chill. "Why did you bring that, Boone?"

"To show to Persely. I wanted her to know that I defended Lucinda."

"You don't need the shirt. I'll tell her what you did."

But my brother would not be convinced. He wrapped the bloody shirt around his handlebars and we got back on our bikes and rode on, listening to the wind and looking behind us anxiously for signs of headlights. But there were no more cars, and we were free, for the moment. As we rode along together, I talked to him, sister to brother. I told him that things had simply gone too far, and that we had to find someone, some reasonable adult, and tell them everything. Boone wanted to know who would listen to us, and who would be willing to get involved.

"I know someone," I said at last. "Someone who's kind and gentle. Someone we should have told a long time ago."

When we reached Lake Shine and the old boat dock, we hid our bicycles and climbed the steep path to Mr. Walt's house. Virginia creepers hung across the sill of his front window, and the living room light was on. Boone knocked on the door and we waited in the dark, each of us mumbling to ourselves, going over once again what we'd say to him. I felt a sense of relief for the first time in months.

Boone knocked again.

"Maybe he's asleep," I said. A feeling of dread was slowly growing in me. Like newly grafted wisteria, it was taking its good time to bloom. Boone and I pressed our faces to the window and looked into the living room. It was orderly except for a newspaper spread out on the coffee table, and Mr. Walt was nowhere to be seen. "Maybe he's asleep," I said. We moved around the left side of the house, around to the back bedroom, and peered into the window once again. Mr. Walt's bed was unmade, but his room was empty. Boone and I followed the oval steps of the flagstone path that led around the house and into the backyard. We stepped between two giant oak trees and saw him.

"Thank God," I said in relief.

Mr. Walt knelt at his wife's grave. His old dog sat next to him.

"Mr. Walt!" I called softly.

He didn't answer. As we drew closer, we noticed something very strange. His hand was stretched out toward the flowers on the grave, but he remained absolutely still, his head bowed as though in prayer or to receive a pat on the head from an affectionate ghost.

"Mr. Walt," I said in a whisper.

Boone touched his face. "He's dead." We knelt down next to him, studying this patient and gentle man whose failed heart had been so caring. We stroked his cold arm, full of sorrow and regret that we couldn't have come earlier. But we could not help him now, and he could not help us. The dog moaned a little.

"We have to call someone," Boone said.

"About what?"

He threw up his hands. "What do you mean? About Mr. Walt kneeling here dead!"

"What good is it going to do him now?"

"He needs to be buried properly!"

"He looks pretty happy to me," I said without irony. "He's where he wants to be."

The dog looked up at us.

Boone stood up at last and pulled me to my feet. "I guess you're right. There's nothing we can do. Let's go find Persely."

"Wait," I said. "Let's get some supplies out of Mr. Walt's house."

"You mean break in and steal his stuff?"

"It's not stealing. He doesn't want it now, and he'd want us to have it if he knew we were in trouble."

Boone turned his face toward the heavens and squinted at the starlight. "Oh, he knows."

We entered the house through the back door and spent the next hour loading all kinds of supplies into a crab sack we'd found in the garage, nonperishables and slightly perishables and bread and flashlights and sheets and blankets and socks and string and knives. Two fishing poles and a sack of oranges. A six-pack of hot Cokes. Toothpaste. We found a machete in the closet and also a few T-shirts that we could all wear.

"We need a gun," I said.

Boone looked at me, horrified. "Why?"

But the answer was evident, and rather than answering him, I began going through Mr. Walt's desk drawers, looking for a weapon. My eye caught something. I held it up to the light. It was an invoice from Pertier's Flowers for a dozen yellow roses. Total: $13.95. Wordlessly I showed it to Boone.

"Do you think . . ." he asked.

Meg waited until Simon went to town, then put on her best dress, her pearls, a pair of panty hose with not a single hole. Her red sling-back shoes. A few minutes later I heard her in her bedroom, dialing the phone. Please, she was whispering, I need to see you. I've been thinking about you. And I know you're thinking about me.

"Maybe Meg's not so dumb after all," I said finally. "And I guess maybe it's true what she said . . . about it not

being Daddy. I guess he was never coming back after all."
And now I remembered Meg on the phone: *I'm sorry
you're not feeling well. Go back to your wife.*

Boone said: "But why would Meg pick Mr. Walt to—?"

"She knew he had a crush on her. And Mr. Walt did have
six children."

"But they all died!"

"Meg just wanted to get the job done, probably. She
wasn't thinking that far ahead."

I gave up trying to find a gun and instead helped Boone
load the supplies into the boat. When we had finished, we
went back to where Mr. Walt was kneeling. Boone
crouched down beside him and put a hand on his shoulder.
"Thank you, Mr. Walt. For everything. And for what you
might have done."

"Don't tip him over," I warned.

Boone whispered a quick prayer for Mr. Walt, then said:
"We've got to take the dog. We can't just leave him here."
The dog was panting slightly. He looked at us with his eye-
brows raised, as if to say, *Did you make him better?*

I grabbed his collar. "Let's go, boy." Boone took hold of
the collar as well and we pulled with all our strength, but
the dog wouldn't move from Mr. Walt's side. Finally we
gave up. We found a big bag of Chuck Wagon in the garage
and dragged it over to him. We filled a bucket with
water and left that for him, too. Then we climbed into the
boat and headed for Never Island.

Chapter Nineteen

Boone turned off the motor just as the tip of our boat struck the first cattails of the shore. We hadn't said a word to each other since leaving the dock; we had been sobered by Mr. Walt's death and by the stark reality of our own situation. I felt vaguely angry with Boone. Somehow I blamed him for fighting with Simon over Lucinda, although in my rational mind I could think of no other option. Shouldn't I be proud that Boone had grown a backbone and saved a brain-damaged girl and an overweight toad? Why my ambivalence? Perhaps it wasn't his actions so much as . . . that bloody shirt, which he had carried with him all the way to Lake Shine and was now bearing across the water like some kind of trophy.

Boone and I hid the boat in the cattails and splashed ashore, carrying the bulging crab sack between us. We made our way up the bank and plunged into the forest, Mr. Walt's flashlight sending a powerful beam before us, lighting up our surroundings so we could see the cross-vines and the skinny trunks of countless pine trees, and also the brown pine needles that were hanging all around us, half fallen from the trees and yet suspended as if in midair. Occasionally we'd walk between two trees that were too close together, and the sack would get caught between them, and our progress would stop until we could pry it out.

We found Persely sitting on the blanket, Indian-style. Not even twenty-four hours had passed since we had last seen her, and yet when she stood up and walked toward us, she seemed years older.

"Hi, Persely," I said, but she made no reply. She was looking at Boone. He dropped his end of the sack. It fell into the brambles and rattled with all Mr. Walt's possessions.

He walked closer to Persely and the two of them stood staring at each other. Persely had that defiant look on her face I remembered from the newspaper photos, but there was plenty of light falling down from the stars and moon, and under this light she seemed sad as well. The night before she had raged like a wild animal—*You don't do shit because you're a fucking chickenshit! You and your little friend God!*—but now she just stared back at Boone in silence. The tension between the two of them hurt my stomach.

Boone threw his T-shirt up in the air.

Persely caught it. She held out the shirt and inspected it. "What's this black stuff on it?"

"Simon's blood. I stabbed him." A tone of anguish and fear and uncertainty and . . .

Persely hesitated a moment. Then she brought the T-shirt to her face, almost as if she were about to sniff that stain.

The hair rose up on the back of my neck.

She smiled at Boone, starlight covering her big front teeth. "Where'd you stick him?"

"In the arm."

"Why not in the heart?"

He didn't answer her. He took Mr. Walt's machete out of the crab sack, unsheathed it and turned the blade so that it glinted in the moonlight. "Step back," he said. "I'm going to hack us a clearing."

Boone's machete came down again and again, sometimes making a thin ringing sound as it struck into rock or glanced at the wrong angle off the slender trunks of the young tallow trees. Persely and I helped to clear away the brush, and when Boone had finally made a clearing suitable for three people, we all got down on our hands and knees and scraped off pine straw and roots and brambles until we felt only bare ground beneath our hands. Boone went back into the forest, returned with an armload of dead branches and proceeded to build a fire.

"How'd he learn to do that?" Persely whispered.

"Boy Scouts," I said. "Until he dropped out. They picked on him for being a saint."

"He ain't all saint," said Persely. Her eyes shone.

* * *

The fire was burning well. I sat half dazed, watching the flames rise up in the shape of palmetto blades. Something buzzed around my head. Crickets sang a faithless hymn. In the distance, waves lapped against the shore. Every now and then I thought I could hear a boat breaking through the cattails, footsteps through the woods, Simon's whistly breath. I felt as though he could materialize suddenly on our island like a demon with neither compass nor clue, but simply the whisper of instinct and the smell of his own blood calling to him from Boone's white shirt.

We were using the stretched-out clothes hangers to roast some Oscar Mayer wieners Boone and I had found earlier in Mr. Walt's refrigerator. I tore off a piece of black wiener and put it in my mouth. It crackled between my teeth. Ashes and flesh. "What are we going to do now?" I asked, and was surprised that my words came out accusatory, frightened. "Look at us. No money. No home. Just the clothes on our backs."

"That's not true," said Boone. "I found ten bucks in the pocket of my jeans."

"Big deal."

"So what?" said Persely. "So we'll run the boat to shore every now and then and we'll steal stuff."

I glared at her down the long crackly back of a wiener. "Yeah, we'll look pretty inconspicuous."

"Inconspicuous," she said. "They didn't allow big words in the West."

I was sick of Persely. Sick of my brother's love for her. Sick of being afraid. "Go to hell, Persely."

"I've already been there, Judge."

"We have to get along," said Boone. "We're all we have. We can't go home after what happened today."

Persely ran the end of her clothes hanger through a pale wiener. "Tell me about it." Her voice was urgent. "Tell me exactly what went on, Boone." The firelight played upon her face in mysterious patterns, like the inkblots she'd been forced to study at her trial.

Boone told his story, and I relived it as I heard it. Lucinda crossed over the road to our house, the twins waved at us from the backseat, bound for Corpus Christi and its crusty glut of new and exotic victims, Simon edged down toward Lucinda at the dinner table.

Boone's voice had a peculiar lilt to it, a singsong that dragged the horror along casually. And now Simon led Lucinda into his bedroom, Boone stepped in front of him, halting the forward progress of his body, Lucinda fell away, Simon seized Boone's throat, Boone stabbed Simon in the arm.

Blood sprayed into our faces.

Persely's pupils had grown large. "Tell me again," she whispered. "Tell me about how you stuck him, and how the blood sprayed out."

And Boone dutifully began again, talking more slowly, his voice rising and falling, his breathing shallow. I listened with growing anxiety, the fire hot against my face, my head swimming, Simon's blood everywhere . . . "Stop!" I shouted, startling Persely and Boone out of their trances.

I jumped to my feet. "It's not a beautiful thing to stab a man! Even Simon Jester, as much as I hate him, too!"

Boone shook his head as if just awakening from perfect sleep. "Alice is right," he said. "God wouldn't want me to take any pleasure in it."

God. It surely had not been a long time since I'd heard that word come out of Boone's lips, but it seemed like forever.

"That's what I'm trying to tell you, Boone!" said Persely. "There ain't no God. And for once in your life, you didn't wait around for him. You grabbed ahold of matters yourself. And you got *justice.* And your stepdaddy deserved it, 'cause he's evil just like my daddy was."

Boone's answer seemed to take all of his strength. "No one is truly evil. God says there's good in all of us."

"Then tell me," said Persely, "tell me what's good about that man."

Boone was thinking about it and I found myself veering over against my will to Persely's side. I didn't want Boone enjoying Simon's blood, but I didn't want him looking for any sweetness in Simon's soul. "There's nothing good about him!" I said vehemently. "He poisoned our dog and he tried to rape Lucinda Laird and for all we know, he killed his other family! I guess Boone told you in his letters that he said his family drowned. But there was always something funny about his story. Of course, our mother fell for it. He could have said that a giant anaconda squeezed his family to death and our mother would have said, 'That's terrible. Wipe your feet on the welcome mat and come on in.'"

"His little boy was beautiful." Boone sighed. "I used to cry, just thinking about him. Who knows how he died, but you can tell from that picture that he was a sweet little boy." His eyes widened. "Hey, wait! I still have that picture. I stuffed it in my pocket." Boone stood up and eased the picture out of his back pocket. He unfolded it and handed it to Persely.

"That's him," he said.

She looked at the picture for a long time, her blue eyes registering nothing but sadness. She handed the picture back to Boone. When she spoke again, her voice came out flat.

"No," she said. "That's me."

Chapter Twenty

I couldn't speak. Persely's words had left me stunned. I drew in my breath and looked through the flames at Boone, who seemed equally stricken.

"What do you mean?" I finally managed.

"That's my picture," she said.

"That can't be you," Boone said. "That's a little boy."

Persely closed her eyes a moment. "Look at it again."

I crowded over next to Boone and we stared at the picture together. Blond hair. Blue eyes. A girlish smile. Persely suddenly snatched the picture from Boone's hand and threw it into the fire.

"No!" Boone cried. He lunged forward and tried to rescue it from the flames, but it had melted already and was winding around a stick. Boone jerked his hand back and watched the picture drip into the fire. "Why'd you do that?" he gasped.

"'Cause that little girl is gone now. There's just me now."

I jumped up, pacing in agitation. "So my stepfather was your father? And his dead wife was your mother? And his dead son was you?"

Persely stared at me. "Yes, ma'am," she said softly.

"You're lying!" But it was all making sense to me in a rush. Simon's hatred of Persely. His first appearance at Hollow Cove, brought on by Boone's ad in the paper. His desperation to have a new child he could "raise right." His obsession with poison and betrayal. *Children will turn on you.*

"Tell us what he looks like," I said finally.

She took a deep breath. "Nasty black hair. Brown eyes. Small and close together. He likes to drink sugar out of the bowl. And when he gets mad . . ." She indicated on her own forehead. "There's a line right here, 'tween his eyes."

"But wait. Your name's not Jester. It's Snow."

"He musta changed it. You said he worked as a counselor at a church, right? You think anyone would want his Bible talk if they knew he was Jeremiah Snow? Whose own girl tried to poison him? You think your mama would have married him?"

"Yes," we answered in unison.

She looked down at her hands. "Boone said somethin' in one of his letters that made me wonder if it was him. But I figured it couldn't be. But just in case, I wrote 'Poison your father' under the stamp. And then, when I come over, and I was sittin' in that closet, and he made Boone smoke my cigarette . . . I heard his voice and I knew then that he was my daddy come back to haunt me."

I remembered the way she looked after Simon had gone back to his room. Her pale face. Her trembling body. *I have to get out of here.*

"Why didn't you say anything, Persely?" I asked. "Why didn't you tell us you were Simon's daughter?" Then it dawned on me. I pointed my finger at her. "Wait a minute! You were using Boone! You were trying to get him to poison Simon, and you were talking about justice for Boone and justice for me, when you really wanted justice for you! You wanted Boone to finish your job, didn't you?"

My brother looked at her. "Is that true?"

Persely didn't answer, and none of us knew how to proceed. I was thinking about Simon's story, about his wife and her terry-cloth robe and her picnic basket, about the storm coming, about his little boy knee-deep in calm water throwing his red-faced tantrum: *NOOOOOOO!* "That story he told about his family drowning at the lake," I said. "That was just a big whopping lie, then?"

More silence from Persely.

Finally my brother said: "Tell us, please. Tell us what Simon and your mother did to you that was so bad they deserved to die."

The breeze picked up and moved the flames of the fire to one side. I started to put another wiener on my clothes hanger, then thought better of it.

"He hated me," said Persely. "He was mean. He hit me. And my mama didn't care. She didn't love me." Persely's voice had begun to take on a lilting, dreamy quality. Persely believed in God back then. She asked him for help and found him silent. If God was the nectar, then nectar was absent from this dry planet. And so Persely turned away from God. And her hatred of her parents grew. The hatred made her feel strong. It felt right to her.

"So here comes fate," said Persely. "Saving me." One day in school the lessons of history turned to Rasputin, how he was seduced and lured to a secret place and given poison cakes. That one word stayed in her mind. *Poison.* Her father, Persely realized, deserved to die that way. And her mother as well. Especially her mother, for knowing and not caring. Persely got the poison easily. It came in a tan-colored box with a picture of a rat on the front.

I looked at my brother. Sweat ran down his face. He couldn't take his eyes off Persely. His clothes-hanger rig had fallen into the fire and now lay across the burning logs, the wiener blackening like the scorched head of a cattail.

"So then I was ready," said Persely. One Saturday, early in the morning, she found herself in the kitchen alone, mixing up a pitcher of Tang. Orange crystals to which she added white ones. Presently her mother came into the kitchen humming, as she always did in the morning. Her father joined them and they all sat down to breakfast. She watched Jeremiah and Mary drink their Tang, saying nothing; her father sipped a third of it and her mother drank the whole glass, and a few minutes passed, then blue skin shallow breathing oxygen deprivation vomiting cramps dizziness convulsions writhing bodies on the floor . . .

A memory I have of Simon Jester completes the story. He's showing us the picture of that blond child and crying. *I loved my boy. I loved him! And he betrayed me!*

* * *

Boone and I sat transfixed for several moments. The story felt so right that the crickets had to remind me how wrong it was. I jumped to my feet. "You're a monster, Persely!"

"Don't say that," said Boone.

Persely looked into the fire. "It's all right, Boone. Maybe Persely is a monster. But she fought the good fight."

"Simon lived through that?" Boone asked.

Persely shrugged. "He didn't drink enough of the Tang, I reckon, and the paramedics got to him in time."

"How?" I asked. "Who called the paramedics?"

Persely was silent. Then she said: "I'm tired of this story."

"Persely, I know Simon treated you bad," my brother said, still looking stunned. "I know how much that hurt you, and for so many years. But did he really deserve to die? And did you have to poison your mother, too?"

"You don't understand," Persely snapped. "She was twice as bad for letting it happen. Like your mama is."

"No," I said quickly. "Meg just doesn't know any better."

"Suuuure. She don't know any better. And you put up with how weak she is. But one day you're gonna wake up so mad that you'll want to kill her."

Boone gasped. "We will not! She's our mother!"

Persely looked up at the stars as if they had murdered their parents and she could turn to them for support. "Just you wait."

I had to ask Persely something. "I don't understand why

if Simon, or Jeremiah, was mad at your mother, he would take it out on you."

"That's easy," said Persely. "Jeremiah wanted a sacrifice."

"A sacrifice?"

"Yeah. The mama's got to sacrifice anything that comes between her and him. Got to stand by and watch her kids get treated bad. That's the only way to prove her loyalty, far as Jeremiah thinks. That's why he killed your old dog. Your mama fought for him. For the first time in her life, too, sounds like." Persely paused. "You said Jeremiah's got some money he keeps in the safe?"

"Yeah," I said. "Ten thousand dollars. He said it's— your mother's life insurance money."

Persely shook her head. "That bastard. He's got no right to have my mother's money."

"What do you care?" I asked. "You hate your mother."

Persely jumped to her feet and glared at me with her fierce, bright eyes. "Shut up! Don't say another word about my mama, or I'll kill you!"

And that's when I realized that I did not trust her story. There were elements of truth in it, but like her father, she was keeping something from us.

Chapter Twenty-one

The fire had died down, but the tension broiled flesh-colored things. I could not take my eyes from Persely, who had sat back down and was stirring at the red ashes with her clothes hanger.

"Do you think we're safe on this island?" I asked at last. "Simon knows you tried to meet Persely at Hollow Cove, Boone. What if he finds us here?"

"He won't," said Boone. "Hollow Cove is way over on the west side of the lake. There's got to be fifty or sixty islands on this lake, and some of 'em disappear when it rains too much."

"Let him come," said Persely. "Boone and I will take care of him."

"Sure," I said.

Boone had edged over closer to Persely. "He has no way of knowing we're here. And besides, Simon doesn't have a boat."

An ash had fallen into his hair. Persely brushed it out, her gesture almost tender. "So are we just going to stay on this island forever?"

My brother sighed. "Let's go swimming," he said finally.

"I told you," said Persely, "that I don't know how to swim. Not like you, you big swim-team star."

"I'll teach you."

"I'll drown."

I giggled deliberately.

"I wouldn't let my mother drown," said Boone, "and I won't let you."

Persely stood up and stretched. "If we're gonna swim, we gotta get naked."

Boone looked immediately bashful. "I can't."

"Okay," said Persely. "Just the drawers, then." She shucked her shirt and pants and stood in her underwear, her breasts bare once again. Boone's mouth fell open and he quickly turned his head.

Persely looked scornful. "You two chickens gonna do it, too? Buck buck buck?"

Boone hesitated, then stripped to his Jockeys. I took off my cutoffs and kept my T-shirt on. The three of us headed back through the woods and down to the water, where the fuzzy old heads of the cattails moved in the slight breeze. We waded in, the moon half full overhead, its chaste glow tickling the waves, urging light into movement. The water so warm it clung to us like oil.

"All right," said Persely. She was up to her waist. "This is where it ends, Bucko. Another step and I'll drown."

Boone approached her cautiously, looking away from her breasts. "I'm going to have to put my arms around you to hold you up." He put his arms around her bare slim waist. "Now just lie forward in the water. Like it's a bed."

Persely leaned forward and pushed up her feet. Her head went underwater. Boone adjusted his arms and she came back out, sputtering.

"I've got you. Turn your head. Straighten your back and your legs."

She obeyed him.

"Now move just your arms. You're going to want your hands to enter the water to the side . . . like this . . . and when they come down like this, they turn again . . ."

I stood in the water, my T-shirt clinging to me. I watched him. I felt soothed by the gentleness in his voice and gestures, and all of my new concerns about him suddenly lost their importance. Boone was still Boone, full of love and patience. He was still a saint and still my brother.

"Persely," he said, "you're splashing too much when you kick."

The wind had slowed down and the moon shone on my shoulders. The lake-bottom silt came up through my bare toes; tiny fish nibbled at me. Not a boat on the lake. Just a wilderness of black water and far, far away, the tiny lights of a tiny town. Somewhere in that direction we had all been tormented and beaten and plotted against. But now we were all alone—those lights could not swim to us.

Boone and Persely were hard at work, his back bent, his

glasses wet, her pale spine washed over by waves, sunfish hidden from my sight swimming under her, their flat eyes dully regarding the cones of her breasts. She struggled and kicked, her long, flailing limbs containing none of the grace her body had demonstrated in its climbing of trees or lighting of cigarettes. I waded out until the surface of the lake touched my chin, then I pulled my feet out from under myself, leaning back until I was floating in the water, my arms and legs outstretched. I let the water rock me, let it rush into my ears until I could no longer hear Boone's instructions to his beloved, just the exaggerated sound of my own breathing and the whooshing sound my hands made as they moved back and forth in the water.

This was the true sound of the lake, every human murmur amplified and then dissolved into the elements. I said my own name, *Alice, Alice,* and underwater the word was haunted and true, sad and disappointed and lost amid the rush of my own breath.

I said *Mother, Mother,* and after a time I said *Father, Father.* With the water in my ears, those two words had the gestures of sunfish, swimming closer and then suddenly darting away from me with no clear motivation at all. I found that I was crying. Tears ran down my face. Around me the entire world undulated in the darkness and—farther across the earth—in the light. People were sleeping and eating and fighting wars and learning to swim. But I was alone.

The next morning Boone summoned all his Boy Scout training and constructed a crude lean-to out of pine branches, securing the rickety contraption with the string

we'd brought from Mr. Walt's house. We spent the day
making our clearing wider and lurking around the island,
moving among the trees like ghosts, the trapped pine needles brushing our faces as we passed through. We dared
not go as far as the bank in case we were seen, but the three
of us did huddle behind a large red oak to peer out onto the
lake, scanning the flat green surface for motorboats, the
game warden or someone else. Someone whose name we
didn't speak.

For lunch we ate blackberries, the tender shoots of
young cattails, crackers and Spam. Boone remembered a
Gilligan's Island episode in which a carton of ice cream
had washed up on the island, and we all looked hungrily
toward the shore.

That night Boone said that to conserve our rations, we
should supplement them with fish. Near a small palmetto
we had buried a package of bologna to try and keep it cool.
Boone dug it up, peeled two tepid slices off the top and
took the boat out to a nearby cove to fish for channel cats.

"I'll go with you," I said.

"No, I won't be long," said Boone, and left Persely and
me staring at each other across the fire. Yellow firelight
swam around her torso, driving shadows from her shoulders to the line of her chin. She hadn't combed her hair after swimming the night before, and now it was more wild
and tangled than ever. All day long I had sensed between
my brother and her some tension I couldn't place, and now
I wondered if she in fact had appalled Boone with her nar-
rative as much as she had me and if, despite his tender
swimming lessons the night before, he was having second
thoughts about her. I myself felt overwhelmed and disoriented in her presence. Her own story had made her seem

like a monster, not just the things she'd done but the smug way she'd described them. And yet there seemed to be a hole in that story, something unsaid. A secret and a pain.

But was looking for the good in Persely as stupid and careless as Meg looking for the good in Persely's father? I didn't know.

Persely hugged her knees. "What are you staring at?"

"Nothing."

She lit a cigarette. Her supply was beginning to dwindle and I imagined her, nicotine-mad, waving down boats and giving us all away: *Hey, mister? You got anything menthol?*

She pressed her lips together and exhaled through her nose. "Y'all sure were shook up last night, weren't you?"

"It was quite a story," I said. "Now what's the real one?"

Persely impatiently took another puff. "I don't know what you're talking about. But let me tell you this, Alice, 'cause I kind of like you, even though you're a smart girl and you're gonna grow up and no man is ever gonna want to hump you." She leaned forward so that the firelight moved around her chin and fell back over her shoulders. "Listen to me, 'cause this is real important. Let me tell you this like a friend. Even if that wasn't my real story—and I'm not saying it wasn't—*no one gives a shit about your real story.* Not your friends, not your mama, not the cops, not teachers, not God. But *you* have got to give a shit. You've got to guard your real story, Alice. If you guard it, it'll mean something. You see?"

I didn't really see then. But I found myself leaning closer to her.

As if acknowledging our new intimacy, Persely took a puff on her cigarette and then held it out to me.

"Smoke?"

"No thanks."

"You ever try?"

"No."

"Want to?" Persely said this almost conspiratorially, with a sudden grin that ate firelight.

"I guess," I said at last, carefully taking the cigarette.

"Wait. Not like that," Persely said. She moved close to me and readjusted my fingers. "See? Hold it like this. All right. Now take a puff."

I filled my mouth with a disgusting taste.

"No, you've got to inhale."

I tried again. Took a deep breath and forced the horrible cloud down into my lungs. I dropped the cigarette and clutched my stomach, hacking and coughing.

"I did that at first, too," said Persely. "But I learned."

Finally I caught my breath. Wiping the spit off my mouth, I glared at her. Whatever tenuous bond we'd had was now broken. "I don't want to learn," I snapped. "My stepfather smokes."

"And you're not anything like your stepdaddy, right? But you think I am. 'Cause I've got his blood runnin' through my body, right?"

"I didn't say that."

"You called me a monster."

"I didn't mean it."

"You sure?"

I hesitated and then I spoke the truth. With great uncertainty, not unkindly. "I don't know what you are."

"But you don't like me."

"I don't like the way you treat my brother."

"I treat him fine."

"It's not right to keep telling him there's no God. You just make him sad when you say that."

She lit another cigarette and waved it at me. "What do you care? You don't believe in Boone's God neither. In one of your brother's letters, it said your god lived in a bush."

I remembered my broken offerings, my unanswered pleas. "Well, that's over with."

"I'm telling you for the last time, there . . . ain't . . . no . . . God. All we got is fate. And if I'm a monster, it's just 'cause I was meant to be."

Smoking that cigarette had affected me. I felt dizzy and my stomach rumbled. Now I looked at Persely and her body seemed to waver. "And I guess Simon was meant to be a monster?" I demanded.

"Maybe. And guess what . . ." She leaned forward again. "Maybe your brother was meant to be a monster. Maybe it's his fate."

I jumped to my feet, horrified. "Don't you ever say that about my brother again! Boone is a saint!"

"So was I, once. Sweet sweet sweet. Remember the picture?"

I wanted to kill Persely suddenly, tear out her hair and claw her face and choke her firelit throat. I took a step toward her, but my stomach lurched again and I turned around and threw up in a clump of bushes. Sinking to my knees, I tried to steady myself. My whole body was shaking, half from the cigarette smoke and half from Persely's words. I'd been wrong to think there was any good in her.

After several minutes I stood up and turned around.

"Got the first-time smoker's blues?" Persely asked.

"I'm going swimming."

"Me, too."

"Suit yourself. I personally don't care if you drown."

"I personally don't care if you drown," Persely mimicked, screwing her face up to mock me.

We walked through the woods silently, enemies again, far apart from each other. Seething. When we found the water, I waded out into it without taking off my clothes. I lay on my back and floated in the warm water until I was alone with my thoughts. Everything was going to be all right. That tension I'd felt all day between Persely and my brother was a comfort to me, for I was sure it meant her hold on him was loosening.

Boone found us floating silently in the cove when he came back from fishing.

"Catch anything?" I asked.

"A little one," he said. He was tying off the boat. "Persely, you shouldn't be swimming." The tension again.

"Don't be such an old man, Boone."

"Old man? Who's an old man?"

He tied off the boat and jumped in the water with all his clothes on, wading toward Persely. "Get the catfish, Alice," he said absently, but he was staring straight at Persely. She stopped paddling around and rose out of the water to face Boone, her hair wet and lake water running down her bare torso.

I waded over to the boat to get the fish, but as I lifted the stringer, my eyes never left my two companions, who were standing in the still water very close to each other. *Tell her, Boone. Tell her you don't love her anymore.*

The catfish began to writhe on the stringer, and temporarily distracted, I looked down at the fish. It was small, no bigger than a pound. "You call this dinner?" I asked, but no one answered. I looked back at Persely and Boone, who were standing together in the water, their bodies copied by moonlight and splashed on the lake surface. His arms around her. Her arms around him. Faces together. Lips touching.

The silence of the first kiss. The exclusive kiss that forever dunks a sister's head underwater. I stood there with my mouth agape. Boone's hand slid down Persely's bare back, stopped in the center and moved in circles. And finally I understood. The tension between Boone and Persely was not contained in the story she'd related, or in the struggles between God and fate. It was simply the anticipation of a kiss.

They kissed again later, sitting by firelight, after the meager catfish had been skinned and cooked and eaten. Its severed head stared at me from the middle of the fire.

"So Boone," said Persely, shooting me a glance, "does all this kissing mean you understand what drove old Persely to make her parents that special drink?"

Boone had his hand on her leg. "No," he admitted. "But God understands you, and He forgives all things. He'd forgive you, too, Persely, if you'd only ask."

Ah, God. The dammed-up nectar of His mystery was once again flowing through my brother's veins. I smiled, for although I didn't really know this God, I preferred Him to Persely.

But Persely said: "Well, guess what? I don't need God, 'cause I don't need forgiveness. I'm not sorry. I'm happy my mama's dead, and I only wish Jeremiah was in the ground, too."

"I don't believe it. The Persely I know would—"

"You don't know me, Boone. And if you did, you wouldn't love me."

Boone put his arm around her. "That's not true!" he said fiercely. "I know your past. And I still love you, Persely."

She gazed into the firelight. "You don't really know what I've done."

"I don't care!" He drew her close to him. "All that time I loved that boy on the wall. I wanted to protect him. It was you, Persely. It was you I loved."

They kissed for a long time.

The fire's heat drifted over to a nearby bush and drew out the faint scent of my vomit. My heart sank as I sat there watching the two embracing and remembering what Persely had said earlier that evening: *Maybe your brother was meant to be a monster. Maybe it's his fate.*

The two of them paid me no heed. While they were still kissing, I found the bloody shirt Boone had given to Persely and threw it in the fire.

Chapter Twenty-two

We decided to ration the food and to stay on the island until we thought of the perfect plan for our eventual escape. The plan that had formed in my mind had Boone and me fleeing to South Carolina to live with gentle Aunt Garnet, the only one in the family and indeed in the adult world who seemed able and willing to protect us from harm. But Boone would go nowhere without Persely, and I would go nowhere without Boone. And, of course, the fact that we were in the company of such a famous and striking criminal precluded the three of us from ever getting on a Carolina-bound bus, or even hitchhiking by the side of a public highway. Nor could we call the police. We were trapped because of Persely, and this state of affairs made me hate her even more.

We rested during the day and we ate the blackberries that grew along the ground, and the soft green tubers of cattails, and tuna, and Spam, and a loaf of cocktail pumpernickel that we had found in Mr. Walt's cupboard. When we dug up the bologna it had turned a cyanotic color, so we buried it again to use as bait for the channel cats, creatures who had historically demonstrated no real fear of food poisoning. We built a fire every night, taking the slight risk that its smoke could be seen above the tree-tops. We grew wilder. Our families were gone from us, they had fallen away and left us with rocks and water and cattails and the miracle of burning wood, and we were never going back.

Boone and Persely continued the swimming lessons, and after a few nights, we both became used to Persely's tendency toward partial nudity and stopped looking away when she walked toward us, shirtless, ready to learn the butterfly stroke. She seemed to revel in Boone's instructions and the feel of his hands around her bare waist. But she didn't seem to make much progress on her form or her stroke.

"You're sure taking your good time learning to swim," I told her once.

She answered me in a low voice: "A girl at the hospital used to tell me to let a boy teach you things. They like that. It makes them feel important."

As the two of them swam, I left them alone, floating on my back. Water under my body. Water between my toes. Water in my hair and eyes and ears and teeth. I spoke the names of the people I'd lost and, my ears underwater, heard their sad echo. *Mother . . . Father . . . Spencer . . .*

We slept in the lean-to, stretching out on the bare ground, Boone and Persely wrapped up in each other, with Mr. Walt's machete near Boone's head. On nights when I was especially angry at Persely's antics, I would drag my blanket into the cover of the pine woods and try to sleep on the spongy ground, insects crawling over my arms. But I was always too frightened to stay away, for I had dreams about Simon coming back for us. The tearing sound of his borrowed boat on the wet bank. His knees parting cattails, water moving up the fabric of his pants. His body moving through the jungle of the pine woods, disturbing the shadows, rattling the leaves. The sound of his voice. The feel of his hands around my neck. But I told myself that he had no real reason to track us down, now that we were gone and out of his way and he had another child he could obsess about—one he considered, for the moment, his own.

As the days and the nights passed, Persely and Boone grew closer. He put the orange flowers of the trumpet creeper in her hair; they shared blackberries and mouthfuls of lake water; under the drifting fog they embraced, half dressed; in the darkness of the lean-to I heard them kissing each other. Once Persely ripped her ankle on a briar and my brother knelt down and put his mouth to her torn flesh, drinking her blood until the flow stopped. I stood aghast. Once I saw his hands on her breasts. Once I saw them half out of the water, lying on the bank, their bodies naked and darkened by the sun.

Boone still told her about God and forgiveness, but if God spoke through him, it was only in a hoarse whisper, full of breezes and cotton. All the while, Persely was telling Boone about fate and tigers and the absence of nectar in the godless world. And I myself, left out utterly and completely, could only watch as they became more and more wrapped up in each other.

Persely and I were sitting by the fire when Boone walked up. He'd been fishing since dusk, wading out from the island and then casting in close to the cattails. He no longer went out on the boat; we were low on gas. He walked toward us out of the forest, his fishing pole in one hand and a portable radio in the other.

"Look what I found," he said.

"Where did you find that?" I asked.

"In the hull of the boat."

"Oh yeah. I took it from Mr. Walt's house. I forgot about it."

Boone turned it on, and discordant static blared. "It works," he said. He fiddled with the dials until a song by the Rolling Stones came on.

"Ahhh," said Persely. Her cigarettes had run out that morning and she was a little jumpy. "I miss music. Every time I escaped the loony bin, some new star would be dead. Jimi Hendrix. Janis Joplin. Jim Morrison . . . I missed all the good new songs. They don't have a lot of dance parties in the loony bin." She looked at Boone. "You know how to dance?"

Boone set his fishing pole against a tree. "No."

"Why not? Don't they have dances at school?"

"Yes . . . but I never went."

"Geez," said Persely. "Come here."

Persely rose to her feet and Boone walked around the fire until they stood together, face-to-face. The possibility of a kiss arose, swooped in and faded away, like a moth suddenly dying of old age.

"Turn it up," said Persely, and the Rolling Stones howled in a bucket of static. "Put the radio down," she added, and began to shake her hips and move her arms to the beat. "Like this, like this."

"Like this?" Boone's arms flailed.

"You're getting it."

Their hair fell into their faces and the light of yellow flames zigzagged on their writhing bodies, Boone swooping toward her and then falling away as though drawn close and then rejected by her temperamental soul. And it was obvious that they no longer had to think about the dance because they were as one with the beat and the crickets and water and moon and stars and blood . . . *If I don't get some shelter, oh yeah, I'm gonna fade away! War, children, it's just a shot away, it's just a shot away!*

I looked at them.

Savages.

I had begun to feel wild myself. Hair growing on my legs and under my arms. My one outfit rinsed out in lake water and full of wrinkles. My own self beginning to take on the scent and appearance of a primitive being, a process begun in our yard back home, with my do-nothing god that ate my sacrificial gifts.

Boone tripped over something, faltered. Persely laughed and caught him. Another song came on and they kept dancing.

* * *

We could have continued like that all summer, just hiding out, living on fish, dancing under moonlight, turning brown in the sun, listening to the batteries die in the radio, lying low during bass tournaments, attempting to poison one another's philosophies and slowly losing our fear of Simon finding us.

But Persely, girl of dangerous surprises, had other plans. Whether it had been brought on by her withdrawal from cigarettes or by her own ghosts, an urge was growing inside of her.

Three nights after Boone found the radio, she threw down a stick she was gnawing in memory of a cigarette and said: "I gotta see him one more time."

Chapter Twenty-three

W ho?" asked Boone cautiously.
Persely jumped up and began to pace. Boone and she
had been cavorting naked in the woods that day, and pine
needles were still bristling here and there in her tangled
hair. "You know," she said. "Jeremiah. Simon."

"Why?"

"I just . . . I don't know. I want to see his face."

"But you know he's your father. You heard his voice."

"I know. But I just need to look at him and make sure in
my mind."

I jumped to my feet to face Persely, my shadow falling
over the fire as if shielding it from the horror of Simon's

name. "No! Are you out of your crazy mind? Listen, we'll get you more cigarettes. Cartons and cartons. You can smoke three at once! But get this idea out of your head! You're the one that made Simon a crazy poisoner, and you're not going to drag us back there!"

"I gotta know," Persely said firmly.

"We go back there and he'll kill us all."

"I'll kill the varmint first."

"You've already tried."

"Shut up!" Boone shouted. "Shut up, both of you! We're not going back there. If we go back, we'll die. I know it."

"I'm going," said Persely.

"Well, I'm not taking you there, honey. It's not safe. Not just for us. For you."

Persely glared at him. "I ain't your prisoner, Boone. If you won't take me, then I'll swim." She plunged out of the clearing and into the woods. Boone ran after her, and I ran after him. When Persely reached the edge of the bank, she jumped into the lake and began to swim awkwardly, her clothes growing heavy with water and slowing her progress. Boone dove in after her. In a few strokes, he reached her. He grabbed her by the ankle and tried to hold her as she clawed and fought him. It was a silent, deadly serious struggle, made up of their histories, of water and black air, of love and fear. I felt like an interloper, watching it. A voyeur to all the sad themes of living.

Persely clawed Boone's face. Pulled his hair. Spat water at him. Finally she stopped struggling, and Boone put an arm around her and towed her back in to shallow water. When he could stand, he embraced her and held her wet body to his, so tightly that they looked like one creature. She shivered and he sighed something into her ear. Persely's body went limp against him. He carried her to the bank, laying her down tenderly, as Simon Jester once laid down our half-drowned mother.

Persely is our stepsister, I thought to myself. *And the daughter of a maniac. And a maniac herself. And the girl my brother loves. And we will die because of her.*

"Okay, Persely," Boone was saying. "We'll go back there. You and me."

"Oh, no," I said, hating both of them. "You're not leaving me on this island alone."

We lay next to one another in the lean-to. Bugs crawled on our skin. Mosquitoes hummed. Another night, and yet things had utterly changed.

"What's the plan?" asked Boone.

Persely shifted next to me. "We steal another truck, somewhere. Then we drive down until we're about half a mile—"

"No," said Boone. "I mean about the driving part."

"What about it? Why can't we drive?"

"Because, Persely—and I'm really being serious about this—you don't know how to drive. You almost got us killed last time. And nothing would attract more attention than you jumping curbs and mowing into buildings."

"Then what do you figure on doing, *honey*?"

"We'll take the bicycles. Remember? We hid them by the docks."

"Humph," said Persely. "First, riding six miles on your

handlebars will kill my ass. And second, people will see me and say: 'There's famous Persely Snow. She's on the loose and looking good.'" The old bragging tone in her voice was back.

"I've thought of both of those things," said Boone. "If you insist on going, Alice, you'll have to ride on my handlebars. You're smaller and lighter than Persely and you won't attract as much attention."

"Thanks," I said. "And my smaller, lighter ass thanks you, too."

Boone looked at Persely. "And about people recognizing you—I have another idea."

"What about it?"

Boone sat up in the lean-to and reached for the machete. "Come outside with me, Persely."

The next night I sat between them in the boat, shivering and furious and full of a dark dread that churned my stomach. I didn't say a word until we caught sight of the dock.

Then I said: "You both have shit for brains."

"Alice, don't swear," said Boone evenly.

Persely turned to me. She wore a baseball cap; her new short haircut made her look younger. "You could have stayed back on the island. Then I would have had a bike to myself."

"Are you kidding? I'm not staying there."

"'Fraidy cat."

"Maniac."

"Cut it out," said Boone. He looked up at Mr. Walt's house. "I wonder if he's still back there."

"I don't care," said Persely. "I don't care about nothing but seeing Jeremiah Snow."

I tried one more time. "Please, Persely," I said in the kindest voice I could muster. "You love Boone, don't you? And don't you see that you're putting him in danger?"

Persely hesitated a minute. She exchanged glances with Boone. "The brat is right," she told him. "I know where you live. Y'all stay here and I'll go."

"No!" he said. "You're not going anywhere without me."

So it was settled. We found our bicycles and began the slow, painful ride back to the house. I was balanced precariously on the handlebars of Boone's bicycle; Persely trailed behind us. Once we saw headlights and had to hide in the cow pasture, but otherwise the long highway was empty, and the streets beyond. We were full of fear and in no mood for talking, but grimly we rode on because Persely couldn't let it go. And because Boone couldn't let Persely go. And because—no matter what the danger—I could not let my brother go.

A mile from our house, in that foreign neighborhood of topiary and soft grass, sudden headlights appeared behind us on the quiet street.

"Run!" I said.

"No," Boone hissed. "It's too late. Running will just attract attention. Just ride real slow and easy. And Persely, duck your head a little."

The headlights didn't pass, but remained behind us.

My body felt cold. "Oh God. What if it's Simon?"

"Just stay calm," said Boone. "Keep pedaling. Everything's going to be all right."

A siren started up behind us, so loud we almost wrecked our bicycles. We looked back and saw that the car had sprouted colored lights.

"Okay," Boone said quickly. "This is our story. We're three kids out on a bike ride."

"A bike ride at three A.M.?" I asked.

Boone ignored me. "And Persely, you're our baby-sitter."

"Are you crazy?" Persely gasped. "A runaway loony girl?"

"It's hard to get good sitters at three in the morning," I said.

"New plan," said Persely. "We're gonna jump off our bikes and run like fucking hell." She looked back at Boone. "Not together but in different directions," she added. "I mean it."

"On the count of three," said Boone. "One, two, three." I leaped off Boone's bicycle. I heard Boone gasp as his crotch hit the bar.

"Boone!" I shrieked.

"Run, Alice!"

Behind me the bicycles clattered as I ran away. I heard the policeman's voice: "Hey, come back here! Stop!"

I ran through the backyards of the neighborhood, through banks of dark bushes and gardens whose foliage felt like fur, among the barking of disturbed dogs, across the rich grass, stumbling on abandoned toys, feeling the soft fabric of a cotton shirt someone had left on a clothesline. I climbed the stiles of a fence, collected splinters and continued running through a quiet suburbia where normal children slept and normal parents dreamed normal dreams. Where kitchen clocks turned. Where ficus plants thrived. I ran through their yards, trampling their flowers, breaking their hedges, tearing their clothes off the lines—a streak of drama staining the banality of sleep. I tripped on something and fell, my arms flying up to protect my face. The ground moved underneath me and swallowed me whole.

Chlorinated water flooded my nose and mouth. I had fallen into someone's pool. I didn't know which way was up, so I swam in a desperately chosen direction until my head hit the bottom of the pool so hard my teeth clacked together. Blindly I used my legs to push up. My face broke the surface and I gasped in late-night air. Not a soul in sight. The newly broken water slapped the sides of the pool as I dog-paddled to the shallow end, found the cement stairs and sat on the third one down, trying to collect my wits while taking deep breaths, rubbing the top of my head, listening. No footsteps. No angry residents. No policemen. No enraged stepfather. No predatory rednecks. No girl struck by lightning. No evil twins. No dead dog. No one.

And I loved this no one, this absence of anyone who could cause me concern or grief, because those two emotions had drained me of energy. That pool was a smaller version of Lake Shine, its own blue-green sanctuary whose chlorine would kill any troublemaking organisms that might thicken an otherwise peaceful evening. I wanted to stay in that pool forever.

Something sticky was running down my face. I touched the liquid and then licked my fingertip. Blood. Persely and Boone were calling my name. I slowly stood and slogged up the stairs, trudging toward their voices in the dark.

They were crouching next to a high brick wall.

"The coast is clear," said Persely.

"Where did he go?" I asked.

"Gave up, I reckon."

"Do you think he recognized you?"

"Nah."

"What happened to you, Alice?" asked Boone. "You're soaked. And you're bleeding."

"I fell into a swimming pool."

"Are you okay?"

My field of vision was strange, and my head ached. "I'm fine, Boone. It's been a lovely evening."

He was looking down the street. "Oh, no," he said. "That cop took our bikes."

"That's okay," said Persely. "It's only a mile or so to your house."

"And how far is it back to the island?" I demanded.

She shrugged.

Boone took her hand. "Let's just go," he said. "We'll walk through the front yards, away from the streetlights. Every time we see headlights, we duck."

And so we proceeded, motley group that we were. Two sneaky teenagers and a soaking-wet girl. Boone was being very protective of Persely and also of me, pointing out stairs, bushes and rocks, and listening for cars and people. Together we trudged through the open moonlight as dogs howled suddenly and stopped just as quickly. We were making our way through a particularly large yard when a light went on in an upstairs window. The three of us dove behind a cement bench and waited, our hearts pounding. I stole a look and saw a face in the window. Wan, thin, distracted, tragic.

My father.

I blinked. My head hurt badly, and the hard bottom of a stranger's pool was playing tricks with my vision. I squinted and looked again.

Spencer Katosky.

He peered out into the night, trying to make out what he couldn't see from that bright room, sensing some danger no doubt, looking from right to left over the lawn and then at the row of ligustrum bushes that divided his yard from the next one. As the roiling swirl of a near-concussion took my guardedness away, a wild longing came over me for him. Persely and Boone said nothing—my brother, no doubt, out of respect for my anguish, and Persely out of some sixth sense for obsessive attractions and lost causes.

Spencer's face left the window and the light went off. My heart sank at the loss of him.

"Let's go," my brother whispered, but just then the door opened and Spencer came out in his pajamas, sweeping a flashlight in all directions as he crept barefoot down his flagstone walkway. Behind the bench we barely breathed, and our eyes followed the beam of the flashlight as it lit up things taken for granted under sunny skies. The flat blades of St. Augustine grass. An old newspaper, wounded by a lawn mower and left to rot. A square patch of impatiens. A red flag lowered on the side of the mailbox.

Spencer's leg shivered a few feet from us. I could see the veins in his feet. His suburban bravery—so little called-for and yet so earnest—broke my heart. And I yearned for this boy who was mild-mannered and kind enough to be startled by some greater badness. I wanted to touch his foot, his knee, his face. He stood there a long moment, then his posture changed so that the movement of the flashlight seemed more like a game than a frightened necessity. He swung it around and around. A boy freed from his bed in the middle of the night. He shone the beam on his bare feet and studied them. Wiggled his toes. Finally, with a sigh, he turned off the flashlight and went inside.

Persely and Boone let out their breath in relief, but I felt none at all. Boone helped Persely up and we walked silently until we came to our street.

"It's not too late to turn back," I said.

Boone shook his head. "We've come this far . . ."

The house loomed colorless in the dark. Strange. I wanted to go running toward it, crying. Throw my arms around my mother's neck. Find my room. Find my shells in the shadow box I'd made in art class. Fetch my broken offerings from the holly bush and put them back together. Dig up Numbhead and bring him back to life and put his toad back in his mouth. Revive the dead bees one by one. Throw a softball in the air. Watch my real father catch it. Find my sheets—newly washed at the time of my flight— and press my face against them.

The three of us crept up to the house until we were crouching under our mother's window, our knees in some fallen vines of yellow jessamine, whose poison can kill in ten minutes.

"Okay," Boone whispered. "Take a quick look."

Persely raised herself up and pressed her face to the window, panting. She crouched back down. "I can't see nothing," she whispered.

"Then let's go," I urged. "It'll be dawn in a few hours."

"She's right," said Boone. "This is too dangerous." He turned to Persely, waiting for her response amid the hum of the air-conditioning unit and the rush of wind through the branches.

"I can't go," Persely said. "I have to see his face. I have to know."

"You can't see anything. They don't sleep with a light on."

Persely turned to Boone. "Let me ask you something. How would y'all sneak out when you were keeping me at Lake Shine?"

"Through our bedroom window."

"Is it locked?"

"You can't go in there. You'll wake him up."

"He sleeps deep. I oughta know."

"I said no, Persely." His voice was pleading.

She gave us a sudden smile in the darkness, her teeth pale against the night. "I've snuck out of a nuthouse seven times. I've jimmied all kinds of locks. I'll be quiet as a mouse. No one's gonna know."

"This just gets better and better," I said.

"If you insist on going," Boone said, "then I'll go with you."

"No," said Persely. "You're clumsy. You make too much noise. I'm just going to take a quick look and skedaddle."

I grabbed Persely's arm and she shot me a hateful look.

"Let me go."

"We're going to get caught."

Persely jerked out of my grip. Boone found my mother's old hive tool in the grass and inserted it under our bedroom window, rocking on it gently until the window moved. Persely slid the window up soundlessly. "Y'all wait over behind that clump of pampas grass," she said, indicating with a tilt of her head an area on the side of the house. "That way if something happens, you can make a run for it."

"I'm not waiting over there," said Boone. "I'm waiting right here."

"Don't be stupid," she said. She looked at me and didn't smile. "Ain't no sense in both of us getting caught. Your sister needs you, Boone."

With that she disappeared into the window, quiet as a slow breeze.

Boone hesitated.

I grabbed his hand. Reluctantly Boone let me lead him to the other side of the towering grass. We waited behind it, expecting Persely to appear any second. The minutes passed. Nothing. Boone began to breathe heavily. I imagined his eyes twitching.

"Oh God," he whispered. "Why did I let her go in there? Why did I do that?"

"She made you do it."

"If something happens to her, I'll die. She's my life."

"Just hold still."

Suddenly a light came on in the window of the sewing room.

"Oh, no," said Boone. He darted away from me and rushed toward the light, keeping his head low. Try as I might, I could not follow him. My throat was icy with dread and my hands were shaking. My brother crouched underneath the window, then slowly raised up for a look. He made some gestures, waved his hands. Nodded. More gestures, urgent ones. He watched some more. Then he returned to his place beside me, behind the tall grass.

"What's happening?"

"Persely's in there," he said, still huffing.

"What's she doing?"

"You don't want to know, Alice. I tried to motion for her to come out, but she's paying no attention."

We waited until my legs began to fall asleep. Boone removed his glasses, wiped them off and put them back on for the twentieth time.

Sudden footsteps to the right of us, and a body flinging itself into our space. I gasped, lashing out blindly.

"Relax," Persely said.

"Where did you come from?" asked Boone.

"The side door. I'm telling you, I'm quiet as a mouse."

"Was it him?"

"It's him, all right. Sleeping like a snake."

"And my mother?" asked Boone after moment. "Did she look all right?"

"Looked okay to me."

Something was in her hands. A trash bag filled with something.

"What is that?" I asked. I could see her teeth again in the dark.

"The money he got off my dead mama."

I gasped. "You took his money?"

"Don't belong to him. It's my mama's."

"Oh, God," I groaned. "That's why you came here, wasn't it? You didn't want to see him. You wanted to steal that money."

"I wanted justice, and I got it."

"How did you get it out of the safe?" asked Boone.

"I told you. I can undo any lock. I'm a damn fool and the best there is. That's from *Hang 'em High.*"

I jabbed my index finger into her chest. "You are going to put that money right back, Persely." My head throbbed and my stomach hurt and I'd had enough.

"She's right," said Boone. "Simon will go crazy when

he sees it's gone. He'll think we came back and stole it. Just leave it under the window. Maybe he'll think some burglar dropped it or something."

"Really?" asked Persely. "Boone, you really want me to do it?"

"Yes."

Her voice was soft, tender. "For you, baby?"

"Yes. For me."

"And how 'bout justice?"

"He'll get his justice someday."

Persely gave my brother a soul-searching look, her eyes gleaming under the starlight. "You're right, honey."

We watched her creep away toward the house again.

"Just drop it right under the window," Boone called softly to her.

Persely stopped a few feet from the window. She knelt down and picked up something out of the grass. Suddenly she threw it at the window. The glass broke.

"Persely, no!" Boone shouted.

"I'VE COME BACK TO HAUNT YOU, JEREMIAH! YA COCKSUCKER!" Persely screamed. "HOPE YOU LIKED THE TANG!"

"Oh God, oh God," Boone panted.

The light came on and the face of Simon Jester appeared at the broken window, his mouth open in shock.

Persely whirled around. "Run!" she shouted, her legs pumping as she sprinted toward us with the sack still in her hands. "Run!"

We ran. Behind us I heard the front door open.

We leaped over hedges. Dashed through briars. Tripped over hoses lying like snakes across the grass. We ran across driveways, stumbled through flowerbeds, collided with bird feeders. Our hands occasionally touched. Out of breath, we threw ourselves behind an old station wagon and crouched there, breathing hard. My wound had re-opened and blood ran down my face. My heart was racing so fast that I thought I might faint.

Boone took his pocketknife from the front pocket of his blue jeans, opened the blade and waited, peering around the bumper for a glimpse of a madman. "Why did you do it, Persely?" he demanded, breathing hard. I could hear the anger and hurt in his voice.

"Because you was giving me orders. Telling me what to do. Like Jeremiah used to."

"Persely," he said, anguished. "I'm not him."

"You and Simon deserve each other, Persely," I said. I wanted to seize Boone's knife and stab her with it.

She pushed me, hard, and I fell backward. "Don't you never say that again," she snarled, "or I'll wring your neck!"

"What are we going to do?" Boone demanded. "Sit here and argue until he finds us?"

To my horror, I began to cry. "Boone, maybe he didn't see us. Maybe it was just her that he saw. Leave her, Boone. It's her fault. Without her, we'd be safe." Tears streamed down my face. "Boone, who do you love? Me or her?"

Boone stroked my back helplessly. "Both of you, of course."

"Do you want me to die?"

"No!"

"Then forget about her! She's caused us nothing but trouble."

"I'm sorry. I can't leave her." He turned to her. "Even though you did a stupid thing, Persely. Even though you weren't thinking of our safety. Just about yourself."

"I'm sorry, Boone," Persely said after a moment.

He ducked his head and looked under the station wagon at the dark street. "You see any headlights?"

"Maybe he's on foot," said Persely.

After awhile I stopped crying and just sat there dully. "How are we going to get back to Never Island?" I asked. "Our bicycles are gone."

"We'd have to walk all day," Persely said. "With you bloody."

"Why don't we just flag down a policeman?" I said. "We haven't broken the law. We could tell him the whole story."

"I'd get sent back to the hospital," said Persely.

"Good," I replied bitterly. "That's the best place for you."

"And anyway, a cop won't help."

"Sure he will. I'll tell him Simon's trying to kill us."

"He won't believe you."

"I'll show him my head. And tell him Simon hit me."

"Don't matter. Won't help a damn bit. So you just go ahead and flag down a cop, *Alice*." Lake Shine had treated my name so much kinder when I had whispered it underwater.

"No one's flagging down a cop," said Boone. "But how are we going to get to Lake Shine?"

For a minute Persely lost her angry expression and regained her careful Cooperesque smile. "Y'all know what's got to be done." She pointed. "See that truck yonder?"

Chapter Twenty-four

We left the truck in a bait-shop parking lot two miles from the lake and ran through the cow pastures the rest of the way. Silently we climbed into the boat and headed for Never Island, watching the sun test the morning first as an orange globe and then as a golden one.

Persely's mood had declined on the drive over. She slumped a little in the boat as we passed the silent coves. Halfway to Never Island, Persely suddenly threw the sack of money overboard, turning around and watching it disappear. Boone and I exchanged glances but said nothing, just letting our quiet sense of doom take a harder shape in our separate bodies. Simon's money, gone forever. We couldn't give it back to him now if we wanted to.

Persely looked at me with a strange expression, one that had nothing to do with a garbage bag full of money that was sinking into seventy feet of water somewhere behind us. She leaned over and whispered to me: "Tell me, Alice, that you didn't mean it when you said me and Simon deserved each other. Tell me you were just mad."

There was no anger or violence in her eyes. Just a look so anguished that it embarrassed me a little. "I didn't mean it, Persely," I said. "I promise, I didn't." She seemed relieved and I went back to ignoring her.

When we reached Never Island, we took the motor off the boat and hid it in a thicket of cattails. Then we dragged the boat up the steep bank and into the forest where it could not be seen from shore. We covered the boat with branches and clumps of pine straw, working in silence, in fear and hostility. We both knew that Simon was sure to come after us now, in search of the stolen money or his crazy lost daughter.

Boone and I were on the same side, for once. Or so it felt to me.

He looked at Persely when we were finished hiding the boat. "Let's go."

We walked silently back to our clearing, briars catching at our clothes, old pinecones cracking under our feet. When we reached the campsite, Boone sat down in a heap on his blanket. Persely sat down next to him.

She touched his hand. "Are you mad at me, Boone?"

He didn't answer her.

"We're trapped," I said softly. "We're trapped here with you."

Before the sun had risen fully, we had all fallen asleep, so exhausted were we by the events of the night.

My brother was at the kitchen table. And he was sleeping so deeply. I shook his arm. Wake up, Boone, wake up. Simon was at the head of the table. Can't you wake up your brother, Alice? Why won't your brother wake up? Meg turned from the oven and her face dissolved and became Persely's. She smiled. Boone is tired, she said. He's very very tired. I looked back at Simon and Simon was Boone. No! I shouted. You can't be Simon! You can't be Simon! Persely said: It's his fate.

I awoke with a start, my heart beating a jungle staccato as I tried to orient myself. That was it. We were on an island. The three of us. I looked over at Boone and Persely. They had awakened and were holding each other.

"I'm sorry, Boone," she was whispering. "I'm so sorry."

"It's okay, Persely. I understand."

"No, you don't, you don't. You don't belong with me. It hurts you to know me."

"I want to know you. I love you."

They began to kiss, clinging to each other.

I sat up and rubbed my eyes as a raw ache moved through me once again. Boone was back with the enemy, leaving me alone.

"I'm hungry," I said.

Boone stopped kissing Persely and looked over at me. "We have hardly any food left."

"Good thing we've got that satchel full of money," I said. "Oh, wait, never mind."

"I'm going to go check out the lake and see if anyone's around," Boone said.

"I'll go with you."

The sun was warm on my face and I was sweating under my clothes. I felt groggy from sleeping in the heat, and my head still hurt where I had hit the bottom of that swimming pool. On top of everything else, my nightmare had left me trembling and dispirited. Boone walked in front of me, ducking under the low branches of trees that oozed sap.

We stood together at the top of the bank, looking out across the clear water and catching sight of a single tiny boat in the distance.

"Probably a fisherman," said Boone. "He can't see us from here."

"I have to talk to you. Sister to brother."

He turned to face me. He looked different. A bit of stubble on his cheeks. His eyes older. His shoulders squarer.

"I don't feel safe here anymore, Boone. Simon will find us here."

"He doesn't have a boat."

"He can rent one."

"He has no idea this island is out here."

"Meg could tell him."

"She wouldn't."

"He knows we used to come here to swim. And he knows this lake. We met him when he was fishing here, remember?"

"So what? This lake is gigantic. It takes two hours just to drive around it. By the time he figures out we're here, we'll be long gone."

"That's what I wanted to talk to you about. I want us to leave this island, and I want to go to South Carolina and live with Aunt Garnet."

He folded his arms. "You know we'd never be able to

get Persely to South Carolina. She's famous. She was on the cover of *Lone Star Monthly* last July."

"She won't be going with us. It'll be just you and me. Like it used to be."

A look of sudden anger crossed my brother's face, and he turned away from me. He picked up a stick and threw it in the direction of the boat.

"We can call Aunt Garnet collect," I persisted. "She'd send us the money. And we'd be safe then. We could hop on a bus and never be scared again. You know Aunt Garnet would shoot Simon if he ever came around."

"So you want me to leave Persely? Just like that?"

"Just like that."

"I love her."

"I'm your sister."

Boone shoved his hands down in the pockets of his cut-offs. I could see a long scratch across his glasses. The waves beat at the cattails. An osprey landed nearby.

"You go, Alice," he said at last. "You should be safe. I'll take you to shore and drop you off."

"I won't leave without you."

We watched the osprey gulp down a sunfish. Boone said, "Then I guess we're stuck."

By midafternoon the sky had clouded over and the rain poured down. The three of us sat in the leaky lean-to, playing poker with cards we'd taken from Mr. Walt's chest of drawers. Raindrops slid down the cards. When dusk came in, the bad weather cleared for a bit. Our dinner that night used the last of the food. It was too wet for a fire, so we sat around the charred logs, Boone and Persely holding hands. Persely's hair was decorated with a crown of trumpet flowers Boone had made for her that morning. We were all soaking wet.

"So what the hell are we going to do now?" I said. "Stay on this island until we die?"

Boone kissed the side of Persely's head. "Let's not think of that right now."

I shivered. "He's going to come after us, Boone. I can feel it."

"I think the island is safe. For now."

"I think you're wrong."

He looked at Persely. "What do you think?"

"For once, I'm gonna agree with the runt. I say let's get out of here."

Boone shook his head. "Not tonight. There's a storm coming. Smell the air. We'll wait until just before dawn and then we'll make our getaway."

That night the heavens opened and poured down upon us. Persely and Boone and I lay huddled together, terrified by the thunder and the lightning and the cracking of branches. Water collected in the declivity in which we camped, flooded the fire site and washed the ashes into the surrounding briars.

Sometime in the night the rain stopped, and we slept. At four in the morning Boone woke us up, and we packed a few soaked possessions and headed for the boat.

It was gone.

Chapter Twenty-five

I saw Persely's look of terror and felt sick myself. My legs were shaking uncontrollably.

"Did the water wash it out to shore?" Persely whispered.

"No," Boone said. "The rope's cut. Simon's scaring us. It's a game to him."

"He knows where we are," I said. "All three of us. Everyone he hates is right here on this island. And no one's going to save us."

We heard the distant thunder of another storm. Boone threw down the rope and stared out into the choppy waves. His wet shirt stuck to his body; raindrops trickled down the lenses of his glasses.

"I say we swim for it," said Persely.

"Right," said Boone. "You're not so good at that."

"Yes, I am. Really."

"Even if you were," he said, "Alice can't swim that far. And with a storm coming . . . we could all be hit by lightning."

I had a sudden image of the three of us sitting on a quilt, our eyes half closed, our backs slumped, someone reading stories to us.

"So we just sit here and wait to die?" Persely asked.

Boone's jaw went hard. "We won't die. We'll fight."

"With what?"

"We've got the machete."

"Oh, that'll help tons," I said. I looked at Persely, hatred for her boiling up in me. I told her: "You did this to us."

All day long it rained intermittently. Thunder rolled, and in the distance, lighting twisted through the sky. We moved pine straw from the forest floor to the clearing, in an attempt to soak up some of the water. When the work was done, we sat together silently.

"Meg must have told him," Boone murmured once. No one answered him. Persely and I locked eyes and she moved hers away first.

Night moved in and the crickets sounded creaky. Another storm was coming. The breeze turned into wind. A drop of water hit my face. I could barely see Boone in front of me, the night was so dark.

"Sweetheart," he said to Persely.

More rain was falling.

"It's so dark," said Persely.

"We'll take turns keeping watch," said Boone.

"Watching what?" I demanded. "I can barely see."

Boone switched on Mr. Walt's flashlight and shone it in my face, but the weak light barely reached me. "We've got this."

"The batteries are almost gone."

"It'll do."

We crawled into the lean-to. Boone put one arm around me and one arm around Persely and we sat there waiting— for what, we didn't know—as the rain beat down harder, dripping through the lean-to and soaking our clothes and washing the discordant notes out of the crickets.

"I think I hear a boat motor," I said.

Boone cocked his head. "I don't hear anything. Are you sure?"

I listened again. "I guess not."

We sat there silently, Boone's arm like a father's around my shoulders, his other arm like a lover's around Persely's waist.

"I hear something! I hear something!" Persely gasped.

My heart skipped a beat.

"What?" asked Boone.

"I don't know. Footsteps or something."

"It's your imagination."

"Don't let him get me, Boone! Don't let him come close to me! Please, please!"

"I'll protect you, honey."

Boone managed to soothe her, and then all was quiet for a few minutes. Next to me I could hear Persely's tortured breathing. Finally she said, "You don't belong with me, Boone. I'm a monster. I belong with Simon."

"Don't say that, sweetheart," Boone murmured, but I myself had had enough. I was soaked through with rain, shivering and terrified. And in my mind I deserved an answer. And so I said: "Just cut all the bullshit, Persely. You're hiding something, and I want to know what it is."

"Be quiet," said Boone, but I could hear Persely inhale, could imagine her lungs filling up with raw, wet air, the fuel that makes a confession.

"I'll tell you," she said. "I'll tell you the real story, but then I can't see y'all no more. I'll just pretend you understand me. I'll just pretend you forgive me."

"I'll forgive you," said Boone. "No matter what." He paused a minute. "So will God." And with those words I imagined Boone's God suddenly crawling out of the dead fire outside and shaking off the ashes as a dog would shake water from his coat. "All right," Persely said at last. And she began to tell us the real story. A little of Simon's story, a little of Persely's story, and many things neither one of them had mentioned. When it was over, I finally understood Persely Snow. And in a horrified way, I understood Simon Jester. But by then we were almost out of time.

Chapter Twenty-six

She grew up with his madness. His countless demands, his faith, cruel and wild, his sudden violence and bizarre punishments. She grew up with an early memory, so vague and dim, of his hands around her neck, tightening. She never told anyone—could have been a dream—but it became a habit, through the years, on those days when the weather was hot and he was particularly crazed, to touch her neck with her fingertips, protectively.

Her mother wouldn't leave him. She was weak, jobless. She needed a man and had fallen under his spell so completely that she seemed more child than mother. Persely didn't hate her mother. Instead she loved her, saw her weakness as something homegrown, starting in the spine and moving outward, and she tried her best to comfort her.

Her mother's great love for her seemed to set Jeremiah off, make him question her loyalty, so this motherly love was expressed mostly at night, a kiss, a murmur, a straightening of the covers. Persely cherished these moments, for in the midnight air, her mother always smelled the most like a mother, without those masking odors of bleach and cinnamon and Murphy's oil soap. Her mother would tell her how paralyzed she felt, and how sorry she was for that weakness. "I don't really love him," she whispered on more than one night. "But I need him. I'd die if he left." Persely would take her mother's hand and try to keep her there, in her room, but soon Persely would be left alone to overhear another argument downstairs.

Over the years, the arguments grew worse, and the punishments grew worse for Persely. All the requisite torments one would assume would come from a man unhinged. Sometimes he locked her in her room, sometimes he wouldn't let her eat, sometimes he left bruises. Persely could feel his hatred for her growing. And her hatred for him. It got between the flesh and blood of father and daughter and made them strangers to each other. Enemies.

No one helped Persely at school. No worried-looking teacher took her aside. In vast hot Texas, this drama was the sweat under the saddle, neither seen nor felt.

Her mother stole into her room and held her hand and brushed her hair back from her face.

"He's a sad man, honey. He feels small. He's threatened by you."

"Why?"

"He wants all my attention. But it's not right. It's not right."

"He's crazy."

"I'm sorry. Do you forgive me?"

"Yes."

"He wasn't like this when I married him."

"I understand."

"Some day we'll run away. We'll go to Kansas City. It's pretty, and the people are nice. So many fountains there, and hardly any men."

Eighth grade marked the greatest change. Jeremiah punished Persely more frequently, more severely, and she learned to be calm and to teach her body the grim lessons of passivity. Stimulus brought no response, his screams brought no effect, bruises were no more painful to her flesh than wine was to the belly of a priest. She began to think of her body as alien, flimsily immortal.

She prayed to God and received no answer.

Fate stepped in.

One day in school she learned about Rasputin, a mad monk with the glittering eyes of Jeremiah Snow. Rasputin was poisoned, imperfectly, with cakes. But others were poisoned better over the following years, and many problems were solved, and many bad people fell away. Persely began to read books. Her knowledge grew. She bought a small yellow box and kept it in her room. Deep down she knew that she could never bring herself to use it, but keeping the deadly crystals in her room and imagining stirring them into her father's drink made her feel better, more substantial, more of the world.

Her mother had lost weight. One afternoon Persely

walked into the kitchen and saw that her mother had set up
a record player on the Formica table and was dancing
around and around to the music of the Andrews Sisters.
Something was flying off her arms onto the floor and the
curtains. A stream of it ran down the white oven. Two
drops flew into the fruit bowl on the single pear. A drop of
it hit Persely in the face, and she put her finger to it and
looked at the blood on her fingertip.

"Mother!"

A Gillette razor blade sat on the album cover between
the second and third Andrews Sisters.

That night Persely's mother came to her room and sat
down on her bed. In the dim light Persely saw three Band-
Aids on her mother's arm.

"Why did you do that?" Persely asked.

"I'm so tired, baby."

"Let's leave."

"Someday we'll go to Kansas City. You know, the mist
around the mountains there is blue in certain lights."

"Let's go now."

"I can't. I can't."

Persely looked over at her shelf. Her box of poison sat
there, between two albums. She thought of her father, dead
on the floor. She thought of the mountains of Kansas City,
the swirl of blue mist. Climbing them with her mother by
her side.

Persely and her mother redoubled their efforts to make
everything just right, to be loyal and true, but Jeremiah's
madness was growing. His rants and his sudden violence.
One day Persely lost her temper with her mother.

"Why do you let him do this?"

"I'm sorry. I'm sorry."

"No, you're not. You don't love me." Persely's voice was loud, accusatory.

"Yes I do, baby!"

"You're weak. I wish you weren't my mother. Then I'd be safe." Persely immediately regretted the words. "I'm sorry," she said. Her mother gave her a strange look and left the room.

Later that afternoon as Persely sat in her room, she heard her mother down the hall, dialing the phone. "Please," she was saying. "My husband's been mistreating my daughter. You've got to send someone over to help us."

Persely sat straight up in bed, shocked, as she heard her mother give the address. She looked out the window and saw Jeremiah in the front yard, raking leaves. Ten minutes later a police cruiser pulled into the driveway and a deputy got out. This was the moment of relief. Of truth. This was the moment when the victims were saved and the demons struck down.

The deputy talked to Jeremiah for several minutes, then got back in his car and drove away.

Marshal Cooper would not have turned his back on her. Marshal Cooper and his kind are dead. They've been buried in their boots, the years have passed, the star they wore on their chest has crumbled down to three points, and their great-great-great-grandsons don't even turn on their sirens at the thought of a girl done wrong.

Persely ran out into the hall and stood facing her mother. Together they listened as Jeremiah came roaring back into the house.

Tears streamed down her mother's face, and in the midst of her own fear, Persely's heart broke for her. Mary had risked everything, just this once, to defy her husband and to protect her daughter, and now she was drained of the will to fight.

Jeremiah thundered up the stairs and seized his wife by the shoulders. "Did you call the police on me? Did you? Did you?"

"It was an accident!"

"An accident?" He shook her. "You have betrayed me!"

Persely edged closer, unsure of what to do, terrified that her father would finally strike her mother.

Mary said: "I'm sorry, Jeremiah."

"Honey," said Jeremiah Snow, "maybe you need to learn a lesson about *loyalty*."

Nothing happened that first night. Nor the second. On the third night, just as Persely was falling asleep, she felt something around her neck. A cord or a belt. She opened her eyes, touched her throat, felt the smoothness of leather. She tried to lift her head, but the leather tightened.

Cooper squinted from the horse. The knot of the noose sat over his collar. You're making a mistake, he said.

She couldn't breathe. Her room, gray in the night, began to turn pitch-black. A red gash broke free at the left side of her vision. The red turned into purple. Persely left her body, floated around the room stunned, wingless, borne along in the air by the currents of the ceiling fan. She floated past her posters of Clint Eastwood and Janis Joplin, floated past her books on the sea and her secret box of poison.

That'll teach you about loyalty.

Sacrifices are incremental. Take a fingernail, you'll want the finger next time. Beat someone up and next thing you know, you might hang him. Kill a grasshopper and next you'll want to kill a fiddler crab. Make a man wear a crown of thorns and then you're running a sword through his side.

From above, Persely saw her father finally let her go. He stood up, looked at her a minute and left the room.

Persely awoke early in the morning. Could it all have been a dream, again? But she had a blinding headache, and when she breathed, her throat hurt. She went to the mirror, saw the red ring around her neck. Touched it. Understood now that her father had meant to kill her. And, given enough time, would kill her. She decided not to tell her mother, who had used up the last of her energy calling the useless police. Instead she formed a plan that would free them both. She tied a bandanna around her neck, Cooper-style, to hide the marks.

That night Jeremiah sat at the dinner table as though nothing had happened. Let's all go on a picnic tomorrow, Mary. There's just been lotsa stress 'round here. The venue chosen was Lake Shine, a fat green body of water upon whose eastern shore, next to the Baptist encampment, sat a state park.

Late the next morning, Jeremiah Snow lounged on the bank of Lake Shine with his wife and child. Bluebird sky, fisherman's curse. The trees were set back, and the sun was high overhead. Potato chips, peanut butter and blackberry jam sandwiches. Orange Kool-Aid for the mother and the daughter and Tang for Jeremiah, for he was the only one in the family who craved its bittersweet taste.

Mary wore a plastic swimming cap to keep her red hair from spilling out. Persely rose from the bank and waded out in the water. Blond hair and blue eyes. Not a boy but a girl. Not three but thirteen.

Come over here and eat your sandwich, Jeremiah called to his daughter, but the girl ignored him. Instead she turned her back to him and concentrated on something she saw in the water, a minnow or a quick-witted sunfish. Her neck was hot under the bandanna. She could barely breathe. Her heart beat wildly as she waited for her father to drink his Tang and die, leaving his wife and daughter free to go to Kansas City. Persely had mixed the potion herself, early that morning, hands shaking. Now she shook all over, knee-deep in the calm water. The sun stood like the law in the sky; the clouds had gotten away from it.

Behind her, Persely could hear her mother say: *Honey, can you open my thermos? The lid's on too tight.* She heard the small whooshing sound of her mother's thermos lid loosening—harmless orange Kool-Aid—and then, a few seconds later, her father's thermos opening.

A new breeze swept in from shore, carrying a bare static, and Persely felt it and recognized it, like the smallest buzz of a sciatic nerve, the most subtle pang of a trick knee. The tension caused by knowing Jeremiah's head must be tilted back at this very moment, and the poison must be sliding down his throat. She heard mumbling behind her but couldn't make out the words. She turned around and waded toward the bank. Her father wore a slightly puzzled expression.

He no longer held the thermos.

Persely finally heard what he was saying:

I'm telling you, it tastes funny. Try it again.

Her mother had his thermos in her hands. Her own thermos was next to her knees. Dutifully she began to drink, gulping this time.

Persely screamed. She stumbled in the water in her haste to reach her mother.

NOOOOOOOOOO! NOOOOOOOOO! A beet-red face and blond curls plastered to her head. Her body trembling violently, her eyes streaming tears. *NOOOOOOOOO! NOOOOOOOO!* No temper tantrum here. Only horror.

The wind rushed through the shallow woods behind her parents. Cars raced along the road that wound around the lake.

No storm was brewing. Not a cloud in the sky, not a whisper of rain or a fragile lick of lightning or a distant clap of thunder.

The storm was inside her parents.

Cyanide was doing terrible things to them. They writhed on the ground. They screamed and moaned. Persely ran toward them, her feet rising out of the shallow water, droplets flying. But her parents were lost in the thunder that oxygen makes when it struggles out of blood cells, the lightning of body processes jerking and failing. She reached her mother, tried to pin her down, but her mother's arms jerked out of her hands. The woman's skin was turning blue. She writhed and clawed and foamed at the mouth.

Persely left her mother's side and ran away from her parents, through the woods and toward the highway beyond. *Help! Help! Somebody help us!*

She turned once, and looked back. Her father reached toward her. *Wait!* He called out the word once more, so softly it was barely a sound.

Wait.

Chapter Twenty-seven

We couldn't see one another's faces. The rain picked up again and leaked through the roof of the lean-to.

"My God," Boone said at last.

Persely didn't answer. In the dark I heard him kissing her. Not on the mouth from the sound of the kisses, but on a smoother and more comforting plane: the forehead or the cheek or the side of the neck.

"So . . ." I murmured. "It happened right here on this lake. Why didn't the papers ever say where it happened? Maybe if we'd known that, we could have figured it all out."

"Persely doesn't want to talk about it anymore," said Boone, but Persely drew a deep breath and said: "Here's the reason, I think. The state park is right next to the Baptist camp, right? And the Baptists pay a lot of money to rent that land. They run all their summer church camps out of there. And guess who owns that land? Guess who rents it to the Baptists?"

"Who?" I asked.

"The mayor. I guess he didn't want word leaking out about what happened right next door. He was probably scared the Baptists would go somewhere else. So he talked to some folks, and it stayed out of the paper."

All the loose ends of this horrible story were coming together in my mind, so quickly and so well that I forgot to listen for footsteps or boat motors or Simon's shallow breathing. But I had to ask one more question.

"After your mother died, why didn't you just tell the police what happened? Why did you pretend you were some crazy monster, Persely?"

"Didn't matter anymore," said Persely. "None of them lawmen were there to save me when I needed it. And besides, I couldn't get it straight in my own mind, what I did to my mama. I loved her so much."

"So your mother died and Simon lived," I said. "That's ironic."

"No," said Persely. "That's fate. Fate made me a monster."

"You're not a monster," I said.

My brother kissed her. No more talk of God from Boone. He remained silent on that subject, and I pictured Boone's God calling to him weakly and sadly somewhere, lost in the sudden complexity of my brother's soul.

"Can I tell you two something? Like a secret?" Boone asked.

Persely and I hummed our assent. Rain slid off our heads.

He took a deep breath, as if tortured by his own words. "You know how the Bible says to forgive? Well, I don't think I forgive Simon."

"That's hardly a confession," I said.

"But I think I hate him," Boone insisted. "For what he did to you, Persely. And I know it's not right, but I think he's evil. And that there's no good in him. No good in him at all."

"You're too hard on yourself, Boone," I said wearily.

"But it's wrong not to forgive."

"So many things are wrong." My eyelids were heavy. "So many things."

"You're safe now, Persely," Boone said urgently in the darkness. "You're with me now. I'll protect you."

"For now," she countered. "Because it ain't my fate to be with you."

"What are you talking about?"

Suddenly she began to cry. The sound of her weeping amazed and devastated me. Boone whispered to her. The wind picked up and I heard the movement of leaves and the far-off sound of the water rushing against the bank.

"Don't you see, Boone?" Persely managed. "I wanted you to be a monster so we could love each other. I couldn't love you with so much God in you because I think God hates me. If there is a God, he's sitting up there in heaven with my mama, and my mama's face is blue."

Boone said, "Your mother forgives you because it wasn't your fault. You're good, Persely. You're good. I love you I love you I love you."

The rain came down harder. Thunder clapped. We could

hear one another's breath. I thought I heard footsteps, but it was only the rain.

Lightning struck close by, and we jerked.

"Do you want to go to sleep, honey?" Boone murmured.

"I'm too scared to sleep. He's coming for me. He's gonna get me."

"Even Simon's not crazy enough to go out on a boat in a storm like this," said Boone. "Just go to sleep. I'll keep watch."

"No," I said. "I'll stay awake first. I slept longer today than you did."

"You sure?"

"Uh-huh."

"All right. Here's the machete."

"Like that would help."

"It will make you feel safer. I don't think I can sleep either, but if I do, wake me up in three hours."

I set down the machete at my side and put my arms around my knees, watching the rain, thinking about Persely and her dead mother and the guilt she had carried around for so long. I was surprised to find that I understood her completely, her fierce protection and forgiveness of her mother. And I understood her murderous urges toward her father. I had never planned to kill Simon personally, but I did sacrifice many toys and two Barbie dolls to that desire. My god hadn't answered me. Not like Persely's had.

Beyond the trees I could hear the waves crashing against the island, and I imagined the rocky banks eroding under that relentless force like a childhood dissolving under unbearable circumstances. Rain dripped down my neck and soaked my clothes. Lightning lit up the sky and then disappeared.

Next to me, Persely and my brother were sleeping. I could hear their steady breathing. The radio was still on, the batteries so weak now that the song drifted out low and plaintive: *There'll be no strings to bind your hands, not if my love can't bind your heart . . .*

I thought I heard a boat. I strained my ears, listening. There it was again. I started to wake Boone up and thought better of it. Just my mind playing tricks on me. More lightning. Thunder in the distance. My own chattering teeth and the breathing of Persely and Boone. The song had declined into kissing its own static. My eyes felt so heavy, and I nodded before I shook myself out of the half-sleep, rubbing my eyes. I felt around next to me until I found the machete, placing it across my knees. Mumbling to myself to keep awake, I counted the thunderclaps. The walls of the lean-to rocked me gently, and in between the lightning, I thought I felt Persely's mouth against my ear and heard her voice whisper: *Guard your real story, Alice.*

I bowed my head and closed my eyes. The four of us, Persely, Boone, Lucinda and I were each astride our own giddy Appaloosa, riding through the cow pasture that led to Lake Shine, no saddles or bridles, just that rocking motion with the wind in our hair and the sky pure blue and my fingers grabbing at patches of swirling blue mist . . .

I woke up squinting, a strong yellow light shining on my face. A voice behind that light.

Got you.

Chapter Twenty-eight

I fumbled for the machete in my lap, but Simon seized it first. I screamed my brother's name and kicked out at Simon, sending the flashlight flying out of his hand, and then a great confusion of shouts and a great struggle and the lean-to collapsing and Persely shrieking and a whirling of water and sound and darkness and stark confusion and a strange, quick bite on my upper arm that left a weakness running all the way down to my fingers.

I heard Boone's voice. "No!"

I broke away and ran through the woods, voices and the crashing of branches swirling around me and the thunder in my ears and things rising up in the night to slap my face, but I kept going, desperately, down into the water, down into the black waves that rushed inside my mouth as if toward some desperate reunion with my throat and lungs.

Boone's voice again. "Alice! Alice!" His hand grabbed mine in the water and then let it go. "Swim! Swim!"

I squinted through the pouring rain. "Where's Persely?"

"She's right here with me. Persely?"

"Boone?"

"Swim, Persely!"

I swam in that churning water, the rain beating down upon me in sheets, its grim music, the sickening snap of lightning, the roar of thunder, the imagined or real motor of a borrowed boat, water choking me, my blue friend turned black enemy. My clothes so heavy, my arms heavy and limp, deaf in the water and half deaf when I lifted my head.

After half an hour the storm began to abate. The thunder moved away, the lightning stopped, the rain went from a swarm of stingers to a bare, sweet mist.

"Persley," Boone said behind me. "Persely, Persely."

Exhausted, I turned in the water. "What's the matter?"

I saw a horrible sudden fear in my brother's eyes. He craned his neck around and I looked out into the sheet of smoothing water. Persely was nowhere to be seen.

"Persely!" Boone shouted. "Can you hear me?" The night was so dark we couldn't see more than twenty feet in either direction.

I treaded water next to my brother and we shouted together. "Persely! Persely!"

My brother clutched my wrist. "She went under, Alice. She was right behind me."

"We'll find her," I said desperately.

Together we dove down, searching through the water as

we had for our mother, not off the shore of a park this time but in a vast sea of darkness, handicapped by terror and by the clothes of dry land. Exhausted, we rose to the surface, caught our breath and then dove down again, searching for a limp body, a stubborn girl surrendered to the elements, an arm or a leg or a patch of short blond hair. Boone's girlfriend had turned into a needle in a haystack, a vast liquid haystack whose gallons were insensate to the desperation of love. Every now and then I would catch hold of something warm only to realize that it was Boone, and that the two of us were grappling under the water together.

I surfaced, letting out my breath. I was having trouble moving my arms and legs.

Boone's head broke the surface next to me, and he spat out water.

We were alone. The stars out now that the clouds had moved away. The marina lights shining in the distance. Our bare feet waving at the lake bottom.

"She's gone, Boone."

"No!" He shouted and went under again. I went after him, my fingers closing around his belt loop. I pulled back violently and he fought me.

We wrestled each other as we rose to the surface, choking and spitting water.

"Stop it, Boone! You'll drown us both!"

"She's not gone." He drove his fist into the water. "Persely! Follow the splash!"

He beat the water again. "Persely!"

"Please, stop screaming. It's no use. And Simon will hear us."

Boone gave me a terrible look. "Simon can burn in

hell." He closed his eyes. In the darkness, I thought I could see tears run down his face.

"I'm so sorry, I'm so sorry," I whispered.

Persely was gone. His love. His crazy famous girlfriend. The little boy in the picture he had grieved over and canonized. The grown-up girl he had kissed and held by the campfire.

"There's nothing left," he said. A wave went into his mouth and he spat it out.

"You're left, Boone."

"You don't understand. There is no me. There is no . . . inside." My brother opened his eyes and I saw them turn hard, as if the chill that slept in the very bottom of the lake had jumped into the soles of his bare feet, risen through his bloodstream and frozen his heart. "Simon will pay for what he did," he said. No more tears. A different voice was coming out of his mouth, one shared by cruel children, hateful husbands, soldiers, pirates, timber wolves and renegade Boy Scouts. It was filled with lightning, poison, the wind of a bent tree. A voice without grace or mercy. It terrified me, more than Persely drowning, more than the thought that Simon was still out there somewhere in the vast waters of Lake Shine. Boone's faith had left him and was slowly drifting down through green water to join a sackful of money, the skeletons of uncollected drowning victims, and the new body—fully whole and perfect—of a blond teenage girl whose hair had last been styled by Boone's tender machete. Did the sunfish see that girl? Did they feel that lost faith? Did they somehow understand that the two things were linked, and were they awed?

"We've got to make it to shore," I said.

My brother glared at me. "I can't. I'm too tired."

"Float on your back."

The water had become still as glass and the two of us floated, under the sky, under the stars, in the deep green water.

Chapter Twenty-nine

Boone and I found the shore at dawn. We staggered out and fell on the bank, drenched and shoeless; we watched the sun rise from the lake's far side. Boone had used his shirt to cover Persely the night before and was now bare-chested. A small cut on his face still leaked blood, and I could see a bruise between his ribs.

I looked down at my own arm and noticed a deep, blood-less gash. Simon must have struck me with the machete during the storm. I turned to Boone to tell him, but something stopped me. I could see something new on his face.

A line in the flesh between his eyes.

I thought it might be a strand of hair, so I reached over and tried to brush it away. It deepened.

My heart sank.

"Are you all right, Boone?"

He gave me no answer, just gazed away into the distance. I wondered if at this very moment he held Persely in his arms, his lips pressed against her neck, his fingers moving down her back. But the line between his eyes told me his thoughts centered on hatred and revenge. Such a short time ago I would have wanted Boone to show a little anger at Simon, but now he frightened me. I wanted to comfort him, to say something about Persely being safe in heaven.

"Boone—"

"Be quiet, Alice."

We got up and walked. It was summertime and no one paid any attention to two kids in wet cutoffs. The pavement felt cool to our bare feet; our hair dried slowly into a sun-lightened tangle.

"Let's go to the police," I said. "Just tell them everything."

"The police are not our friends. They hated Persely."

"But she was a—"

Boone seized me and threw me on the ground. He leaped on top of me, pinning my shoulders down.

"She was a what, Alice?" he snarled.

I looked for signs of gentleness. Love. Found nothing but his red face and his blazing eyes. I began to cry, and he released me but didn't say he was sorry. He helped me up, but I no longer walked by his side. I followed a few steps behind him, watching him. All day long we trudged—in circles, perhaps—as our clothes dried and our stomachs growled. Children passed us on their bicycles. Boys wrecked on their skateboards. Teenage girls lay out on towels in their front lawns, catching the sun's rays, while their younger sisters played on Slip 'N Slides.

Boone saw a pickup truck parked by a convenience store. He stopped, staring at it.

"What's the matter, Boone?"

He picked up a rock and, before I could stop him, hurled it through the back window. The glass shattered and fell into the truck bed. Boone grabbed my hand and pulled me along as he ran.

We reached the edge of town and slowed to a walk. I caught my breath. "You didn't have to do that. It was just a pickup truck."

"Could have been a Snow Hunter," Boone said through his teeth, in a way that meant not to talk about it further.

Here the streets were set up ragtag, warehouses next to tiny office buildings, flower shops next to vacant lots. The sun had grown hotter; when we crossed the streets, our bare feet were tender on the hot asphalt.

"What are we looking for?" I finally asked.

"A church. A lot of them are empty during the week."

"What day is it?"

He looked at the sun as if at some great yellow calendar. "Tuesday, I think."

"What are we going to do in the church?"

"Sleep. Get out of the sun."

We found a church off an old side street, a tiny structure with faded red brick and stained-glass windows of various saints. A single live oak loomed in the front yard, its branches spreading out to the street and over the roof. The sign out front said:

SUNDAY'S SERMON: HOW STRAIGHT IS YOUR PATH?

"Catholic," Boone said. He tried to open the double front doors. They were locked.

"Let's go around the back," he said, but the back door was locked as well.

Boone looked around and found a small stone. He picked it up and stood turning it in his hands.

My bare foot had found a briar, and under the midafternoon sun, I worked it out of my flesh. I nodded at Boone's rock. "What are you going to do with that?"

"Break a window."

Already throwing rocks at God.

"You can't."

"Why not?"

"It's God's house."

Boone stared at me as if I had just inspired some tenuous memory of someone he barely remembered. "It's our house now."

"Don't do it," I said in a stronger voice. It was as if that church were a living thing, helpless and weak, and I was guarding it for Boone so that it would still be alive and waiting for him when he came to his senses.

Boone pushed me aside and threw the rock. The window shattered, and I looked around quickly to see if anyone had noticed. The streets were deserted, the sun motionless, the shadows in place on the grass. From inside the church poured silence, no alarm made up of the high-pitched voices of startled angels. Boone brushed the broken glass from the sill, then reached inside and unlocked the window, drawing it up. "Come here," he said, knitting his hands together and offering the pair of them to me. "Put your foot in here and hoist yourself up. Watch the glass." I slid through the window and fell to the church floor in a crouch, the smell of carpeting and penned-in prayers hitting my nostrils. The church was dark and warm. Red carpeting and pews lined with red velvet. Along the walls on each side were stained-glass windows, each with a different pose of Christ's execution. His face anguished. A spear in his side. Nails through his hands and feet. A crown of thorns. On the wall behind the choir pews was a giant sculpture of Jesus on a giant cross. His head was bowed. His ribs protruded.

I let Boone in the door. He closed it behind him and locked it again, and we walked down the aisle together and sat down on the first pew, looking at the podium where the minister would speak, and up at the man frozen on that cross.

"Nice place to break into," I said.

He shrugged. The light from the stained-glass window played on his bare chest. I looked up at the bare-chested Jesus.

"You meet the dress code here," I told my brother.

Through the broken window in the back of the church, I heard the far-off sound of children playing. My arm had begun to hurt again where it was cut.

"How do you feel?" I asked Boone.

"Fine." His voice sounded flat.

I pointed to a place between his ribs. "Your bruise hurt?"

"Not really."

I hesitated. There was something I'd wanted to ask him all day long. "Are you mad at me?"

"For what?"

"For falling asleep last night when I was supposed to keep watch."

"No. I should have been keeping watch. But I never really thought he'd—"

"How do you think Simon found us?"

He licked his lips and put a finger between his eyes as if to adjust his missing glasses. "Fate."

"It's not your fault, Boone. What happened to Persely."

"Don't say her name."

"It's not your fault."

"You know whose fault it is."

"Whose?"

He stared straight ahead. "His."

"Jesus' fault?"

"No, stupid. Simon's." When he said the name, its hiss cut through the dank odor of the church. "He killed her, Alice. She wouldn't have been in that water if it weren't for him. And you know what? I hope he finds us."

"Why?"

"Because I'm going to kill him."

His tone frightened me. "Don't say that in a church."

"I'll say it in a church and I'll say it to Jesus." He rose to his feet and climbed the stairs to the choir benches, jumped up on one and then leaped from bench to bench until he reached the wall where the patient man hung on the cross with his fingers curled. My brother pointed up at Jesus and shouted: "Do you hear me? I'm going to kill him! Because there is no you! There is no you!"

"Stop it!" I shouted, defending this alien God with whom I shared no history. "Stop yelling at Him. It's not His fault!"

"He let it happen!"

"Leave Him alone!"

Boone just stood there with his finger pointing. Finally he let his arm drop. He stepped off the bench and walked back to the pews. He lay down on one and stretched out. "I'm tired, Alice," he said, and fell asleep.

I sat there watching him as the afternoon darkened outside and some of the darkness began to leak into the church. He frightened me, his new voice and the new expression on his face and his murderous, uncontainable grief over the girl he couldn't save. The saintliness of Boone had drained from him, leaving the same minatory silence the beeyard held when all the colonies died. The absence of motion, sound, nectar.

For so many weeks I had been afraid for my brother's life, but now I feared for his soul. I used to imagine it as a giant pink air cloud drifting in his body, giving him greater buoyancy in lake water and on a pogo stick. I imagined his new hatred for Simon—understandable as it was—as a poison drifting through his bloodstream, headed for that sweet soul in a thickening sludge. Curare to paralyze it. Strychnine to stretch it out in a ghoulish spasm. Cyanide to turn it cold and blue.

I looked up at the wall at Boone's former friend. And I prayed to him, as earnestly as I had once prayed to my pagan god buried in the sharp green leaves of holly. No open moonlight, no humming of bees, no grass beneath my bare feet, nothing broken in my hands. *Please, give me back my brother.*

We hid in the church for two days, drinking out of the bathroom sink in the sacristy behind the choir and sleeping during the day and at night as well, for there was nothing else to do. We had no home. The island was no longer ours. And the lake water was ruined with the final breath of Persely Snow.

"Someone's going to see that broken window," I said to Boone. "We need to start making plans about where we're going."

But Boone would not make plans. He wouldn't talk to me at all. Sometimes I watched him sleep, and even in that unconscious state, the line would reappear between his eyes, as though he was dreaming of an old grudge or plotting his revenge.

My head felt better, and the wound on my arm had grown a scab that was wide in the middle, but my stomach ached from not eating. I was afraid I was going to starve to death in a big scarlet church with my mad brother.

Finally I'd had enough. "Boone, we have to get some food. We haven't eaten in three days."

His eyes were open, but he didn't answer me.

"Please."

"All right." He rose slowly from the pew and ran his fingers through his hair. "Let's go."

"Where?"

"Never mind."

I followed him down the center aisle, noticing for the first time my body's dank, stale odor, like someone buried wet. I reached up to touch my hair and found it a tangled mess. Boone opened the doors and I blinked in the light. We stood in the live-oak shade for a few moments, adjusting to the world, and then we started walking. It felt good to be in motion. Around us, the summer continued. Kids and dogs. Sprinklers. Green grass. Fathers in Bermuda shorts and thongs, hoses in their hands, spraying down gardens. Mothers on lawn chairs, drinking lemonade. Squirrels squatting on their haunches. It all mixed together. It was everything and nothing. And I felt that we were walking in hallowed light, as though we had God's attention, the God who paid Boone no mind when he believed but was now peering at us, full of the sorrow of being forgotten.

We found a Stop-N-Go.

"Act natural," said Boone.

"So I shouldn't point out the machete cut?"

We walked inside. The man behind the counter was middle-aged and tired-looking, with a scraggly goatee and horn-rimmed glasses. His slicked-back dark hair had the beginnings of a ducktail, a style he'd smuggled through the decades and kept for himself. He was smoking a brown cigarette. The smoke of it arced away from the side of his cash register.

He regarded us suspiciously.

I looked over at the newspaper bin and noticed the headline: IDENTITY SOUGHT FOR BODY OF GIRL PULLED FROM LAKE SHINE. I looked away quickly, but Boone had already seen it. He picked up the paper and stared at the headline. For a brief moment I caught a flash of the old Boone. That sadness for hurt things.

"You kids reading or buying?" said the man behind the counter.

The look disappeared from Boone's face. "Reading. What's it to you?"

"You're supposed to wear a shirt in here."

Boone's lip curled. His hands clenched.

"Don't make trouble," I whispered.

"You kids," the man said with a frown. "You're getting worse every year. Like that Snow maniac."

"You don't know anything about that girl," said Boone.

"What a wacko."

Boone took a step toward the man and I grabbed his arm. His muscles tightened beneath my fingers.

The man shrugged.

Boone turned down the aisle and I followed him, hungrily looking at the mayonnaise and mustard and the tuna cans and the sardines, the lunch meat. Everything looked good. Red Hots. Candy cigarettes. Mars Bars. Pixy Stix. I felt dizzy with famine, reduced by the days of hunger, certain that my body would soon devour itself.

Boone was crouching now and I held my breath as his fingers found a can of Vienna sausages, then another. He motioned me down beside him, taking the cans and tucking them into the front of my pants and then carefully pulling my T-shirt down over the bulge it made. He straightened up and motioned to me.

"Walk behind me," he whispered. "Just walk out of the store and act natural."

I walked behind Boone, watching the man at the counter. He glanced at us, looked out the window, took a drag of his cigarette.

I reached the door and pushed it open.

"Hey," the man said.

I looked at him blankly. "Yeah?"

"What you two got there?"

"Nothing."

The man came around the counter and stared at me a moment, then looked at Boone. "Let me see your hands."

Boone showed him his hands.

"How about your little friend? Move out of the way so I can see her."

"Why?"

Just then a can of Vienna sausages fell down through my shorts, hit the floor and rolled several feet on the dirty tiles.

"I see," said the man. He took my arm.

"Don't touch my sister," Boone said warningly. He pulled the man's hand off me. Some other shoppers had entered the store and stood staring at us.

"You're in trouble, son." The man tried to grab him, but Boone moved out of the way and punched him in the side of the head. One of the shoppers gasped. The clerk and my brother struggled for a moment before Boone let out a great cry and pushed him hard against the store window. "Ow," said the man. He held the back of his head.

"Come on," Boone told me. He took me by the hand and pulled me out the door, knocking some people aside as he rushed me out. We ran across the parking lot and down the street. Behind us we could hear loud voices. We turned a corner and then we slowed down, not walking and not running, still holding hands.

"You're hurting my hand," I said.

He let it go.

We turned down an aisle between a hardware store and a watch shop, hurrying to the street beyond. We stopped and looked around, our breath coming fast from our days without food.

The world seemed normal. Cars passed by. Dogs barked.

"You think the coast is clear?" I asked.

"Maybe."

Boone and I sat down on a curb. I noticed his left hand was bleeding between the knuckles.

"Did you have to hit that guy?"

"We got away, didn't we?"

"I never thought you'd hit anyone."

"You heard what he said about Persely."

I didn't want to get into an argument about Boone's lost love, so instead I reached into the waist of my shorts and pulled out the remaining can of Vienna sausages, the label slippery with my perspiration. "Got this."

"Better than nothing."

I cracked the top, which made the wet sound of a bone breaking. Boone and I divided the sausages between us, eating silently. When we were finished, we split the warm juice.

"I'm still hungry," I said.

"We'll go somewhere else."

"No way. I'm not doing that again."

"Then how are we going to eat?"

I froze.

A squad car had pulled around the corner and was coming our direction, lights flashing.

"Run, Alice!"

A policeman jumped from the car and chased us. We ran down an alley between two buildings. At the back of the alley was a tall chain-link fence. Boone hit the fence and climbed it like a monkey.

He paused at the top. "Come on, Alice."

I put my feet and hands through the links and started to climb. But I was exhausted from hunger, fear and the heat.

The policeman ran down the alley toward us.

Boone moved back a little and turned to look at me, stretching his hand down. "Come on! Grab hold!"

I felt the policeman's hands on me. He pulled me off the fence and held my struggling body in his arms. "Got you." He looked up. "Now you just climb on down here, son. I've got your sister."

Boone looked down at us, and I noticed for the first time what the policeman must have seen—a shirtless boy in faded cutoffs. Dirty hair and punk hatred.

"Go, Boone!" I said.

He hesitated. Sighed. And climbed down.

The cop took one of my arms and one of Boone's and walked us to the squad car. He stood us up against the side of it, facing him.

"You kids think it's fun to steal?"

"Necessary," I said.

Boone said, "You taking us to jail?"

The policeman studied us a minute.

"Go ahead," I said. "Take us to jail."

"Hmmm," said the officer. He looked as though he desperately wanted to teach us some wise, patient lesson we would one day pass on to our own children. "You know what, kids? I'm gonna give you a break this time. I'm gonna take you home."

"I'd rather go to jail," I said.

The officer put us in the backseat and closed the door. The back doors had no handles.

"Persely could have gotten us out," Boone said softly.

"Persely?" the cop said, starting up the car. "Persely Snow?"

"No, he didn't say Persely," I said quickly, hoping to avoid another confrontation. "He said parsley could have gotten us out. My brother can break out of any restraint armed with only a sprig of parsley."

"You've got a smart mouth," said the cop. "Where do you kids live?"

"I don't remember," I said.

Boone gave him our address, and the cop put the car in drive and stepped on the gas.

"Why did you tell him?" I hissed at my brother.

"I want to go home," Boone said, looking straight ahead. "I need to see Simon. We have things to settle."

"You're crazy, Boone," I said. I leaned forward. "We're not safe at home."

The cop adjusted the air-conditioning. "Really?"

"No," said Boone. "She's making it up. Take us home. I want to go home."

I ignored my brother. "Our stepfather wants to kill us."

"And why is that?" asked the cop.

"Because he's crazy."

"Really?"

"Be quiet," Boone said.

"And he beats us," I said. "He's hit me and Boone lots of times."

"Got any bruises?"

"Not at the moment."

"My sister's a liar," said Boone. "Our stepfather is a wonderful man, and I can't wait to see him again."

"Oh yeah?" I pulled my sleeve back and lifted my arm so the cop could see it in the rearview mirror. "See that cut? That was made by a machete."

"Ohhh," said the cop. "Not just a knife, but a machete, huh? Look, kid, I'm not calling you a liar, but it sounds like a pretty convenient story. Why didn't you go tell it to someone before you were caught stealing from a store?"

"We didn't think anyone would believe us."

The cop turned the corner. "Tell you what. I'm going to have a talk with your father."

"Just like Persely's cop did," I mumbled.

"What?"

"Never mind." I sat back and crossed my arms, utterly defeated. My death now seemed sure, and although I dreaded the moment, I felt a curious appreciation for the world passing us. The good neighborhoods and the bad ones. The neatness of topiary. The colors of a crepe myrtle. The way mimosa trees spread shade like chicken feed around a yard. The waving tails of dogs. The bright red of a Big Wheel that a little boy was racing down a sidewalk. I would miss bright colors. I'd miss shade and sun and lake water. I would miss Spencer's face. I would miss Poland on a map.

Clipped lawns. A snow cone melting on the sidewalk. The clouds in the blue sky. I had once lain in Lake Shine, green water buried in my ears, my breathing loud, as I watched these same clouds go by.

Boone glared at the back of the man's head. "You lawmen," he said. "You're not worth nothing."

The cop ignored him.

"You're not about justice. You're just a bunch of homos."

"Shhhh, Boone," I warned.

The cop said nothing. He braked for a stop sign.

"Turn left here, homo," said Boone.

"Shhhh."

"Queer. Faggot."

The cop finally spoke. "Someone should teach you some manners, boy."

My brother leaned forward. "Persely Snow is free from you. She won. She beat you."

When we pulled into our driveway, Meg was sweeping

it clean, her belly a little bigger than it had been the night we left. She looked up in alarm when she saw the squad car. The cop let us out and she came waddling toward us.

"My babies! My babies!" She threw herself on me, and once again I was engulfed in her motherly scent. I could hear her labored breathing and feel the baby, huge, against the hollow of my stomach. "Alice," she whispered, "I was so worried. You've been gone so long. I was so afraid I'd never see you again."

She released me and turned to Boone, holding her arms out to him. He backed away from her.

"Don't touch me," he said.

She looked bewildered. "Why are you saying that, baby?" she asked, still reaching for him. "Don't you love your mother anymore?"

Boone just glared at her.

"Son," said the cop, "have some respect."

The front door opened, and Simon Jester came out in a pair of chinos and a white shirt. His hair neatly combed and gathered. An ordinary man and a harmless father.

Simon smiled when he saw us. "Found them scamps, did you, Officer?"

"I'm sorry to say that they were caught taking food from a convenience store," said the cop.

"Boone," Simon gasped. "I can't believe that. You were raised better." Tears sprang to his eyes, and my blood chilled at the spectacle.

"Go to hell," said Boone.

"I have some questions for you, sir," said the officer politely. "I've already got it pretty much figured out in my head what's going on, but I'd like to talk to you a moment."

"Meg," said Simon. "Why don't you take Boone and Alice in the house while I figure this out with the officer?"

Boone and I followed Meg into the house and she poured us some Kool-Aid while we sat down at the table. Her hands shook, and when she came over and handed us our glasses, I could see drops of punch speckling her arms and her dress. Her face was very pale. She moved to sit down and then changed her mind and just stood there, watching us drink.

"How is it, kids?" she asked softly, as though afraid that the wrong proportion of tap water to grape powder would show, once and for all, her failure as a mother.

"It's perfect, Meg," I said.

"Who cares how it is?" Boone asked. "Who cares about anything?" His forehead had grown that crease again.

"I care, son," Meg whispered. "I know you don't think I do, but I love you kids more than anything."

Boone stirred his Kool-Aid with a finger but didn't drink it. The look on his face frightened me. "More than anything, Meg?"

"Yes."

In the silence I could hear Simon outside, talking to the officer. Lying through his teeth.

"Is that why you told Simon where Never Island was? Because you cared about us so much?"

Meg gasped. "Is that where you were hiding?"

"Yes," Boone said. "And Simon came for us one night, in the middle of a storm. With a machete in his hand."

"No!" She looked horrified.

"You told him where to find us."

Meg picked up the pitcher and tried to pour Boone some

more Kool-Aid, but since he hadn't drunk any, it just over-flowed onto the table. I watched my napkin turn purple.

"I told Simon about Never Island when we were dating!" Meg cried. "I had no idea he'd remember. But in the back of my mind, I wondered if maybe you were there. I almost called Mr. Walt—"

"Mr. Walt's dead," said Boone.

My mother dropped the pitcher. It shattered on the floor. Her hands flew to her stomach and we knew, once and for all, that our mother had slept with that endlessly fertile, endlessly tragic old man.

"Mr. Walt's the father, isn't he?" I asked, my voice much kinder than my brother's.

She stared down at the broken glass. "Don't say that, don't say that! If Simon finds out . . ." She looked like she might faint, so I stood up and helped her into a chair.

Boone ignored us. He drummed his fingers on the table. "Simon's out there bullshitting that cop. No one's going to do anything to help us."

"Simon's just upset," said Meg. She was talking faster and faster. "He just gets mad in the heat you know it reached eighty-five degrees today but everything will be fine you wait and see but please son no more baby talk let's just keep that a secret just among ourselves and then everything will be fine and we can all be—"

Boone's hand came down on the table with a loud slap. "Are you out of your mind, Meg? Everything is not going to be fine! That man tried to kill us!"

Meg stared at him a long moment. "Maybe," she said, "he was just trying to scare you. He's calmed down a lot. And he's so happy about the baby. It's coming soon."

Boone jumped to his feet. "And what kind of life do you think that baby's going to have? What kind of life do we have? What kind of life did Persely have?"

"Persely?" she asked.

"Persely was his daughter, dimwit! Simon Jester is Jeremiah Snow. He tried to kill his own daughter. That's why she poisoned him!"

Meg was shaking her head. "That's just a crazy story, Boone. His family drowned."

"His family didn't drown! *Our* family is drowning!"

Meg rose shakily to her feet and started to walk out of the kitchen. "I can't hear this, I can't hear this."

Boone seized her dimply arm and made her turn to face him. "You mean you don't want to hear this. You're going to let your husband kill your own children because you can't stand to be without a man."

"No, honey!" said Meg. "No one's going to die. We're all together again. We're a family now!"

Boone was still gripping her arm. "Maybe Persely was right the first time she told her story," he whispered. "A mother who won't protect her kids doesn't deserve to live."

"Boone," I said, "let her go."

Tears were running down Meg's face. "One time when I was ten years old, I forgot to feed my dog and my daddy tied me to a tree all day in the front yard. And my mother didn't stop him. But I forgave her. She didn't know any better."

Boone's face was bright red. "That's no excuse."

"Boone," Meg said, pain in her voice. "My arm!"

I had no choice. I got between my brother and Meg and pushed him as hard as I could.

He let go of Meg and looked at me, shocked. "Alice?"

I took advantage of his confusion and kept pushing him, down the hall and into our room. I gave him one more push and he fell backward on his bed and lay there, panting.

"You were hurting her," I said. He didn't answer me and so I added: "You're asking too much from her. After all these years, you're asking too much."

"She doesn't love us."

"Yes, she does. In her own weird way."

I heard sudden footsteps coming down the hall. The bedroom door slammed behind my back. A key turned in the lock. I grabbed the doorknob and tried to turn it. "Simon locked us in here!" I let go of the handle, rushed over to the window and raised the shade. I gasped. The window was boarded up so that no light came through. "We're trapped," I said, turning toward my brother.

Boone didn't get up from the bed. He lay on his back and looked at the ceiling. "Maybe Simon is trapped. Maybe Meg."

Beyond our bedroom door, I could hear Simon moving around the house.

"Who knows what he's doing?" I murmured. "Probably poisoning everything in the house. Even the toothpaste."

"It doesn't matter."

"Are we going to die?"

"Someone is."

"Boone, I'm scared."

"Don't be scared, Persely," he said vacantly.

"I'm not Persely!" I shouted at him.

He blinked but said nothing.

I went over and sat beside him. I touched his face, stroked his tangled hair. Traced the line between his eyes with my index finger, trying to smooth it out. I didn't know what I feared more—that my stepfather would kill Boone or that Boone would kill someone himself.

"Boone, if this is our last day on the earth, please do something for me."

"What?"

"Come back to me. Be my brother. Be the old Boone."

"I am your brother. I am Boone."

"No you're not. You're someone else."

He watched my tears impassively. "I can't help being who I am. It's my fate."

"Bullshit."

"Persely's dead, Alice."

"I know."

"She was right behind me. I turned and when I looked back again she was gone."

All afternoon we waited in our room, listening to Simon pace through the house. The floorboards squeaked. Low mutterings came through the walls. The room had cooled a little when we heard the lock turn again.

Simon opened the door. "You two," he said. "Go help your mother fix dinner." He was smiling a little, and I could see the challenge in his stare.

Boone got off the bed and walked up to Simon, looking straight into his eyes. "I'd be glad to," he said.

"Put on a shirt first, boy. Learn some manners." Simon left the room abruptly.

"Okay, Boone," I said. "Here's the new plan. We pretend to help with dinner, then make a break for it out the back door."

"No," he said. "I'm not leaving."

"I won't leave without you."

"Then stay."

"You're being stupid. You're going to get me killed."

"Well, I'm good at getting people killed." He turned to leave, and I started to follow him out of the room. He turned around and touched my arm. "You stay here. *I'll* help with dinner."

The look on his face so frightened me that I backed away from the doorway and sank down on the bed. He closed the door behind him. I couldn't move. I felt pinned to that bed, so I simply sat shivering, listening to the noises in the kitchen. Doors opening and closing, the clatter of lids on pots. My stomach hurt. Finally Boone came back into the room and said, "Dinner's ready."

When I entered the kitchen, I saw that Simon was dishing up the rice. A quick knot of fear formed in me, and I looked at Boone questioningly. He looked away.

Everything looked poisoned to me. The wild rice. The zucchini. The breaded chicken strips. The mint in the tea. The last of the sunlight coming through the window. The sweat on our faces. No one spoke. The tea glasses were already on the table. Simon began setting down plates.

Meg wouldn't look at me. Her face was ashen. She turned around to stir something on the stove, and her big stomach swept a towel off the oven door. Simon picked up the towel and kissed Meg on the side of the head as he straightened back up.

"Careful, darling," he murmured.

She didn't answer him.

We all sat down at the table.

Chapter Thirty

"The salt's clotted," Simon remarked. He shook the cellar hard over his zucchini, but the salt wouldn't pour. He shrugged and looked down the table. "Funny how things get ruined," he said. His eyes met Boone's. They held each other's gaze.

I could see a line between Simon's eyes. A line between my brother's.

Meg picked at her food and said nothing. I wondered if she was thinking about Mr. Walt, or worrying about Simon, or remembering Boone's horrible words to her earlier that afternoon.

"So, Boone," Simon said, "quite a week you've had,

huh? You didn't even thank me for talking you out of trouble with that cop."

"You're good at that," said Boone. "Handling things. Telling stories."

Simon didn't take his eyes from Boone.

Boone wiped off the sweat above his lip.

"Where's the money?" Simon asked.

"It's at the bottom of the lake. With your daughter."

Simon laughed. "I don't got no daughter."

"Not anymore. But you did. Jeremiah."

"That ain't my name."

"The hell it isn't."

"You believe everything a poisoner tells you?"

Boone's voice was full of hatred. "You killed her. You chased her off that island, into the storm. She drowned."

Simon scratched his head and looked puzzled for a moment. He glanced at my plate and then at Boone's and said: "Why ain't you eating your food, kids?"

I looked down at my dinner. The zucchini looked dry as a grave.

"You want us to eat?" said Boone. "We'll eat. We'll drink. It doesn't matter anymore." He took his glass of tea and took a big gulp.

"Stop it!" I cried, jumping out of my chair and trying to grab his glass. He caught my arm and held me away as he threw back his head and kept drinking.

"Please," I whispered. "Don't do this."

Boone slammed the empty glass down on the table and sat there huffing and glaring at Simon. "Sit down, Alice," he ordered.

I obeyed him, looking at him anxiously, alert for symptoms. Dilated pupils, facial tics, tremors, discolored patches on the skin?

"Thirsty?" Simon asked him.

"Yes. You?" Boone said challengingly.

"Why, yes. Yes, I am." Simon picked up his glass of tea and drank. A little of it ran down his chin and started a dark puddle on the tablecloth.

Arsenic concentrates in the hair and fingernails. Phosphorus poisoning loosens the teeth. Toxaphene causes hemorrhages in the brain.

Simon set the glass down hard. "That's good," he said.

"I'll pour you some more," Meg volunteered, sounding tearful.

"Don't bother, honey."

I looked at Simon.

I looked at Boone.

Both of them were red in the face. For what seemed like hours, I watched them glaring at each other, fire in their eyes.

"Boone," I said softly, in a whisper that filled up the room. "Don't be stupid."

"Yes, Boone," Simon mimicked. "Don't be stupid. And eat your food."

"You want me to eat my food? You want me to?" asked Boone. He took a big forkful of rice and then another, jamming it into his mouth, then two or three forkfuls of zucchini. He growled, his cheeks puffed.

"That's right, boy," said Simon. "You eat. And you eat too, Smart Girl. Both of you go ahead, you little traitors. You fucking brats. Because I've got a little story to tell you. A story about betrayal." He paused, looked at Meg. Looked at us.

Boone was leaning in closely. To hear Simon's words or the pattern in his breath?

"Once there was a man. A good man. Didn't never do nothing wrong but try to keep his daughter in line. That was hard. She was . . . what do they call it? Prodigal. One day this man was trying to teach the daughter—that's all, just trying to teach her. Well, the man's wife called the cops on him . . ."

I looked around the table. Boone was trembling, Simon's eyes were dancing and Meg was white as a ghost. Which one was dying?

Did the tea smell normal? Or was that the ghost of an almond?

All cyanide antidotes are poisons themselves.

"Every betrayal," said Simon, "calls for a sacrifice. And a betrayal like that—getting the cops called on me—called for a big one." He paused, took another bite of food. "The wife had to pay. But the sacrifice wouldn't die. Crazy thing showed up at breakfast with a bandanna around her neck."

"You tried to kill your daughter?" Meg gasped.

"Shut up, Meg. I'm talking."

I felt the blood drain from my face, but I could not leave my chair. Tears were running down my cheeks. I did not want to live without my brother. I took a big forkful of zucchini, put it in my mouth and washed it down with three gulps of tea.

Meg was shaking her head. "You're Jeremiah Snow, aren't you?"

"I said shut the fuck *up,* Meg. There's Bible talk going on, and I won't have you interfering." He paused and drank the last of his tea before he spoke again. "So I figured I'd just bide my time and wait for a chance again. This time I'd do it right. 'Cause I wasn't gonna let my wife get away with calling the cops on me. But I hadn't counted on Persely. Not only did she *live*, that little asshole tried to turn the tables on *me*."

Simon tittered a little and looked up at the place on the kitchen wall where her picture used to be.

"I'd seen that box with the rat on it when I snuck in her room. Didn't really think nothing of it. Then I caught a whiff of that Tang in my thermos, out there on the lake. It smelled like death. It smelled like the wine at the Last Supper. Suddenly it all come clear to me. It wasn't Mary that needed to learn a lesson. Not as much as Persely. And who did Persely love more than anyone in the whole friggin' world?"

When chloral hydrate enters the bloodstream, oxygen is the banished third party.

I found my voice. "You did it," I said. "You killed Persely's mother."

Simon shrugged. "It was so easy. Mary started rolling around in the dirt and I started rolling around, too. Acting. I used to be a car salesman, you know. Not only did Persely lose her mama, she had to live with thinking she did it! And I got ten thousand dollars to boot."

"Persely died thinking she was a monster," Boone whispered. "She died without peace."

"Perfect, ain't it?" said Simon. He paused to spear a zucchini slice. "Now here comes the last part of the story. And this is beautiful. This is Christian justice. This is the hell that filled up after they nailed God's boy on the cross."

We all have our ghosts, Marshal.

Boone was leaning in closely. To hear Simon's words or the pattern in his breath?

"You see," said Simon, "a good man always gets a little hint that his own betrayal is on the way. It's a little something God gives to his special people. So I knew a long time ago, Boone, that you were a traitor. I knew it when I first caught sight of you on Lake Shine, looking for Persely."

Boone said nothing.

"She ruined you. She turned you bad. Now I can never trust you again. But that's okay. I got a new kid on the way. A boy. I know it's a boy. I can feel it. And this boy is gonna be raised right. He'll be loyal to me."

"No he won't," said Boone.

I was feeling sick. I pushed my plate away.

Simon pointed his finger at Boone. "You put something in my drink tonight, didn't you?"

I froze.

Maybe it's his fate to be a monster, Persely whispered by firelight.

"Didn't you?" said Simon.

"No," said Boone.

"Oh, I think you did," said Simon. "Just like your crazy girlfriend tried to do way back when. And somehow the glasses got switched around and you poisoned your own stupid self. Accidents happen, you know."

I gasped. All the color was fading from Boone's face.

"Stop it, Simon!" I cried. "You're just trying to scare him."

Simon smiled at me. "Good thing that cop saw the way your brother was acting this afternoon," he said. "He'll make a good witness."

Boone's face was ashen. Sweat had formed on his brow and was running down his nose. His breathing was ragged.

I jumped from the table and ran to him, seizing his cold arm and shaking him.

"Boone, Boone," I said.

He didn't look at me. He didn't blink.

I released my brother and rushed for the phone.

I was dialing when Meg spoke.

"Put the phone down, Alice."

Chapter Thirty-one

I turned around, astonished.

"What?"

"It's too late," said Meg. She was wiping her eyes.

"You're damn right it's too late," said Simon.

I stood there, the phone in my hand, one finger still pointing as if to dial.

"You're all right, son," Meg said to Boone.

Boone's face was still ashen. "I am?" he whispered.

She turned to Simon. "Boone told me about you today. About the things you'd done. And at first I didn't want to believe him. I just wanted us to be a family again. But my son never lies. And so I watched you tonight when you were setting the table. I saw you put something in Boone's drink."

Simon looked surprised. He started to say something and then fell silent. He glanced down at his glass. It was empty but for the ice.

"I wanted to have faith in you, Simon," Meg continued. "I wanted to believe. But Boone's right about you. You're a monster. And I don't want to be a monster, too."

It was finally beginning to dawn on us that Meg had switched the tea glasses once again. Simon's face had turned white. Or even slightly blue.

I put the phone down.

"But Meg," Simon said, sounding almost pleading. "What about our boy? You're going to let him grow up without his daddy?"

"Oh Simon," she said. "Mr. Walt's already dead."

Chapter Thirty-two

Accustomed as they were to the sufferings of tiny creatures, the twins were overjoyed at getting to see a grown man die on their neighbors' front lawn. An ambulance arrived within ten minutes, but there was nothing that could be done. And so Simon Jester left our lives in the same position that Meg had joined his: on his back, arms akimbo, face quite blue.

Meg had finally protected us. We were safe now. There would be no more sacrifices.

* * *

Dead bees, dead dog, dead stepfather. The police had no idea where to start. They talked to all of us, even Mrs. Laird across the street, who went on about her bad life instead of giving any details. They talked to the twins, too, who refused to cooperate with the inquiry at hand, instead confessing solemnly and with great detail to their own little crimes, although they insisted that the hermit crab from Corpus Christi died of natural causes.

I lied for Meg, and even Boone lied, saying that Simon had simply gotten confused about which glass he'd poisoned. But Meg told the truth. Told it almost proudly.

Her story defied the imagination. A man whose daughter once tried to poison him poisoned his wife instead, then took on a new identity and tried to poison his stepson, only this time his new wife switched the glasses and he himself drank the deadly mixture. The police shook their heads. They arrested Meg and dusted the tea glasses for fingerprints. They sent samples of Simon's blood to the lab. Eventually they dug up Numbhead and tested his body for poison. And Numbhead shouted *murderer, murderer* at the equally dead Simon, with a vehemence the hound had never possessed in life. The grand jury wouldn't indict Meg. They believed our testimony that Simon had tried to poison Boone. And what Simon had done to Numbhead made them truly hate that man.

Finally Meg was released, and we were left to go on with our lives.

Which were not without mystery.

The girl they'd pulled from Lake Shine was identified two days after Simon died. She was the cheerleader from Oak Ridge High School who had disappeared there two weeks before. Her parents wept on television and Boone stared out his bedroom window, wondering.

Lake Shine is deep and holds its secrets in the silt. Some bodies are never recovered.

Persely sightings continued for years. But nothing substantial. She had become a ghost, a rumor. And if the mud contained her footsteps, if a sudden scratching at the window was full of her impatience, I could never know.

Five years after Persely's disappearance, an article on her appeared in a local magazine. Included with the article was a picture that had never before been released to the press. A pretty girl smiled from a chair in her room. Behind her head, trophies crowded a shelf. The caption read: "Persely Snow, captain of the girls' swim team, sits with her trophies in May 1968."

Swim team? I stared at the article in wonderment.

Persely Snow leaned forward in the light of the camp-fire. "A girl at the hospital used to tell me to let a boy teach you things. They like that. It makes them feel important."

As for Boone—he turned out just fine. Long after that final and horrible showdown, he told me that he had gone to the garage that night and retrieved a box of rat poison, meaning to stir it into Simon's tea. But at the last minute he simply could not do it. And this was the brother I knew and loved.

He returned to his faith, taught its lessons to our little brother, Sam. Pale and sweet, the boy was born later that summer in an August characterized by the bold and continuous blooms of the crepe myrtle—whose blossoms and roots, as far as I know, are harmless when ingested.

Boone almost never spoke of Persely Snow again, which meant either the subject was simply too unbearable or Boone knew something I didn't—that maybe there was still a wild girl out there, dancing through cornfields at midnight, sleeping in silos, smoking pilfered cigarettes, cherishing memories of a clandestine visit to Kansas City, weeping sometimes, a savage misunderstood girl becoming a woman under the open skies. Surely if this were true, he would have found her by now, whispered to her, *Persely, you are no monster. And God says that everyone is fated to be innocent, if you wish this to be true.*

Perhaps Boone set her conscience free this way, under cover of darkness. Perhaps she never came back into the world, stayed wild as a choice.

And perhaps as the years passed, this savage misunderstood girl and this saintly misunderstood boy sometimes met each other in the dark of night for a single dance, one uninterrupted kiss, a little nectar in the parched stomach of the buzzing world.

Turn the page for a preview of
Kathy Hepinstall's new novel,

PRINCE OF LOST PLACES

coming soon from G. P. Putnam's Sons

Chapter 1

The detective hated it when people looked at his face. A sideways glance and then another, longer one, directed at the scar. Reddish pink, in the shape of a leaf. When he opened his mouth to floss his teeth, the leaf would narrow out into another shape, one he hadn't yet named. He'd had a fight in a bar one night, dead drunk, and someone had stabbed him in the cheek. Usually he wore a beard to cover the scar, though every now and then he'd shave it off, hoping that somehow people's glances had returned to normal. Yet here was another man, in the open doorway, shaken by grief and worry but still registering open curiosity—surprise, even—for a single moment before he turned his eyes away.

"You're the detective?" the man asked.

"Yes."

"I'm David Wells."

The man in the doorway was dark-haired and hand-some, and had a few days' worth of razor stubble on his face. The detective shook his hand and followed him into the living room. The man did not ask him to take a seat, but instead slowed his steps and moved to the side. The detective was used to people acting like this, deferring to him, as though he could ascertain the whereabouts of a loved one from the angling of the venetian blinds, the imperfections in the wainscoting, the position of a lamp. He obliged the man, moving about the room, looking at the fireplace and the deep-blue sofas, the chintz curtains that hung motion-less over the window. A single painting covered half the wall above the mantel. It showed a vast coastline, a churn-ing ocean, a glob of sun up in one corner that had spilled a drop of yellow into the blue sea, leaving a dollop of green. In the far distance of the picture he could see the tiny figure of a horse and rider.

"Martha bought that," David said, "at one of those starving-artist sales. She'd sit here in the mornings, drink her tea and look at it. I don't care for it much myself."

The detective nodded, put his hands in his pockets and said nothing. His fingertips touched an old wrapper at the bottom of one pocket.

David turned and led him into the kitchen, where the sink was piled high with dishes, mail spilled from the tabletop, and the answering machine blinked with a steady red purr. "Sorry for the mess," he said. "I'm not much for the bachelor life."

The detective shrugged in response, but his eyes took in

everything even as he heard the irony and slight twang of anger in the word *bachelor*. The mess in the kitchen of a true bachelor had the feel of permanence, and if dishes were piled in the sink, they had an inherent stability, like statues or trees. Here, pots were still on the stove, stacked on top of one another, sending out the aroma of dried chili. This man probably kept his office neat as a pin. But to restore order to the room his wife once dominated would be the first step in acceptance; David Wells was far from that state of mind.

He followed David through the dining room, around to the mahogany staircase and up to the second floor. David stopped in front of the bedroom at the end of the hallway.

"This is my son's room."

"Duncan?"

"Yes."

The window shade was up, and sunlight fell on the pattern of the twin bed against the far wall. It was a typical boy's room, an assortment of stuffed animals and posters and computer games. Puzzle boxes were stacked on a plastic desk; an action figure, posed on the top box, brandished an orange scepter.

The detective opened the door of the closet and studied the contents. "Did she pack his clothes?"

"Some of them. And a few of his toys. I don't know if she took any of his soldiers. He had so many." David opened a drawer and pulled out a handful of little green figures. "There," he said, as though they were proof of something. "There, there." Suddenly he threw them against the wall. They fell to the ground in their various poses.

The detective said nothing.

"She's sick," David said. "Her mind has left her. She's

in no condition to be wandering around somewhere." He picked up the soldiers and put them back in the drawer.

They went across the hallway to the master bedroom, which was large and sparely decorated: some rosewood furniture, a couple of table lamps, a flokati rug. The detective toed the edge of it as David sat on the bed.

"I can't believe they're gone," David said, his voice faltering. "I mean, one minute everyone's here. And then you just wake up one morning and…that's it. It makes you wonder about God. Do you believe in God, Detective?"

The detective shrugged, walked over to the end table, and picked up a framed picture. "When was this taken?" he asked.

"Three months ago."

The detective looked at the picture and saw another version of the man before him. His smile was quiet and confident. His hair neatly combed, his tie straight. The woman next to him was pretty and small. She had her face turned at a three-quarter angle; her eyes shone. Nothing in her expression suggested a plan to abandon ship, leave the house empty, turn into nothing, vanish. And the boy. Not so much posed as captured in the middle of freeing himself from the restraints of sitting for a portrait. His mother, no doubt, had just arranged his arms and he was in the process of rearranging them. His hands flying out at odd angles. An open mouth, caught in the middle of some screeching remark designed to foil the shutter at the moment of perfection. Two seconds after this picture was taken, he was off his mother's lap and on the other side of the room, bounding toward something more curious. The detective remembered taking his own son for family pictures, years before. To boys, portraits were slivers of church. Boring, with a reverence directed at something unseen.

He set the picture back down on the table. "I'm going to need to look through your wife's papers—any letters, diaries. Any old prescriptions. Canceled checks. Credit cards. I'll need to get the phone records for the last month or two. I have to know where she worked. Her habits. I need to talk to her friends. I need to get a complete description of the vehicle, tires, tail light pattern, bumper stickers, all that."

David nodded but he seemed resentful, as though he'd let a stranger take hold of his chin and study his watery eyes. "You used to be a cop?" he asked.

The detective stiffened. Maybe David Wells knew a little bit about his story. Maybe he was trying to even the score a little. Loss for loss.

"Yes, I was. A few years ago."

"Why'd you become a detective?"

He didn't answer.

"I hear you're good at what you do. The best. I hear you have amazing insight into people. That you're a chameleon when you're on a case."

"Maybe. But I never turned a color my ex-wife could appreciate."

David Wells didn't smile. "I'm not just hiring you to find her. You need to bring her back. I don't care how much it costs. I don't care what you have to do. I'm hiring you because I heard you're the best."

The detective thought of the woman in the picture and the boy. Between them they had such vitality. No wonder the house seemed dark without them.

"She's very fragile," said David. "She was a good mother.

Still is, the way she sees it. I love her. You ever love someone who's crazy?"

The man was trembling. His words were too fast and running together, and his eyes held a strange light. Stress, thought the detective, or maybe something more.

"I don't know if I've ever loved someone who's crazy," he said at last. "When I'm in love, I guess I'm pretty crazy myself."

Chapter 2

I thought I'd feel different, watching that old station wagon burn. My husband, David, had bought it second-hand six years ago, after we had Duncan. That car was good to us, and I could not have imagined even a month ago that I'd be standing next to my boy in the middle of the desert, watching the flames, under starlight so strong I could see the seats blackening. I suppose that as a wife I felt a little guilty, but as a mother I felt exhilarated. I had soaked some newspapers in gasoline and put them in the front seat and lit them, as my child watched from a safe distance away. Then I ran, huffing and puffing, unsure of the progress flames would make in a durable family car, or if the whole thing would go off like a bomb and lift me high above the cholla cactus and prickly pear. When I reached Duncan the fire was burning bright. He stood motionless. I thought he was going to ask me what I was doing, but he didn't. He was probably the only person left in the world who still trusted me. I sat down cross-legged on the cool desert ground, pulled him onto my lap, and together we watched the fire move through the car. When the gas tank blew, the station wagon raised its back end as though bucking in a rodeo full of sensible family cars, and Duncan let out a single loud cry that contained no fear—more of a war cry, really—and I knew he had never been so proud of me, the fact that I had destroyed something so big, and in such a big way. His father could have taken him to a million baseball games and never achieved the same effect. I could feel his heart beating fast through my body, the wind blew the scent of gasoline on us, and right behind it the sweet scent of creosote flowers. I always thought the word *creosote* meant something that came from a chimney. Apparently, though, it is also the name of a desert shrub. The old man, my co-conspirator, once told me that out here in the desert, creosote hangs in the air after a summer rain. If I ever were to cross his path again, I would tell him that an act of arson could release that same fragrance.

As the fire lost its power, ashes began floating out of the wreckage, circling over our heads and dropping down on us. My clothes turned black here and there, and when I rubbed my nose I felt my fingertip crush a piece of ash and coat my nose with my abandoned life. Back in Ohio, they thought I was mad. Doctors and neighbors and even my husband, who at that moment was no doubt in the midst of some scheme to track me down.

But the tales of my madness were lies. I was utterly sane.

Centuries ago, the Rio Grande was strong and wild; it fought limestone on its way to the sea, and then sank down tame enough for our rubber raft. This was our second day on the river, and my son lounged on the other side of the raft, facing me as I paddled. In the canyon walls around me, I saw the decorations of a peaceful spring: prickly pear and ocotillo, and mud nests full of baby cliff swallows. Most of the flowers were unfamiliar to me, and although I used to run a flower shop, there were few parallel species I could think of in Ohio. Duncan was humming a little song. I couldn't quite make out the melody, something he'd learned from a jingle on TV, or a Tejano tune he'd picked up from the car radio as we drove through Texas in the night.

We entered a narrow gulf between two high canyons, and a blanket of shadow briefly fell over the raft before the river turned a corner and we floated out into the sunlight. The shallow rapids carried us from one shore to the other, bumping us against Texas and then Mexico. "Isn't it amazing, Duncan?" I asked. "Two totally different countries, all within a few yards of each other."

"I want to get out!" he begged. "I want to go to Mexico!"

"No, honey, we won't be able to stop for a while."

He sadly eyed the foreign shore not five yards away. I stretched out my bare foot and nudged his knee.

"You're not bored, are you?" I asked. "I mean, you should be sitting in school right now. Learning fractions or maybe how to spell, or painting a cow or something. That would be really boring, huh? But you're special. You get to ride down a river with your mommy. How many boys your age get to do that?"

"None," he said. "Although Tommy's father has a farm."

"I hear the farm is in foreclosure."

"What?"

"Nothing. You're having fun, though, right?"

"Yes, Mommy." His dimples were so pronounced that they made me feel even guiltier. I had lied to my son. Not a little white lie but a bald-faced black one, as vast as these canyons. But the color was coming back to his face, a bit. He had looked so pale back in Ohio.

"I'm worried about him," I told David, a few days after the tragedy.

"I'm worried about you," he said. "Very, very worried."

"What if he's wounded? Traumatized for life? How can I help him after what he's seen?" I was trying to wash the dishes as I spoke. My hands were shaking. I felt something stab me, and when I lifted my hands out of the water, one of my knuckles was bleeding. David came up behind me, caught my arm, and held it high as blood ran down.

"It's all right," he whispered in my ear as he guided me to the bathroom. "Stay calm. Stay rational."

This was my calm. This was my rational. I abandoned David and his advice, turned instead to a river and its course into the middle of nowhere.

"Mommy!" my son now exclaimed, and I followed his pointing finger. The head of a tiny swallow appeared in the round opening of a mud nest. "It's a baby bird!" Duncan tried to get to his feet.

"Sit down, honey! That's a swallow. Did you know that

giant birds used to fly over this river, and their wings were big enough to stretch over our pool back home?"

Duncan's eyes turned glassy. He covered his face.

"The big birds are gone now, honey," I said quickly. "They're fossils. Fossils can't hurt you."

I had packed carefully. I had canteens and insulated blankets. I had polypropylene rope, Ensolite pads, wool clothing, iodine tablets, dried food, moleskin, scissors, twine, a fishing pole, a deck of Old Maid playing cards, and an anaphylactic shock kit. I had a Coleman stove, a broken railroad watch, two old Hollofil sleeping bags, a hunting knife, flashlights, carbide lanterns, canned beets, Mars bars, John Denver music, matches, and Spam. I had a portable CD player that ran on batteries. I had one back-pack full of nothing but long-burning candles. And I had directions down this river, whispered to me and committed to memory. For the past day and a half I had looked for landmarks. A fishing camp on the Texas side. A narrow is-land that split the current into two channels. The remains of a pump house, whose ladder was still attached, and missing several rungs. Petroglyphs on a dry arroyo. A sharp bend in the river. A canyon in which two boulders, shaped like the heads of cows, created a class II rapid.

"We have everything we need, son," I told Duncan con-fidently, my voice perhaps a bit too high, my words a bit too fast. "We have our own food, and we can always eat off the land. Juniper berries, yucca blossoms, century plant hearts."

"I want spaghetti."

"Duncan, you will finish your century plant hearts or you will get no dessert."

He stared at me.

"That's a joke," I told him.

He gave me a smile that meant my attempt at humor, not the humor itself, was amusing, then wiped the sweat off his face. Duncan was supposed to be sitting in his first-grade class right now, which was held no longer in the main building, but in an extension building made of corrugated tin, out back across the west side of the playground. When the teachers wrote on the blackboards, the sound echoed through the tin, and when the children were let out at recess, they only had to run ten feet to get to the monkey bars.

All across the country, first-graders were writing on tablets. Teachers were pacing the classrooms. Gym coaches were blowing their whistles. Janitors were pushing buckets of soapy water slowly down the hallways. And the smell in the buckets was vaguely that of hospitals. It trailed through to the classrooms. The children sniffed it and thought of sick days, humidifiers, and ginger ale.

My son was a truant, drifting down the river with me.

One day last fall, when class was still held in the main building, someone from Duncan's school called me. He had fallen off the monkey bars and cut open his chin. I rushed over to get him and take him to the doctor, a man with a cheerful face whose glasses kept sliding down his nose. He put three stitches in Duncan's chin and smiled at my son's story. Duncan told him he had been racing three other boys to see who could reach the top of the monkey bars first. A group of children had gathered to watch. Duncan was first to reach the top. He won.

"And you fell?" asked the doctor.

"No," he said, suddenly shy. "Not then."

He fell when he turned around to see if Linda was

watching him. Linda was the girl who lived next door to us. In that doctor's office, decorated with posters of the Muppets, I imagined the scene. Duncan straining to catch a glimpse of her in his moment of triumph, his fingers slipping, knees falling through the bars, the world turning upside down and his teeth clacking as his chin hit metal. That is love, son. Losing your grip at the very moment of victory. Blood instead of kisses.

"Was Linda watching you?" asked the doctor.

"No," said Duncan, ducking his head, the stitches giving him the look of an older, more world-weary boy. "She was watching a race on the slides."

My muscles were starting to ache from moving the oars all day. The water had turned calm and my son was asleep, his face pointed up at the shifting clouds, his eyelashes long and blond. I myself had slept very little, filled with the fear that my husband would catch up to us.

Before we ran away, David's job was to find oil. He was good at it. He could find oil in a Zen garden. Around the office in our home there were pictures of him wearing a hard hat in Algeria, standing in the rain in Dubai, meeting with the president of the Philippines. David looked regal, his hands clasped behind his back, his expression polite. He didn't care that much for niceties. People bored him, I thought. I used to stare at those pictures when he was away, imagining myself in those exotic locales.

I knew that he was looking for us, and as carefully as I thought I'd covered our tracks, I was daunted by the task of eluding his pursuit. I pictured him pacing around our kitchen, speaking urgently into the phone, interrogating a neighbor or the teenage girl who helped me out at the shop.

On the kitchen table were saucers and plates and pieces of paper on which he'd written down notes, clues and theories. I would have loved to have my husband in this raft with us, wearing madras shorts and no shoes on his feet. But his presence here required his sanity, which was gone, perhaps for good.

D uncan awoke as we passed an arroyo whose dry walls contained the giant oyster fossils I'd been told to look for, a sign that we were very close to the cave. Carrizo cane lined the river. Between the cane and the canyon walls lay a stretch of rocky land, bristling with mesquite trees. I felt a breeze against my face and remembered an old John Denver song, something about flowers, and the wisdom of children.

"John Denver was a misunderstood genius," I told my son. "Like your man, Barney."

"I hate Barney!" he shouted with sudden vehemence. Duncan was at the age when he deeply regretted loving Barney and would rather not have been reminded of the hours he once sat in front of the television, awestruck.

"Who do you love now?"

"You." He knew he'd said the right thing, the perfect mother-son thing, and he grabbed his feet and rocked back against the side of the raft, pleased with himself.

"You're good." I could feel the horrors of Ohio leaving me as the canyons of Texas and Mexico hovered on either side of us like protective parents, a mixed marriage that produced clean wind, ocotillo flowers, swift water, and cinnabar.

This desert didn't spend its time dreaming up new dangers. Flash floods, scorpions, rattlesnakes, frostbite, loose rocks, mountain lions, heat stroke, the barbs of the cholla cactus, the sharp edges of lechugulla. For centuries, mothers here knew what they were in for. They weren't sideswiped like the mothers in Ohio. I would teach my son to be careful. I would say, "Duncan, beware of five-sided leaves and snakes with shovel heads. Don't put your hands in strange places. Don't bother creatures that warm themselves on rocks. Drink lots of water, and don't ever sleep in a dry wash. Do you understand, son?"

And he would nod.

He was a good boy, most of the time. So timid in his crush on Linda that it broke my heart to see it. Even at six years old she favored gauzy, delicate dresses and carried around a white, shell-covered purse. She had the face of an angel, flyaway blond hair, and a way of walking that demonstrated a belief that the world could be conquered so easily; it was a vast stupid place in love with pretty girls, and the rewards were endless. She would pace up and down the sidewalk, pushing a carriage full of Knickerbocker dolls. On the occasions when she pushed too hard and the carriage turned over, her dainty shrieks would send Duncan racing out of the house, where he would perform doll triage as she stood by, barking orders at him. I wanted to tell my son not to fall for girls like her, that she and her dolls were trouble, that she would always be the boss and he the servant.

Duncan had a set of army men he played with on the driveway, dividing them into platoons, sending them on secret missions. They were brave men, stoic in their fixed positions, and the afternoon would fade as they advanced inch by inch down the driveway, past puddles and pine leaves and discarded toys. Linda would come out in her gauzy dress and interrupt his games. She would stop the army and assign the soldiers to duties of her own choosing, which had nothing to do with battle. Once she even took a pair of fingernail scissors and cut off a soldier's arms, taking away the plastic hands and the gun they held, too.

"Look what you did!" Duncan protested. "He can't fight!"

"He doesn't need to fight," Linda said calmly. "He's in love."

I wondered why my son couldn't stand up for himself. *Put that soldier here*, Linda would say, *and that one over there. Make the soldiers guard my dolls.* Sometimes she would take an interest in one of the plastic men and slip it into her purse and with her bring it home to live, captured, on her vanity table or in the bottom of her closet. There came a time when I had to go next door and explain to Linda's mother that Duncan's battalion was so ravaged that it no longer could protect its flank.

The boat bumped another boulder, startling Duncan.

"It's okay, baby. We're almost there. I packed three of your soldiers. I knew you'd want them."

He crossed his arms and cast his eyes downward.

"What's the matter, honey?"

"Nothing."

"You miss Daddy?" My heart sped up at the question.

"Not yet." He was used to David's being gone. Once David went to Saudi Arabia for three months, and when he returned, he looked shocked at the way his son had grown. I used to wonder if Duncan was different from other boys because his father was away so much. Maybe something about the way a father grabbed his son and roughly tickled his stomach instilled in him the confidence to keep his toy soldiers from being stolen by a blond-headed girl.

"I miss Linda," Duncan said. His eyes filled with tears, and I realized my mistake. The mention of his soldiers reminded him of her, that blond-headed, pretty little thief.

"Oh, honey," I said, putting down my paddle and reaching over to touch his cool face.

Linda had been dead for nearly three weeks.